BLOOD AND DUST

J.C. PAULSON

Black Rose Writing | Texas

ISBN: 978-1-68433-880-1
PUBLISHED BY BLACK ROSE WRITING
www.blackrosewriting.com

Printed in the United States of America
Suggested Retail Price (SRP) $20.95

Blood and Dust is printed in Chaparral Pro

For Ken
who, in another life,
would have been James Sinclair.
All the love.

BLOOD
AND
DUST

Chapter One

June 1882

Blood spattered the blacksmith's shop, dotted the goldsmith's bench and smeared the pointed tools of the trades.

My blood. Smithery's like that.

Someone else's blood, thick and slippery, spewing over my dining room table and spilling in an arterial waterfall onto the floor . . . I had not signed up for that.

The table provided the cleanest surface on the property, the one place I could fathom slicing the leg open. Amputation presented itself as the only option; the gunshot had shattered the shinbone, exploded veins and ground the meat into hamburger. No doctor, me, but even I could see the limb was done for. So was my patient if it did not come off soon.

"Hold on to him, Bert," I said. "Hard."

"Where?" Stone blind, Bert needed me to navigate.

"Right here." I took his hands and placed them on the man's thigh. "Don't move."

The patient's name, as far as I could determine, was Alexander. Drunk as six sailors and in more pain than I could imagine, he babbled it out as if cotton wool lined his mouth. He had probably puked a few times, from whisky and agony. Dry as dust, that tongue; I would guarantee it.

Just as well he was pissed up. Maybe his blood alcohol level, along with the few drops of laudanum I had scavenged from the dead doctor's clinic, would keep him compliant long enough for me to remove that leg from the knee down.

I placed a piece of wood between his teeth and told him to bite down, but he moaned and gasped. Screamed, occasionally. The wood, of course, would fall out.

"Alex, for fuck's sake, grind on this," I said for the tenth time, replacing the stick. "You don't want to bite off your tongue too."

Finally, I got a slight nod. Okay. Progress.

I had also stolen a scalpel. What the hell, right? Doc Arlington would never use it again. Stropping it on my thumb, and shocked to feel how dull it was, I took it to the shop for a serious honing before heating it in the forge. A good slosh of moonshine made it as sanitary as I could possibly get it.

All of that preparation had taken longer than I had hoped, so the poor bugger on the table had been writhing and bleeding like hell for a good half-hour, all told. Time to get on with it.

"Okay, Bert, here we go."

"Ready, James. I'm holding on."

Truth to tell, I had taken a swig of moonshine myself. I had good hands, steady and sure. I could make a perfect horseshoe, or a knife that sliced paper, or the most delicate golden wedding ring a girl could want. This leg problem stretched my expertise, so I needed liquid courage. Steadied me a bit.

Who else would do it? No one within forty-five miles. By horse and cart. It would take two or three days, maybe more, and Alexander would be dead by then.

The leg had to come off at the knee, to avoid muscle removal or sawing bones. I sliced the skin six inches below it into three strips and folded them back. That did not go over well with my patient. He thrashed and yelled, his eyes rolling in his head despite the laudanum; but Bert held on like grim death. I loved that man. Best partner ever, eyesight problem notwithstanding.

Blood flew like spit and flowed like syrup. I tied him up tight with a tourniquet, but it did not do the whole trick. Shit. After all this, would he just up and die from blood loss? How much could he stand to lose? Like I said. Not a doctor.

The other big problem was the real threat of slipping on the dark red sea now covering my dining room floor. I snapped a towel off the stack of linens I had put on the table and threw it under my feet. Maybe it would help keep me upright.

Carefully, quickly, I severed the tendons that held the tibia and fibula in place. That went well, considering. I poked around a bit and figured out where all the blood poured from, then sutured up the ends of the veins and arteries. I had stolen the medical needle and thread, too. Finally, the skin flaps: I pulled them down and over Alex's new stump, sewing them up snugly.

Civil war surgeons could pull off a relatively simple amputation in two minutes. I had read about it in a newspaper somewhere while still down east, a couple of years back. I was not quite so fast, it being my first real surgical procedure, but I had done my best.

By now, Alexander, whoever the hell he was, lay there twitching in complete shock. What do you do for shock? I wondered. Newspapers and book learning were not helping me with that issue.

"Don't you fucking die on me now," I told him, leaning up to speak right in his ear. "Not after all this. Don't you dare fucking die. I'll make you a nice leg if you just won't die."

He did not say anything, of course.

"Are you done, James?"

"Oh, sorry, yes. You can let go now, Bert. Be careful as you step away. The floor's slippery."

"Someone's coming," he said.

I could not hear anything, but I knew better than to question him. I saw, he listened.

Sure enough. Ten seconds later, the door flew open.

Standing there were two blazing eyes, blue as the summer sky, snapping with fury and fear. And a wobbling gun, trained right directly on my torso.

The sun glowed behind this apparition, and let's face it, I did not expect someone to walk in just then. Plus, the firearm had my full attention.

Therefore, it took a few seconds before I could appreciate that the eyes and gun belonged to a woman. The rest of her shook with emotion under a flowered calico dress thin as butterfly wings and the palest lavender from too much laundering. I noticed this, even in my confusion, because the body underneath was slim and round and soft and quivering.

She spoke first.

"If he dies," she said, "you die."

Chapter Two

Toronto in 1880 bustled from morning until after dark under the power of some eighty-five thousand souls, mine among them. Served since mid-century by three rail lines, the eastern Canadian city had pretty much exploded over the last thirty years. You could feel it breathing heavily, working busily, fornicating like crazy.

In the developing madness, some eighteen years ago, I was born. The folks, James and Caroline Sinclair, were Scottish immigrants who sought the proverbial better way of life in Canada. Da was a mechanic and Mum a midwife and Jill of all trades. She sewed clothes, babysat kids, baked wedding cakes — you name it. Whatever brought in a few extra dollars, she would do it. If she did not know how, she would learn.

She had five mouths to feed, and labour problems followed Da around in the churning political climate of a city trying to settle itself. Often out of work, he would be picketing or drinking while Mum picked up the slack, birthed babies and had some herself.

Fucking heroic genius, my mum.

Two sisters came along first: Mary and Catherine, boom, within ten months. Not long after, named for the paterfamilias, came me — James Davidson Sinclair, Junior. Breeding became a problem after that. Mum had two miscarriages, and that was it for the family expansion project.

Just as well. Times were tough enough without more Sinclair progeny running around. I do not think Mum saw it that way, though. She loved babies.

I managed to get in a few years' schooling before being put to work. Da took me on as an apprentice at fourteen, minutes after my voice changed. Mum would not stand for me being pulled away from my education entirely, though. She had been rather a lady of letters back in Scotland, thoroughly versed in literature, poetry, music and various other areas of knowledge. Her relatively wealthy father had been horrified when James Sinclair Senior stole her heart and whisked her off to the colonies. It really had been a mad thing for her to do, but here we were.

And so, every night after work, we would read and do sums, and she would tell me heroic tales from history. Every chance she had, she dragged all three of us young Sinclairs to musical and other artistic events.

Work came less easily to me than learning at first. Tall for my age but stringy, job one was to build some muscle. Lifting wheels and hoisting tools required a fair amount of strength, so I ran every day and repeatedly lifted anything heavy lying around our shabby apartment. By sixteen, still a tad skinny and having stretched to six feet, I nonetheless could hold my own in the shop.

The benefit to apprenticing for Da — apart from contributing to the family coffers — was that I learned about steel. How to bend it, reclaim it, bang it and make it into something shiny and new. Few things in my life had been shiny or new. I liked shiny and new. A lot.

One day, I slipped a little piece of metal into the pocket of my overalls. I stared at that little bar of gleaming promise for weeks. Then I beat it up. I heated it up. I hammered at it some more. When finished, it looked more or less like a ring. Round, but dull.

On the way home, I popped into the hardware store and picked up a sheet of sandpaper that cost me a couple of cents. Slipping into my room, really just a partitioned area of my sisters' shared bedroom, I sneaked my project out of my pocket and had at it.

The sandpapering actually worked, after a fashion. The dull metal began to shine and reflect the light peeking through the filthy window. Mum washed those windows with all the elbow grease she could muster, but she could not get at the outsides because we were on the third floor. Sunlight filtering through the glass stained the air a pale sepia.

I shook and panted with the thrill of having figured it out myself. I made a ring. I made it pretty. No one told me how; it had just happened.

"Mum," I said later that night. "Here."

My trembling fingers unclenched with an effort, revealing the ring resting in my palm.

"Jem," she breathed. "What on Earth is this?"

"I made it for you, Mum."

"Oh, Jem. It's beautiful."

"Try it on, Mum."

She reached out, delicately plucked the ring from my hand, and slid it over her fourth finger on her right hand. Unerringly, she knew where it would fit best. It was just a slender band, but it did glow.

"But how?" she asked.

I explained that I had taken a tiny piece of scrap metal from the shop and played around with it until it turned into something. I heated, hammered, shaped and burnished it.

"Oh, dear," she said. I did not like the sound of that. "Does your father know about it?"

"Uh, well, no."

Frankly, it had never occurred to me that it might be a problem. Realization tumbled through my suddenly terrified brain. Basically, I had stolen that tiny bit of steel. He would be livid.

"I just wanted to make you something nice, Mum."

"I know, dear. Let me see what I can do."

She tried, but the minute my father saw the ring, he lost his mind. Still outweighing me by something like sixty pounds — he was a big man — and fired by fury, he hauled me by the ear down three flights of stairs and out into the minuscule, filthy back yard. Not for nothing had Toronto been known as "Muddy York" in its early days.

He was in his cups, which did not help. He beat the hell out of me, yelling the entire time. Windows flew open around the enclosure from the neighbouring apartments; heads peeked out, their owners wondering who was making all the damned noise.

"You bloody fucking little thief!" he screamed. "I'll teach you to steal, James Davidson Sinclair!"

He had never been this crazed before, the bastard. I'd endured plenty of cuffs and smacks, but not a full-bore, holy-hell beating like this. I stayed as silent as possible, emitting only oofs and grunts, and that did not please him either. Damned if I would give him the satisfaction of hollering.

Finally, exhausted, he stopped and slumped against the dirty brick wall of the building.

"Get out of my sight."

I stumbled away with blackened eyes, bruised ribs, cuts on the forehead and cheeks and shins. If it were not for my mother, I would have left that night and never, ever come back.

He took the ring, of course, before flinging himself out of the apartment and back to the pub. Mum, weeping, washed my face and back and bandaged up what she could.

"My sweet boy," she crooned. "My poor, sweet boy. It will be all right. All right, now."

Then I did break down. I cried in her lap until the violent fucker who was my father came back some time later, weaving so heavily he bounced off the walls of the stairwell.

I had to get out of that mechanic's shop. I could not look at him day after day anymore. How the hell I was going to extract myself from an apprenticeship to my own father, I had no idea. But now I knew what I wanted to do. It had to happen soon.

CHAPTER THREE

Before James Senior became a serious drunk, before his ambitions were torn away from him like flayed skin, he had his moments.

The morning after my beating, I lay aching on my cot, staring up at the single shelf that held my few trophies. Among them sat a tiny train locomotive, intricately carved from a block of wood and painted bright red. An engineer, no bigger than a fly, leaned out the window, the brim of his hat poking out over his crooked arm.

Much too old for toys, I could not part with the locomotive. Da made it for my sixth birthday, and I am here to tell you he did not make or give me very many presents.

That is when it hit me, like a fat slap from a fish's tail. Da had not beaten me because I had stolen a scrap of metal worth next to nothing. He had beaten me because I had made Mum a special gift, a gesture that would never have occurred to him. At least, not in recent years. I had shown the bastard up, and he did not like it. It reminded him of who he used to be. Who he could have been.

As the toy locomotive attested, the man had some talents. He was incredibly good with his hands, even if they were also brutal. I began to realize I had probably inherited, or at least learned, those skills from him — minus the brutality. In many ways, I was a mama's boy.

From the moment I clapped eyes on my precious toy, I loved trains. Smoke-belching, stinking, somewhat terrifying things they were, but they symbolized power, excitement, human advancement and travel. Not that I understood that at the time, apart from the excitement. As I grew, I would go to the train yards whenever I could to absorb the thrill of being surrounded by engines and people and dreams.

Dreams of what, I had little idea. Where did the trains go, exactly? I gathered not very far, at least not yet. The railway had just begun its expansion to the west, a wild and unknown territory — the thought of which filled my gut with a sweet, shuddering terror.

Stories filled my ears and imagination of heathen tribes, crazed prospectors, brave explorers, animals that could tear you apart with one massive swipe of the jaw. Was it all true?

Would I ever find out?

I finally eased my scraped, bruised legs over the side of the bed. Sitting up, I immediately found I had a diamond-splinter headache and could barely move my left arm. But I would be damned if I would let on to Da, and double-damned if I would stay home from work.

"Morning," I mumbled to my parents, who were eating a skimpy breakfast at the table.

Da turned bloodshot eyes on me and returned his gaze to his food without a word. Mum's sad, smudged eyes lingered on my black-and-blue face, and she managed a small "good morning."

She scraped back her chair and motioned for me to sit down, then went to the stove and filled a bowl with oatmeal. I ate it through clenched teeth. Not a word passed among us. My sisters would have eased the tension with their chatter, but they had left early for their child-minding jobs.

I asked myself again how I could possibly get through the next few years working with Da. Hunched over my breakfast bowl, I stole glances at his stony face and swore to myself again that I would somehow get away. The main problem, even more daunting than finding other work and a place to stay, was leaving Mum.

• • •

In the weeks that followed, I avoided home as much as I could. I would rise early, work hard, stay late and wander the streets until my body neared collapse, starving and exhausted. Mum played along, leaving a hot dinner in the oven or a cold one in the icebox.

Apart from curt instructions and interactions at work, Da and I seldom spoke. I had nothing to say to him, and it seemed he dodged me as well. It did not occur to me until much later, but I think he was ashamed. He rarely looked me in the eye. Whether because he had beaten the hell out of me, or because I had been a better son than he was a husband, I was not sure.

I took different routes on my evening tours of the city, craving the whole, wide, bizarre experience. Some nights, I would simply go down to look at the trains, and occasionally I would pick up an hour's work for ready cash. Other nights I would amble past the stores, peering in the windows and dreaming of being able to afford trinkets and warm clothing for Mum and Cath and Mary.

Still other nights, I would end up on the tantalizing, brain-muddling, body-awakening street where prostitutes emerged from dark doorways to touch and tease me. I had no money for such intriguing pursuits, but I also felt shabby when they approached me. I thought of what Mum would say if I capitulated. I did not like the words ringing in my ears.

"Those ladies," Mum had once said, "are down on their luck, my Jem. No self-respecting woman would do . . . what they do, with men they don't know, if they didn't have to. Mark my words, son, they're crawling with disease. Do you want to pay them for giving you a sickness? Do you want to be one of the men robbing them of self-respect? No, you do not."

No, if she was going to put it that way. No, I did not. Still, I felt the sting of arousal as they crooned at and flattered me, using language I had never heard fall from a woman's lips.

Sex, however, increasingly became an obsession. How did a young man — which is how I viewed myself — manage to relieve the agony of desire, if not with a prostitute? Young ladies of my acquaintance, and there were few enough of them, were unlikely to participate in a rousing session of erotic love.

A year or so of this kind of torture slowly passed. Sexual frustration, little comfort at home, and the ongoing tension of working with my father in the machine shop made me want to jump out of my skin.

On a wild night, as the icy wind whipped off Lake Ontario, I walked past the closed shops along the street toward home. My hands and face were numb from cold, and I strode along with my arms wrapped around myself, trying to keep from freezing. Focused on making it home before losing a toe to frostbite, I barely glanced in the store windows.

One window, though, caught my attention. It offered a view into the jeweller's shop, a beacon in the gathering darkness, with wares displayed in spotless glass cases. Yet I barely noticed these glories, because my eyes were riveted on a sign bearing in large black letters the words, "Goldsmith needed. Inquire within."

CHAPTER FOUR

"Sit down, young man," said the goldsmith. "Let's see what you can do."

The ten most glorious words I had ever heard came from the lips of one Graham Tattersall, master of the gleaming arts and in my eyes nothing less than a god. I ran to his shop after work the next day, praying it would still be open. Huffing from the mile-long dash, I tidied my hair with both hands, opened the door and stepped in.

"What can I do for you?" he had asked, scrubbing filthy hands on an even filthier scrap of fabric. "Looking for a little something for your girl?"

With all the confidence and respect I could infuse into my voice, I said, "Sir, I am here to inquire about your job as advertised in the window."

"Do you have any experience?"

Of course that would be his first question. I had to decide right smartly whether to tell the truth. After all, I had a tiny bit of experience, didn't I?

"Not really," I admitted. "I did make a ring for my mum once, out of steel."

"Did you, now." He paused and cocked his head at me. "How did you manage that?

"I took a wee piece from the machine shop and heated it up. I hollowed it out pretty nicely into a ring. Then I sandpapered it, so it looked shiny."

He peered at me over his jeweller's loupe, clamped rather precariously to the side of his glasses. Apparently I passed early muster, because the next words he uttered were those glorious ten.

I found myself seconds later seated at a goldsmith's bench, featuring a metal tray, a chewed-up looking chunk of wood sticking into my face, and various tiny tools arranged neatly in a small rack. I had no idea what to do with most of them, but a few seemed fairly self-explanatory.

Tattersall thrust a slender silver bar into my hand. Silver. I could not believe it. I had never before held a precious metal or stone. It shone with promise in my palm.

"See if you can do something with that," he said.

He gave me a few tips — like taking care not to overheat it — and simply went back to work.

I decided to try another ring, working from my limited knowledge. Carefully, I heated up the bar, bent it and figured out how to meld the ends together. I found a tool that looked like it might do in place of sandpaper and gave it a good rubbing. It gleamed. It was more or less round. I slipped it on my finger.

"Ah, sir?" I asked tentatively, sometime later. "Do you want to see what I've done? I don't want to ruin your silver."

"No, son, I don't need to see it until you're finished," he said. "I can hear everything I need to know. Carry on. It needs to be smooth, round and shiny. You're not quite there yet. Take that hammer on your right, give it some whacks, and see if you can make it perfect. Round and perfect."

I had never seen anything like this hammer. Made of walnut, its head was covered in soft rawhide. I picked it up, examined it with great curiosity, then gave my project a gentle thwack. That did nothing, so I tried again with greater force.

"That's better," Tattersall said.

Aha. I smacked the ring a few more times, trying to achieve that perfect roundness. Once I thought I was close, I burnished it again. Tattersall stood up and came to peer over my shoulder.

"Not too bad, young man. Not too bad. What's your name?"

"James Davidson Sinclair Junior, sir."

"Well, James Junior. It's not perfect; no, it's not. But it's a damn sight better than anything I've seen from any other applicant in the past two weeks. When can you start?"

I stared at him in disbelief. Did he just offer me a job? As a goldsmith?

"I guess I'm not sure. I have to give notice at the machine shop, sir." And find a place to live, but I did not say that out loud. "Two weeks?"

Tattersall considered, then nodded.

"That'll be fine. Glad to know you are working, and responsible about leaving your employment. You could come in Saturdays for now, if you'd like. And Thursday evenings. I'm often open until seven Thursdays; not everyone can come in during the day."

"Yes, sir. I'd like that. Thank you, sir."

"The pay won't be great at first, James Junior. You'll have to make me a little money before I can afford to give you decent wages." He named a sum. "Can you live with that?"

Good question. How little could I live on? I had no idea what rent would cost, nor how I would feed myself. At the moment, I didn't care.

"Yes, sir. When would you like me to come in next?"

"Saturday. Eight in the morning. See you then, James Junior."

I thanked him again and rushed out the door before he could change his mind. I had two weeks to figure out where I was going to live, and how to scramble out from under my father's authority and wrath.

And tell Mum.

I could not back out now, nor did I want to. Job one was to find a home, and frankly I had no idea how to go about it. I could simply wander around checking signs in boarding house windows, in the same way I found the advertised job, but that seemed a haphazard approach.

I headed for the coffee house where the boys tended to hang around after work. A couple of my older mates lived alone, and I figured they could point me to an empty room somewhere or at least give me some advice.

Jack Malone and Gerry Spriggs were in a deep and heated conversation when I entered the dusty, dim shop a few blocks from Tattersall Goldsmiths. Jack worked on the railway; Gerry was also a machinist's apprentice — at a competing shop, but we fooled around together just the same.

"What are you fighting about?" I asked, slipping into a chair next to Jack and giving him a light, obligatory punch in the shoulder. I nodded a greeting at Gerry.

"Hey, Jem," Jack said agreeably. "There's another strike coming at the railyards. The Mail reported it this morning. I'll be on the picket line again, but we have to show those bastards they have to pay us what we're worth."

"And I'm sayin' the bastards will just find someone else to come in and do the work instead of you. The union's wrong this time. I tell you they're cuttin' off their noses to spite their faces."

"What'll it mean for the machine shops, Gerry?" I asked.

"Dunno yet. Less work from the yards, for sure. If the shop's men are in the same union, they'll have to go out too."

Maybe moving on was not such a bad idea after all. If Da had to strike again, or if business fell off, I could slip Mum a few dollars . . . assuming I could afford to.

"Listen. I have to ask you a question, but you have to keep this quiet."

"Yeah, sure, Jem," Jack said, but I did not get the feeling he was appreciating the importance of keeping my secret.

"I mean it. You have to promise you won't say anything to anyone. Okay?"

"What's going on, Jem? You sound serious."

"I am. Promise."

They crossed their hearts. I could not hope for more, so I jumped in.

"I got a new job."

"Y'what?" Gerry said.

"I did. And I need a new place to live. You two know of anywhere?"

Jack and Gerry nodded wisely. Both knew my father and his temper. The implications of leaving his shop were clear.

"It has to be cheap," I said, unnecessarily.

"Not a lot of palaces around here anyway," Jack said. "I think there's a spot in my boarding house. It ain't very fancy, I warn you."

"I don't need fancy. I need a room with a bed. And somewhere to cook."

"Landlady does the cooking, Jem. It's room and board. You get a room with cold water, bed, dresser, chair. She'll draw a hot bath once a week."

I mulled that over. It did not sound too bad.

"How much?" I asked, warily.

"Thirty bucks a month, with the hot water."

"Where is it?"

"Down Dundas way. Where's this new job?"

"On Yonge. Tattersall Goldsmiths."

Jack's eyes looked like they might pop out of his head.

"Y'mean jewellery?" Gerry asked.

I nodded, and a grin I had been valiantly trying to suppress broke through my control.

"Well, that'll make a change," Jack said. "When do you start?"

"Saturday, part-time. Got two weeks to get sorted out."

"Okay. Want to come and meet the landlady, see what she's got?"

"Yes," I breathed. "Can we go now?"

Jack laughed at my eagerness.

"Sure. Let's go. Want to come, Gerry?"

"Nah, I'll see you later. Say eight?"

"Sure, see you later."

Off we went to the boarding house, maybe fifteen minutes away on foot. Excitement churned my stomach. I was really doing this.

Chapter Five

Auntie Vogel's Boarding House sparkled. It seemed incongruous and impossible, considering seven large single men lived there, but the floors in the small foyer shone, the walls had recently been washed and not a speck of dust could be seen.

The large brick building housed a small neighbourhood grocery on the main floor, the landlady's quarters on the second, and four rooms on each of the third and fourth. One was open to let.

To me, I hoped.

Auntie Vogel herself was pushing fifty, I thought, judging by the stark streaks of grey in her hair. Tall and tautly muscled with rather severe lines around the mouth, she terrified me.

Until I looked more closely into her large brown eyes, flecked with amber and soft with sorrow. There was more to Auntie Vogel than her physical presentation told the beholder.

Jack had knocked on her private door, and she answered immediately.

"What do you want, Jack? Need a bath?"

"No, Auntie. I wanted to introduce you to someone. This is James Sinclair. He's a friend of mine."

"Ma'am," I said, unsure of how to address her. Auntie seemed far too familiar. "How do you do."

"I do just fine, young man. To what do I owe the honour?"

"I'm looking for a room, ma'am. Jack here says you may have one to let."

"That may be true, to the right person." I watched her size me up. "Are you the right person, James Sinclair?"

"Yes, ma'am, I think so. I'm hard-working and I don't cause any trouble."

"And can you afford it?"

That sent the butterflies in my gut racing, but I steeled myself and said, "Yes, ma'am. I will always pay you the rent, on time, no matter how hard I have to work."

An eyebrow quirked upward.

"What do you do for a living, James?" she asked.

"I work in a machine shop, but I'm about to become a goldsmith."

"Are you, now? Tattersall's or McLeod's?"

"Tattersall's, ma'am. I also help out at the train yards when they need extra hands."

"I hear they're striking again."

"Yes, ma'am. But they can't stay on strike forever."

She considered me for a very long time, arms crossed over her chest — arms that bulged almost like a man's. This woman worked hard, physically hard. I wondered if she had a husband.

"Would you like to do some work for me, as well?" came the surprising question. Likely not a man in the picture, then.

"I — I would," I stammered.

"All right, then. Twenty-five dollars a month and I'll throw in the bath if you can help me a bit with the heavy lifting."

I could feel Jack tense beside me, and apparently so could she.

"Now, Jack," she said. "You're not hardly reliable enough to help out around here. Too many late nights. But maybe young James is. We'll see. So, James Sinclair. When will you move in?"

"Would next week be all right, ma'am?"

"That'll be fine. Tell Graham Tattersall to send me a note about your impending employment or to pop in for some tea. And call me Auntie."

•   •   •

That turned out to be the easy part. As I suppose I knew it would be.

It took me four days to generate the courage to face my mum and tell her my plans. We had had a quiet dinner that night; Da was in the pub drowning — or perhaps fuelling — his fury over the strike. While I dreaded delivering my news to Mum, she dreaded Da coming home drunk again. At least I had this chance to speak with her alone.

Rarely home at that hour, I tried to help out when I did appear. I carried the supper dishes to the sink and filled it with soapy water, hoping that doing chores might smooth the upcoming conversation. I washed and she dried, while my sisters did the general tidying up.

"Mum. I have something to tell you." I could not go on.

"Yes, Jem?" she said, weary encouragement in her voice.

"I've, ah, I've decided to try a different occupation."

"What on Earth do you mean, son?"

"I've apprenticed myself to Graham Tattersall."

"The jeweller?" Mum's eyebrows furrowed together in amazement.

"Yes. I want to be a goldsmith."

"I know, Jem. It hasn't escaped my notice. Have you spoken to your father?"

I shook my head. Obviously, I had been avoiding that conversation even more than this one. Mum gave me a sad smile. We both knew how he would react when he found out about all this.

"Mum, I can't live here. You know Da. He'll kick me out anyway, after I quit the machine shop. And besides, Tattersall's isn't on strike. At least I'll be bringing in a bit of money."

She considered this for a moment. "Maybe Da will let you stay in that case," she said, hope clearing her voice. "It makes sense to scatter the eggs from the basket."

"No, Mum. I can't see it. But I won't be far, and I'll visit you every week. I promise."

She broke down. Her face fell into her hands, and the sobs she tried to swallow made her shoulders shake. Tears sprang into my own eyes, and I took my poor weeping Mum into my arms.

"I love you, Mum. But I have to do this. I just have to."

"I know," she snuffled into my shirt. "I will miss you awfully, Jem. Awfully. But you are growing up. You're getting so big. And you're almost eighteen! I canna stop you. You're — you're almost a man."

Shocked at this self-proclaimed revelation, she backed away and looked into my face, then reached up to touch the whiskers sprouting on my cheeks and chin.

"You were my baby. You are my baby. Such a beautiful baby boy, those big brown eyes staring at me as if you'd never seen me before, every time I'd pick you up and cuddle you."

Another sob escaped her as tears poured down my face; but Mum had not endured immigration, living with my father, grinding work, three babes and two miscarriages for nothing.

She gave one, sharp nod, wiped at her eyes and said, "All right, then. Have you found a place?"

"I have. Auntie Vogel's Boarding House. It's a fine, clean place. And she says I can help her with the heavier chores for reduced rent. I should have a bit left over to help you."

"When will you go?"

"On Sunday."

Logistics took over the conversation. We agreed I would slip away with my things, then return later to confront my father. Quitting the shop could wait a bit; the strike would delay that necessity. But I would have to tell Da.

• • •

I rose at first light on Saturday, anticipating my first day of work at Tattersall's. Sleep had come sporadically that night as I dreamed happily of diamonds and gold and the elegant women who would wear my beautiful jewellery.

My threadbare clothing might not live up to expectations at a jeweller's, but I did my best. I scrubbed my skin with soap and water until it turned red. I tugged on dark trousers, pulled on my cleanest, whitest shirt and combed my hair carefully.

Slipping out the door, I managed not to wake the household but still tiptoed down the first flight of stairs before putting on my shoes. Damned if I would ruin the day — the first of my new life — by having a confrontation with my father.

Tattersall's was not yet open when I arrived, a little breathless from excitement. I wandered down the street as it came to life in the thin morning sun, feeling every vibration of rattling horse and cart, every thump of barrel and box as supplies were delivered to the shops. People appeared from every direction, from around every corner. The very air rang and hummed and sang. This was now my street.

I turned back toward Tattersall's; it was nearly eight o'clock and I wanted to be Johnny on the spot when the boss unlocked the door. I was not, however, the first to arrive. A young woman had beaten me to it.

Unless she was an angel. I had never seen anyone so fair, so delicate. She appeared to be dressed in gossamer, swirls of whites and golds and blues, below a heart-shaped face so pale and upswept hair so light that she seemed to shimmer before me. Aquamarine eyes smiled as I approached the shop, which reassured me she was actually human and not an apparition.

I nodded politely, and she nodded back. We waited together in a brief uncomfortable silence until she gave a small cry of distress.

"Miss?" I said. "Is something wrong?"

"I seem to have misplaced my necklace," she said, clutching at her throat. "I came to have it repaired, but where is it?"

Her loss presented a thorny problem. I could hardly peer into her bodice to see if the offending piece of jewellery had landed there. If it had, I certainly could not pluck it out. At the same time, modesty would, I assumed, prevent her from fishing around under her fichu. And yes, I knew what a fichu was. Mum had sewn more than a few of them for local ladies needing to fill in their decolletages.

Neither did I know whether a woman worked at Tattersall's; unlikely. Perhaps the shop offered a private place in which to seek her necklace? The thought brought beads of sweat to my brow.

"The store will open any minute," I said, trying to sound comforting. "I'm sure Mr. Tattersall will be able to provide a solution."

"Perhaps you could just take a peek?" she said, drawing aside wisps of hair escaping her chignon and indicating the side of her neck. "It might be caught in the fabric."

A small spasm of doubt gripped my stomach. I hesitated, but the girl, for she was little more than that, gazed up at me with pleading eyes. I leaned forward with a shallow bow and peered at the indicated spot.

"I'm sorry," I said, "I don't see anything. If I may ask, why were you wearing it if it required repair?"

"Oh, I'd simply lost a small diamond. It was not really broken, you know. Or at least, I didn't think so. Thank you, Mister . . .?"

"James Sinclair."

"Are you a customer of Tattersall's?"

"I work for him, Miss . . .?"

"Oh dear, how rude of me." Her eyes twinkled, belying her comment. "Alice Garrison. Pleased to meet you, Mr. Sinclair."

Finally, Graham Tattersall unlocked the door. Saved.

"Good morning, James Junior. And good morning, Miss Garrison. You have met, then."

"Miss Garrison was just telling me she may have lost her necklace, sir."

"I see. Were you wearing it?"

"Yes."

"You'd better come in."

Tattersall gestured for Alice Garrison to lead the way, then turned to me with a strange expression, a quirk to the corner of his mouth. His face told me this was not the first time Miss Garrison had arrived at the goldsmith's shop in distress. I had no idea what that meant.

Chapter Six

Mr. Tattersall escorted Alice Garrison to the back of the goldsmith's shop, where she might seek her necklace in relative privacy with the aid of a mirror. Returning, he gestured to the bench I had briefly occupied the day I came to apply for the job.

"This will be yours, James," he said. "We will begin with a few lessons in jewellery repair."

He handed me a large gold gentleman's ring, bent and twisted well beyond wearing.

"As you can see, this has been brutally damaged," Tattersall said, sighing, and I felt his pain upon seeing his work so afflicted. "We must bring it back to its round and shiny original self, if possible."

He described the process of heating the ring and beating it back into shape. The rest I already knew; burnish the hell out of it until it shone like the sun itself. I nodded and bent my head to begin when the young lady emerged from the back room, flushed and tittering.

"I am such a silly goose," she said. "Here it is, Mr. Tattersall. You see? A diamond has fallen out. Can you replace it for me?"

"Of course, Miss Garrison. If I have one just the right size, we can have it repaired for you by Monday or possibly the next day. Let me have a look. Would you like to take a seat?"

"Oh, yes, thank you. I am quite exhausted. I felt I must be here early; I was ever so worried."

But Miss Garrison did not take a seat. She tottered to my bench and looked over my shoulder — which was distracting in the extreme. Not only could I smell her perfume and feel her breath on my neck, but she observed me doing a job I had never done before.

"I see you're working on Papa's ring," she said.

"Am I?"

"Yes. He dropped it the other day, and a horse and cart got to it before he could."

"Ah. That explains why it's in such bad shape." Literally, I added to myself. This ring was squashed.

She laughed, a sound like Christmas bells tinkling over a field of snow.

"A ring is no match for a horse's hoof," she sang.

"Clearly."

Miss Garrison then found it necessary to touch my arm, evidently a show of confidence judging by her next words.

"I know you can fix it, Mr. Sinclair."

Tattersall, thank God, returned from his desk with the diamond wallet he had been rummaging through.

"I think, Miss Garrison, this will do nicely," he said, displaying a tiny white gem for her approval.

"Oh yes, that looks beautiful. Thank you, Mr. Tattersall. Please put it on Papa's bill for me, will you? When should I pick it up?"

"Perhaps Monday afternoon? Five o'clock?"

"That would be perfect. Thank you. Goodbye, Mr. Tattersall, Mr. Sinclair."

She gathered her gossamer in one hand, smiled graciously, and swept out the door. I gaped for a moment, then turned back to the devastated golden band I held tightly in a clamp. In my peripheral vision, I saw my boss shake his head slightly, as if in disapproval. Again I wondered what had just transpired; certainly more than I could guess at. It had seemed like a normal interaction.

I put Miss Garrison firmly out of my thoughts and turned them fully to her father's ring.

Two hours later, I presented the relatively round item to the master. He took it from me, examined it closely through his loupe, and pointed to a small pit in the gold.

"Massage that out of there, James, and I think perhaps you've done it." He looked up and gave me a smile. "Not bad for your first day."

"Thank you, sir."

As the day went on, customers came and went as I attacked one repair after another. I had never set a diamond before, so Tattersall himself took on the Garrison necklace.

Being Saturday, Tattersall's closed at five instead of at seven. By then, I had unsquashed Papa Garrison's ring, sized two rings down and one up, and repaired a chain's clasp.

I had never been happier.

• • •

"You're not quitting the machine shop, James," my father said the next day.

"I am, Da. I'm sorry, but I want to be a goldsmith. Besides, the shop is under strike action."

"I am your father, and I say you're not quitting." He rose from his lumpy chair to glare at me. "Do you hear me, James Junior?"

"I do, but I'm nearly eighteen, Da. I can do what I want."

That infuriated him, as I suppose I knew it would. His arm shot out, hand fisted; but I was faster than he, if not as strong, and had grown substantially since my last serious beating. I caught the punch in my hand before it landed on my chin and stared back at him, right in the eyes.

My defiance caught him by surprise. He did not attempt to hit me with the other hand, but simply stood there for a moment, breathing heavily. I could not decide if I felt relieved or devastated to see him disarmed.

"Get the hell out," he said, menace dripping from the words.

"I will," I said, dropping his hand.

As I turned away, he smacked me on the back of the head, hard enough to snap my face forward. I whirled, ready to battle it out, but he stepped away from me, out of reach. I gave him a nod, an acknowledgment that I had won this round, and went to pack my things.

They were few enough. Mum and my sisters crept into my partitioned room, silently weeping, and hugged me hard. I slipped away, then, never again to live in my parents' home.

I landed on Auntie Vogel's doorstep half an hour later, torn between the grief of leaving Mum and the excitement of starting my new life as a man.

"Hello, James Sinclair. I was not expecting to see you for another week or so."

"Hello, ah, Auntie." The honorific did not yet fall easily from my lips. "I'm afraid I've had to leave home a bit early. Would it be possible . . ."

"To move in early?"

"Yes."

"Come in, James."

CHAPTER SEVEN

My room was spotless, in keeping with Auntie's obvious passion for cleanliness. Was she also godly, I wondered? I had seen no evidence of iconography; no cross hung over the mantel, no Bible lay open on her desk or table. Even so, I pledged to watch my language.

Minutes after being invited to stay, I settled in with my few possessions, hanging them in the closet or tucking them into the drawers. Now what? I had not thought further than this moment. A crushing loneliness stabbed my heart. I already missed my family, a scant hour after leaving.

Then came the clanging of a bell, loud and persistent. Dinner, apparently, was ready.

I clattered down the stairs and realized I had no idea where I was going. Standing uncertainly in the foyer, my nose finally told me which door to approach. This choice was confirmed by the arrival of two other boarders, who stopped short when they saw me.

"Hello," said one. "I'm Pete Masters. You must be the new man."

"Yes. James Sinclair. Nice to meet you."

"And you. This is Harry Simpkins."

Handshakes all around, and a three-man dive through the door. My stomach had not been full for twenty-four hours, and the aroma of Sunday roast beef made me salivate. Jack was already at the table along with two other men, whom he introduced as John and Martin. Apparently the other two boarders were at work; she would save their plates in a warming oven, I was told.

Bread and potatoes were already being passed around as Auntie swept in with a massive tray bearing the meat. A girl of perhaps fifteen followed her carrying a gravy boat in one hand and a dish of beans and peas in the other. It looked like a feast to me. I could not remember the last time we'd had beef at home.

While we devoured Auntie's delicious meal, little conversation flowed for the first few minutes, as you would expect from a gathering of six young and very hungry men. Once our stomachs were partly full, the chatter began — about strikes and work and bosses and general Toronto news. My tablemates avoided talking about women. I guessed their reticence was due to a great respect for our landlady, and later learned I was right.

She ate with us, and so did the teenage girl — Connie by name. The meal finished, every man at the table picked up his plate and bore it to the kitchen, and of course I followed suit.

"Is there something I can help you with, Auntie?" I asked, having delivered my utensils to the sink.

"Not tonight, James. I think the other boys are going out. You should go with them, have some fun. Tomorrow you can help me with the baths and some wood chopping."

"Come out with us, James," Jack encouraged me. "We're off to the pool hall."

"If you're sure, Auntie."

"I am. Off you go. Have a good time. Remember your curfew, gentlemen. Eleven, no later, on a Sunday night."

"Yes, Auntie," Jack said, something like reverence in his voice. "We'll behave."

She had them well-trained, I thought, as I pulled my coat on. The reasons for Auntie's iron grip on her boarding house and its residents bore further investigation.

"Hey Jack," I said as we hurried down the muddy street, trying to race ahead of the icy wind. "Tell me about Auntie. Seems to me you really like her. Since when do you behave?"

Jack laughed. "Did you enjoy your roast beef?"

"God, yes. It was fantastic. Is the food always so good?"

"Yep. Best boarding house food in the city, as far as I know. You were lucky to get that room, you know. I'll tell you more when we get to the hall. It's too damned cold to talk out here."

We clattered into the dim space, the six of us making a boisterous noise as we ordered beer and descended on a table. While the other four played the first game, Jack told me what he knew about our landlady — much of it, he warned, based on rumour and conjecture.

She had been married once, a long time ago, but her husband had died very young. His passing left her with the house and a little bit of money: not enough to live on, but sufficient funds to keep her business. She had been considered a beauty, at one time . . .

"She's still very pretty," I interjected. "In a strong kind of way."

"She is. Shut up, Jem. Do you want to hear the story or don't you?"

"Sorry. Go on."

"She never remarried. The rumour is that she fell in love again several years after her husband passed, but the man was a wanted fugitive. He was either captured, killed, or got away somewhere, somehow. No one knows, and Auntie never speaks of it."

"Oooohhh . . ." escaped from my lips. A mystery. How fascinating.

"She's been alone ever since. Apart from us, of course. She's a very tough lady. If you don't follow the house rules, you're out. But if you do, she treats you like a son. Great food and lots of it. When we get sick, she takes care of us. The house is always warm and clean. And everyone knows she runs a good house, which doesn't hurt us, either. The girls know she keeps us in line, and so do the girls' parents." Jack grinned. "Easy to get a date. We're known as Auntie's boys."

"What are the house rules? She hasn't told me yet."

"Well, there are the curfews. We have to be in by eleven on Sundays, and ten on weeknights. Midnight on Fridays and Saturdays. We take our dishes to the kitchen after meals, and weeknights we're expected to help wash and dry on a two-at-a-time schedule. Our rooms have to be tidy; no dirty clothes on the floor. No approaching Connie or the other girl for a date. And we have the run of the house and the yard, except for the basement. We're not allowed to go down there."

"Why not?"

"No idea. Just not allowed. So we don't. Partly out of respect, but partly because we don't want to get kicked out. Auntie's is a great deal, James. Don't fuck it up."

"I won't."

But my curiosity was piqued. What was in the basement? Would I ever find out?

Pete appeared right in front of me, holding out his cue. Apparently, he and Harry had lost the game.

"Your turn," he said, with a wry grin. "See if you and Jack can beat those bastards."

• • •

Since the machine shop had closed due to the strike, I presented myself at Tattersall's early the next morning. I had not quit my job yet, but there was no one at the shop to resign to.

Tattersall looked surprised to see me but waved me into my chair.

"Glad to have you, James. Thomas is ill, so I can use another pair of hands."

He handed me two rings that needed sizing, and I fell to my work with joyful focus.

Until Alice Garrison reappeared. She swanned in, her flowing dress a pale green this time, and greeted my boss effusively.

"Am I too early, Mr. Tattersall? I am just so anxious to have my beautiful necklace back. And Papa was wondering about his ring, as well."

"No, no, Miss Garrison. We're ready for you. James here has fixed your father's ring, and I've replaced your diamond. I'll just get them for you."

He turned to the table bearing the finished work and brought forth the jewellery for her inspection.

"Oh, Mr. Sinclair," she breathed. "You are a hero. Look at Papa's ring! It's perfect. He'll be so pleased."

"Thank you, Miss Garrison."

"You're ever so welcome. Papa will be by to pay you, Mr. Tattersall. I hope that's all right?"

"Yes, yes, of course."

"Well, goodbye then." She smiled at me. My stomach lurched. "Goodbye, Mr. Sinclair."

Off she went, and I took a very deep breath. Tattersall shook his head and returned to his bench. What was it about Miss Garrison, I wondered, that seemed to baffle him?

The day went on unremarkably after that. Tattersall's did not lack for customers; it was busy, even on a Monday, and by five o'clock I had long since forgotten about Alice Garrison. We packed up our work and tucked the little items into the monstrous safe. I followed Tattersall out the door; he locked it and left me with a wave. "See you tomorrow, James."

I headed in the opposite direction toward my new home, feeling lighter and happier than I had in months. The delicate work, compared to the heavy lifting and noise and filth of the machine shop, thrilled me to my soul; and the thought of returning to Auntie's for a hot meal — and plenty of company — warmed my heart.

I almost ran into her. Absorbed in my thoughts, I paid little attention to the people on the street. That said, she seemed to appear out of nowhere, a fur-lined cape flowing behind her with a vaguely royal flourish.

"Oh, Mr. Sinclair. How nice to see you again."

"Hello, Miss Garrison. Are you on your way home?"

"Yes. Just doing a little shopping. And you?"

"Yes, on my way home for dinner. I hope you have a very nice evening."

I also hoped to carry on, but she placed a hand on my arm and fluttered her eyelashes at me. Hell. What was I supposed to do? I could hardly just walk away.

"Perhaps you could escort me? I would very much appreciate it. These streets . . . you never know who you might encounter."

I doubted someone would abduct her right on Yonge Street, and also wondered why she was alone. Did the Garrisons not have servants? But it would have been ungentlemanly to turn her down, so I offered her my arm.

"Which way?" I asked.

"Oh, just down here. It's not very far. Thank you so much, Mr. Sinclair."

She talked incessantly about her necklace, her father's ring, the weather and the latest concerts she had attended. I was grateful for her patter; I had no idea what to say, so I just nodded occasionally as we walked along. Alice

Garrison was lovely, and my heart pounded in her company, but she was also a chatterbox and an enigma.

Fifteen minutes later, due in part to our slow pace enforced by her high-heeled boots, we arrived at the Garrison home. Mansion, really.

"Well, here we are," she fluted cheerily.

Then she turned to me, smiled, stood on tiptoe and kissed my cheek. Stunned as I was, my peripheral vision nonetheless perceived a curtain flutter in a window.

She whirled around before I could react and hurried up the path to her front door.

Chapter Eight

"She what?" Jack asked rather loudly when I confided the events of the afternoon just before dinner. "Up and kissed you in the street?"

"Right here," I said, pointing to the spot on my cheek.

"What did you do?"

"Nothing. Kind of surprised me, and I could hardly kiss her back."

"True. You want to watch yourself with that minx, James. Her father is one of the richest and most powerful men in the city, if not the province. I'd bet you're not quite what he's hoping for in a son-in-law. No offence."

Obviously, I thought. None taken.

"What if she does it again?"

"I don't know, but unless you're really interested — and stupid — I'd steer clear."

That night, I helped Auntie heat the water for the baths in massive copper kettles on the steaming stove. She bustled about, stacking clean towels on the kitchen table, and occasionally casting me strange, furrowed glances. After twenty minutes of this, she finally came out with it.

"I'm sorry, James, but I'm afraid I overheard you speaking with Jack. About the young lady."

"Oh."

"Miss Garrison, was it?"

"Yes."

"She's taken a shine to you, then. I assume you met her at Tattersall's."

"Yes. She had a broken necklace — well, it was missing a diamond — and brought it in."

Auntie stopped bustling and braced herself against the table, arms crossed.

"You are a lovely young man, James. Tall and dark, handsome and strong and kind. Perhaps she can't resist you. But maybe there's something else going on? You're hardly in the same social group. Is she trying to enrage a suitor? If so, watch your back. She's a prize, and no mistaking. Do you like her?"

My face blazed red from the heat of the kettles, and from Auntie's assessment of my personal assets. But she made me think. Did I like Alice?

"I don't know, Auntie. I really don't know her. She's very pretty."

"She is that. She is also under the age of majority, James, so watch your step."

I spluttered some sort of agreement to her warning. But I felt shock at her suggestion that I might attempt intimacy with this gossamer girl. It had not occurred to me. Nice young ladies of her standing would never engage in premarital sex. Would they?

"Have you met George Garrison?" Auntie asked, breaking into my thoughts.

"No. I've fixed his ring, though."

"He's a daunting son of a bitch. Big, rich blowhard. And ruthless, which is how he got to be so rich. I want you to be careful, James. You're one of my boys now."

• • •

Miss Garrison, thank God, did not appear the next day. Nor the next, nor the next. I relaxed a bit, although I constantly worried and wondered about what might happen if and when I saw her again. Marriage could not possibly be on her mind. What did she want from me, then, if anything? Maybe she gave me that kiss simply in thanks for walking her home. After Auntie's and Jack's warnings, I rather hoped so.

The days fell away like pearls slipping from a string. The strike wore on, and I fairly forgot about quitting the machine shop. I loved working for Tattersall, especially when I compared it to the misery of my previous job. I learned something new about goldsmithing every day from my patient, kind and encouraging mentor.

In the evenings, eating Auntie's delicious dinners in company with several other young men may have been the most fun I had ever had, especially when we went out on the town afterward. My fellow tenants and I daily devoured enormous helpings of beef roast, pork chops, whole chickens stuffed with sausage and bread, and other succulent dishes.

I worked hard for Tattersall and for Auntie, but also played hard. Every Sunday, I would manage an afternoon visit with Mum and sometimes my sisters. I could spare a few dollars after my rent was paid — Tattersall had given me a raise in short order — and slipped them to my mother. I did miss her terribly, but life proved so much easier away from the parental home, I never once regretted my decision to leave.

Life burbled along in this fashion for some time. I thought that, just possibly, things might turn out all right after all. The only missing piece was female companionship. Nineteen by now, I wanted to look for a wife or at least a girlfriend but had no idea how to go about it. I may have been one of "Auntie's boys," but first I had to meet some young women to approach for dates.

Aware of this lack, Jack and my other housemates, along with Gerry Spriggs, began dragging me to places where the fairer sex would also appear. That meant musical events, coffee houses and staying out of the pool hall at least a couple of nights a week. Nice young women did not play pool or drink beer.

Off we went one Wednesday evening to a classical concert at a nearby church. I would have rolled my eyes, but I was promised a banquet of beauties. A string quartet played Bach and other notable composers, but I barely heard the music. Beauties there were indeed, and they were legion.

I must have looked like a complete idiot, staring around the room as if I had never seen a female human before. Jack leaned over at one point, put his hand under my chin and lightly tapped it.

"Don't drool, Jem," he whispered. "Self-confidence is key. Don't let them see what you're thinking."

"Right," I answered, and smoothed my face into an expression of devil-may-care.

"That's better," Jack said, his chest quaking with suppressed laughter.

Tea and sweets were invariably served after these musical events, rare opportunities for young people of both sexes to reasonably get together and, well, evaluate the options. I accepted a large mug of sweet, milky black tea and a chocolate treat, and surveyed the room.

Miss Garrison was not part of the bevy of at least twenty lovely girls. I breathed and managed to plaster a smile on my face. But how in hell was this done? Was it protocol to simply approach a pretty girl? Or did one have to be introduced? How had I missed this piece of crucial social understanding?

Jack, after procuring his own refreshments, walked over to me and said under his breath, "Relax. You won't have to do a thing. Just wait."

He nodded at a group of four young women in animated conversation a few yards away. To my extreme and complete surprise, every pair of eyes either flicked or glanced in our direction.

"They're talking about you," Jack said. "Guaranteed."

"Me?"

"You. You're the new meat on the hook. And obviously they like what they see."

How he knew all of this was entirely beyond me. He would soon be proven right. Slowly and inexorably, the feminine huddle inched its way toward us. Jack did his part and stepped backward slowly, a foot at a time, while feigning uproarious conversation with Gerry and me. Pete joined us, and we had a full team to take on the upcoming battle of wits.

It took a few moments, but Jack finally, and very gently, bumped into one of the encroaching beauties.

"Oh! My goodness, I am so sorry," he exclaimed to the tiny blonde morsel. "Are you all right? I hope I haven't spilled your tea."

Very smooth, Jack, I thought sarcastically. But it worked.

"No, no, sir. I'm quite all right. Thank you for your concern, Mister. . .?"

"Jack Malone, at your service. May I introduce Pete Masters, Gerry Spriggs and James Sinclair?"

They did the predictable things. Simpered a little, nodded, blushed, said hello.

"I'm Clara," said the morsel. "These are my friends — Bets, Sarah and Meg."

Oh, Meg. Nutmeg, I thought: her hair was a soft brown, matching her chocolate eyes. White arms, soft yet slim, emerged from her short-sleeved dress. The tiniest hint of breast swelled from her bodice. I stared helplessly.

Then she looked up at me and must have seen the look in my eyes: she blushed, a delicate pink creeping into her cheeks. Never in my life had I wanted so badly to touch anyone. My brain was on fire; what could I say to her?

"Did you enjoy the concert, ladies?" asked Lothario Jack, bringing forth the obvious and perfect question.

"Oh yes," said Clara. "I did. Did you?"

"Beautiful. May I refill your teacup?" Jack responded, imbuing the first word with double meaning. Brilliant.

"Oh, very kind. Thank you."

Jack gently took Blonde Morsel by the arm, leading her away to the refreshment table. So that is how this is done, I thought. Now to cull Lovely Nutmeg from the group. I cleared the emotion clogging my throat and prepared to speak, but she beat me to it.

"What did you think of the concert, Mr. Sinclair?"

"They are very good musicians," I replied. Mum, fortunately, had exposed me to music over the years, so I did not feel like a complete idiot expressing my opinion. "I prefer more rousing music, though."

Her laughter confused me at first, but the sound was warm, rich, titillating. "Just like a man. Do you prefer Beethoven? Mozart?"

"I do."

Our conversation from there came easily, lightly. I felt as if I were falling.

At the end of the evening, I screwed up the courage to ask if I could see her again. Perhaps coffee, or a walk by the lake on a warmer day? She agreed, and smiled, and gave me her address, suggesting I send a message with a possible time and day. I said I would do so, and very soon.

"It was lovely to meet you, Mr. Sinclair."

"James. Please call me James."

"All right. James. And call me Meg." She smiled again and was whisked from the church hall in a flurry of coats and scarves and friends.

I would send the message soon. The next day. If I could wait that long.

Chapter Nine

Infatuation is not conducive to paying attention. At work the next day, I dropped my rawhide hammer, lost (but later found) a tiny diamond, and overheated solder I was attempting to flow into a ring.

"What is the matter with you today, James? You're normally reasonably co-ordinated," Tattersall said, exasperation in his voice.

"I'm sorry, sir. I will do better."

"Let me guess," he said. "A young lady? I hope it isn't Alice Garrison."

"No, sir."

"No it isn't a young lady, or no it isn't Miss Garrison?"

"The latter, Mr. Tattersall."

"Ah. So it is a young lady."

I sighed. Not much missed Graham Tattersall's notice. I supposed he was familiar with the ways of love and courtship, having been a jeweller for thirty years.

"I'm afraid so, sir."

"Do you have a date with this lovely person? I assume she is lovely."

"She is, sir. Very. No, I don't, not yet. I admit I've been trying to write a message to her in my head."

"Hence the dropping of things. Well, get on with it, James. Maybe then you can focus on your work." But he smiled at me sympathetically, taking the sting out of the last words.

"I'll do so on my break. Thank you very much, sir."

The message duly sent an hour later, my state of mind remained in upheaval. Now I had to wait for a response. How long would that take? Hours? Days? Forever?

It proved to be about twenty-four hours. The next day, a faintly-perfumed missive arrived at the goldsmith's shop, agreeing to coffee and a walk on Sunday. Two days to wait. My guts had never been so full of flying insects in my entire life.

On Sunday, I scrubbed myself raw in the bath, ignoring the rising issue of arousal. Guilt almost overwhelmed me, because this would be the first Sunday since leaving the family home that I would not see my mother. But the spring bloomed, and the allure of seeing Meg again overcame thoughts of abandoned responsibility.

I walked to her home, fortunately not more than half an hour away, bearing a tiny posy. Approaching the front step, I almost lost my nerve . . . and then her father opened the door.

"Are you James Sinclair?" the man asked.

"Yes, sir."

"Well. Hm. You'd better come in so I can take a look at you."

I do not know why I did not expect a good going-over before being allowed to escort Meg away from the home. In fact, I should have been surprised her parents would even consider letting her leave the house with, really, a stranger. In we went, to meet Meg and her mother sitting rather pensively in the living room.

"Hello, Mr. Sinclair," Meg said, quite shyly, as I handed her the posy. "Thank you so much; this is very kind. May I introduce my parents, John and Marion Blackwood."

"It's very nice to meet you," I said. I hoped they did not notice the small quaver in my voice.

"Tell me, James Sinclair. What do you do?" asked the father.

"I'm a goldsmith, sir," I said, sounding proud to my own ears. "I work for Mr. Tattersall over on Yonge."

"And do you live with your parents, young man?"

"No, sir. I live at Auntie Vogel's boarding house."

"Do you, now. Are your parents in the city?"

"Yes, sir, they are. I see them every week." Not quite true, of course, but I really did not want to dive into a conversation about my father.

Marion Blackwood nodded at her husband. A good sign?

"Well, young man, you will stay in public places with my daughter, at the coffee house and the boardwalk, and behave yourself. If you have not returned by five, I will have the police out to look for you. Are we clear?"

"Yes, sir. I will take very good care of her. I promise. And we will be back by five."

Passed the test. I helped Meg on with her coat, and we escaped down the path as demurely as possible. A block away, Meg exhaled and gave a small giggle.

"I'm sorry about that. Father can be very protective."

"As he should be. If I had such a beautiful daughter, I would be too," I said — gallantly, I hoped.

"That's very sweet, James." She blushed again, which drove me wild. Those pink cheeks were almost more than I could bear. "May I take your arm?"

Damn. Was I supposed to offer? I thought that would be forward, but I had no idea.

"Of course. I'm sorry."

"Don't be."

She slipped her slender hand through the crook of my arm, and my head reflexively ducked for a moment at her touch. Oh, Meg, I thought. How can you be so lovely?

We walked in companionable silence for a while. Despite the effect she had on me, I also felt remarkably comfortable in her presence. She was easy to be quiet with.

Eventually, though, we started to chat. At first, we commented on the first robin pecking at a lawn not yet quite free of dirty snow; and on a group of obnoxious boys clattering down the other side of the street.

Once in the coffee shop, I could not bear it any longer. I asked her about herself.

She was eighteen. She attended a private college, with the intention of becoming a teacher. She played piano — rather well, apparently. She loved music, which explained her regular attendance at the city's many concerts. She had a younger sister.

Then it was my turn, and I told her about my family, leaving out the bad bits; how I had worked in a machine shop and occasionally at the train yards, but was now apprenticed to Graham Tattersall; that my parents were from Scotland, and that I had two sisters.

"What made you decide to become a goldsmith?" she asked. "It's not a very common occupation."

"I'm not sure. I've always liked shiny things. Women look pretty in jewellery. And I think I could be good at it."

My own reticence fell away, and I told her about making the steel ring for Mum, hammering it and polishing it until it shone. She rewarded me with an amazed expression, her pink lips forming an O of surprise.

"And you thought of that all by yourself?"

"I — I guess I did."

"That was so sweet of you. Did your mum like it?"

"Yes, I think she did." Now I had to change the subject, and fast, or I was going to blurt out all the terrible things my father had done. "Would you like to go for a walk now, Meg? Are you finished your coffee?"

"Yes, I am, and that would be lovely."

Outside, the wind had come up, forcing us to clutch our coats tightly. I had not planned for inclement weather, and suggested we walk inland instead of toward the lake. It would be freezing by the water.

At the next corner we made our way toward a small park, somewhat sheltered by trees, and behind a small open shed, she stopped and turned to me. Significantly shorter than I — well, I am tall — she was forced to look up at me, exposing her long throat with its delicate, creamy skin.

Even before she said anything, my breath caught in my own throat.

"I know you won't ask me," said pretty Meg, her pleading eyes looking directly into my own. "And I hope you won't think I'm a terrible hussy. But I would very much like you to kiss me, James."

"Oh, Meg, I want to. But what would your parents say?" I looked around to see if anyone was observing us. "Would they be angry?"

"Perhaps. Perhaps not. I don't know, really. They're very good people. But I am eighteen. And it is only a kiss."

Plenty of folk married at eighteen or nineteen, I thought. And it would be only a kiss.

And so, I lowered my head and gently placed my lips on hers, already slightly pursed in anticipation. She tasted like honey and coffee and flowers and wind; her mouth felt like slightly damp rose petals, excruciatingly soft and silky. After a moment, I drew away and regarded her, to see if her gaze would betray her feelings.

"Was that all right?"

"More than all right. Again, please."

The first contact was sweet, innocent, delicious. The second kiss was different altogether. Her tongue slipped between my lips, tentatively at first; and then we were on fire. I pulled her against my body, feeling her breasts pressing into my chest, her entire body quivering against me. I perceived her reaction even more than my own and wondered what — or if — she was thinking as our mouths made love.

My senses reeled as I gave up trying to read her mind and gave in to the sensation of her lips on mine, her tongue entwined with mine. It was my first erotic kiss. Was it hers?

Humans must breathe, and we finally released each other, but Meg remained enclosed in my arms.

"So that's what it's like," she whispered, as if to herself, and answering my silent question. "I'm . . . I'm glad it was you, James."

Speechless, I tried to come up with an appropriate response to the compliment, even as my body groaned and tightened with desire for this delightful, beautiful girl.

"Yes," I finally said, inadequately. "I am too, Meg. Very glad."

Reality began to bang a drum in my head. I surreptitiously checked my watch; quarter to five. I had to get her back home. We could not be late; if we were, another date would be out of the question.

"Beautiful Meg, we must go. Your father will kill me if we're not back in fifteen minutes."

"Oh!" she cried. "Oh yes. It would be awful if . . ."

"If I couldn't see you again."

"Yes . . . oh, James . . ."

I kissed her again and smiled to break the mood — to keep us on track. We hurried along, arms entwined, until we reached the end of her block and

I released her, almost dying inside. I walked her to the door, worrying a bit about her very flushed face.

"Say it was the wind," I suggested.

"Am I pink?"

"Very pink. May I see you next weekend?"

"Yes. Yes, please. Thank you so much for the . . . for everything."

She directed a longing look at my lips, then turned, flew up the steps, opened the door and disappeared inside. Right on time.

CHAPTER TEN

Had he asked, I would have presented Lucifer with my soul to see Meg again the next day, but it was impossible. Instead, I put my head down and worked my backside off, tearing off ring sizings and building settings with fervour.

Despite flinging myself into my job, the week dragged on. Concentration only went so far in staving off the recurring memory of that second kiss.

Jack and Auntie noticed my dreamy state at home and teased me — mercilessly and gently, respectively. I found I had the capacity to blush, more or less perpetually. That is what falling in love for the first time does to a man. Turns him to jelly.

Saturday finally came. Tattersall and I bagged up all the little bits of gold, the diamonds and sapphires, the partly finished rings, and locked them securely in the safe.

"I trust you will have a nice Sunday," he said, giving me a meaningful look.

"I hope so, sir. Same to you."

He grinned and indicated for me to precede him out the door. Tattersall turned left and I right, ready for pork roast and a rousing night at the pool hall.

Two blocks into the walk home, there she was: Alice Garrison, shining in the late afternoon light, standing all alone by a shop doorway. I considered dashing across the street to avoid her, but mentally slapped myself for being a coward. When I reached her, I gave her a smile, a nod and a good evening. She stepped out into my path and put a hand on my arm. Damn.

"May I speak with you privately, Mr. Sinclair?" Her voice was plaintive, her eyes pleading.

"Certainly, Miss Garrison. Is something wrong? Are you all right?"

Instead of answering, she took me by the hand, led me around the corner and dragged me into the alley, which was alarming in the extreme. If anyone saw me with her under these circumstances, what would they think?

Before I could gather my wits, she placed her hands on my chest and stood on tiptoe, her lips reaching for mine. I suppose I instinctively lowered my head, which proved to be a bad move, because we were suddenly kissing. A few seconds later, horrified at myself, I broke the embrace.

She looked up at me with a small pout and said, "I hear you've been seeing Meg Blackwood."

"Where did you hear that?" I asked, buying time. Why would she care?

"Oh, around. News travels, Mr. Sinclair. May I call you James? I was hoping, you know . . ." and she raised her eyebrows at me.

"I'm sorry, I don't understand, Miss Garrison."

"That you and I might . . ."

Holy God. She had to be kidding. Why would the daughter of a Toronto baron of industry have any interest in a poor machinist's son?

"Miss Garrison, I don't think that would work out very well, would it? Your father . . ."

"I don't care about my father," she cried with heat, and flung herself at me again, burying her face in my chest. "I want you. I want you to take me away. We could run away somewhere, maybe to the West, and live happily and have babies and . . ."

I think I went into complete shock. What had spurred this outburst? What had I done to attract this coddled slip of a girl? I felt like a heel, but I pushed her away from me to look into her streaming face.

"Miss Garrison. I'm afraid it's out of the question. I don't have enough money laid by to make that kind of a trip, and certainly not enough to start a family. And frankly, you don't really know me. Nor I you."

"I do know you! You're terribly handsome and kind and gentle. Isn't that enough? We'll fall in love and have a wonderful life together."

I do not know how I extricated myself from her grip. It is not easy to do such a thing gently.

"I just can't," I gasped. "It's . . . not reasonable, Miss Garrison. I must go. I'm very sorry."

I ran. How do you address such a ridiculous plea? It was not something we could discuss in a reasonable way. I was not remotely interested in her idea, either, largely because I had fallen for Meg. Besides, how old was Alice? Sixteen? They would have the police chasing us, and I would be charged with kidnapping. No doubt about it.

Completely winded by the time I reached Auntie's, I dragged myself up the front steps and up to my room. Dinner loomed in half an hour; I had to compose myself before I faced my roommates and particularly Auntie. She could smell a problem from the kitchen.

Sucking in huge breaths helped. My heart finally stopped banging in my chest, and I went to the sink to wash, throwing handfuls of icy water over my burning face. I had never been so confused.

The dinner bell rang, followed immediately by the sound of doors opening and slamming shut, and the noise of heavy feet clattering on wooden steps. Jack called loudly to Pete, making plans for the evening. I pasted a bland look on my face and peered at myself in the mirror. My eyes betrayed my confusion, but it was time to eat. If I did not appear, someone would certainly come looking for me, or at least shouting.

"James! Where the hell are you?"

Sure enough. "Coming!"

Down the stairs I went, practicing my calm face. My arrival in the dining room brought a little cheer and a round of "finally" and "glad you could join us." They were teasing me. I loved it, and I grinned back at Auntie's other boys.

Moments later, Auntie herself came in, bearing a monstrous platter of roast pork and potatoes. She gave me a sharp look, quirked an eyebrow and returned to the kitchen to fetch the salad and bread.

"How was your day, James?" she said as she sat down.

"Fine, Auntie. Busy."

"Mm hmm. And yours, Jack?"

"Great, thanks, Auntie."

She went around the table, asking each man about his day. But I knew she did not buy my answer. I could see the disbelief in her face. Was I really so easy to read? Or was the woman endowed with special powers? Either way, she trapped me in the kitchen after the other men had delivered their plates and utensils.

"Can you help me with something, please, James?" she asked. What could I do? It was part of the low-rent deal.

"Of course."

I stayed behind, shifting nervously from one foot to the other, trying to decide if I would tell her the story of Alice. She dispatched Connie to gather dirty towels and got right to the point.

"What's happened, James?"

"What do you mean, Auntie?"

"Don't 'what do you mean' me, James Sinclair. I can see it in your eyes. They've gone black and wild. Practically rolling in your head. Talk."

"I don't know if I should, Auntie."

"Something to do with a girl, then?"

Reluctantly, I nodded.

"You're afraid that telling me would be disrespectful to the young lady."

"Yes, I guess so."

"You haven't . . ."

"No! Of course not." I felt the blood rushing to my cheeks.

She released an enormous sigh of relief. "Well, thank goodness for that. And yes, I believe you, James. You should see your face. Are you all right, though? You have me right worried."

"I'm all right, Auntie. Thank you."

"If you want to talk, I'm always here. And I am a vault, James. I would never tell anyone. I hope you know that."

"Yes, Auntie. I know."

"Off you go. If you change your mind, I'll be up when you return. I hear the boys getting their boots on. Hurry up."

• • •

I managed to have a good time that night with the boys, although I tossed restlessly in my narrow bed until the wee hours, replaying the encounter with Alice and anticipating seeing Meg in the afternoon.

I slept in and finally rolled into the kitchen mid-morning to rustle up a cup of coffee. Bacon and fried eggs had been left in the oven, and a pastry awaited on the counter. Auntie was definitely the finest landlady on Earth.

I had to see Mum. I could not go two weeks without seeing her, and I had fifteen dollars to give her besides. Da was not home; she had sent me a message to come by along with that information. I found my former home incredibly depressing. I hugged my poor mother and visited over tea for an hour. When I left, she held me close and told me she loved me.

That left slightly less time for Meg. I raced to the Blackwood home, explained and apologized for being a little late, and we retraced our steps from the week before — drinking coffee, wandering through the park and kissing madly behind the little open shed. It was heavenly, but I felt a flash of guilt when remembering kissing Alice the day before. It had not been my fault, but still.

We arranged to meet again the following Sunday. As we did, I wondered how I could advance this relationship. I had no clue. Perhaps the Blackwoods would invite me for dinner one day. I could only hope.

Wandering home, I relived the sensation of Meg's kisses. Birds emerging from the winter gloom chirped everywhere, and my spirit lifted. I would figure out a way to avoid Alice Garrison, while getting closer to sweet, beautiful Meg.

An elegant carriage stood in front of Auntie Vogel's boarding house. I could see it from a block away. It sure as hell did not belong to anyone I knew. Maybe Auntie had a gentleman caller.

As I walked up the steps, I heard a massive baritone voice yelling at the top of its owner's lungs, and I suddenly knew, as sure as my name, that my life was about to change. Immediately. Cataclysmically.

I would have bet every cent I had on that voice belonging to George Garrison.

Chapter Eleven

"Where is he?" the enormous man shouted at Auntie Vogel.

"I don't know, George. Calm down, damn it. Do not yell at me."

"I'll yell if I bloody well feel like it, woman. When he returns, you tell him I will be coming for him. With the police."

"What on Earth has happened, George?"

"Sinclair has been intimate with my daughter," he said. "I'm going to kill him. Unless he goes to jail first. Do you hear me? When he gets back, I expect you to deliver him into my hands. Am I clear?"

"I think I'll need better evidence than you blowing your top, George. Now get out."

I stood paralyzed on the porch, trying to decide what to do: plunge into the living room and punch Garrison for being so rotten to Auntie, or hide in the bushes until he decided to stop ranting and leave. Neither seemed like a good option. The first was stupid and the second cowardly, not to mention devoid of gallantry.

Connie took the decision out of my hands. She had crept alongside the east wall of the house and appeared silently at the edge of the porch, frantically waving her arms to get my attention. My peripheral vision caught the movement, and I snapped my head to the right. Connie gestured wildly for me to follow her; I shook my head, suddenly determined to confront Garrison and deny his — and Alice's — allegation. But the girl's eyes widened in alarm, and her gesticulations became agitated.

Thumps could be heard inside, like a cane hammering the floor in emphasis. Garrison's voice became louder, which meant he was approaching the front door. In fear, I fled, following Connie to the back of the house.

"That boy's life is over," Garrison announced to Auntie. "Mark my words."

The door flew open, and the man stomped down the exterior steps.

"Expect a visit from the police tonight," he called over his shoulder.

We'd reached the back door, Connie and I. She pushed me into a closet, finger to her lips, and shut me in. I heard Auntie call to the departing Garrison, although her words were lost in the muffled confines of my temporary prison. Then I felt the door slam shut. A moment later, Auntie arrived in the kitchen.

"Where is he?" Auntie asked of Connie.

"In the back closet, ma'am."

"Good girl. Well done. Be a dear, run upstairs and gather his things. You know where we'll be."

"Yes, ma'am."

Gather my things? What did that mean? Oh my God, was she going to kick me out? Did she believe Garrison, even though I had promised her I had not defiled any virgins? She appeared to believe me, at the time.

She flung open the closet door. Fury painted her face in a mask of red and white; her fingers had clearly been thrust through her thick hair, which stuck out wildly at the sides.

"Did you overhear, James?" she asked.

"Yes. Some of it. Auntie, I swear . . ."

"I know. I do know, James. I believe you. Come out of there."

I slunk out, embarrassed at the accusation despite Auntie's belief in me.

"Are you evicting me, Auntie?"

"Not exactly. Well, yes, in a manner of speaking. Come on. We don't have much time."

"What do you mean?"

"George Garrison never makes empty threats. The police will be here shortly. Now come on, follow me. I'll explain everything once we're there. Hurry."

She gave up waiting on me, grabbed my hand and led me out the back door. To the left I saw a hatch I had not noticed before, half-covered in dirt and vines. She leaned down, unlocked it and pulled it up to reveal a set of stairs that ran crookedly down into the earth. A black void obscured whatever awaited at the bottom.

"We could do this from inside the house, but I don't want anyone to see you're home," she explained. "Now go. I will be right behind you. I must close the hatch."

Bloody hell, it was dark. Auntie left the hatch open for a few seconds so I could get my bearings, then closed it as quietly as possible. Forever went by, as I felt for every next step with tentative feet.

"You're all right, James. Just keep going. I'm here."

Finally, there were no more steps, and I landed on solid earth, blind and baffled in the utter darkness. I felt Auntie arrive beside me, then reach around me to the wall. After a moment of searching for something with her hand, she gave a small 'ah' and tugged on a knob. A tiny door opened to reveal a small tunnel, faintly lit from the end.

"In you go. Mind your head."

In a full crouch, I crept carefully over the root-laced, uneven ground toward the light.

"When you see the door at the end, open it and go in."

I did not see the door at first; it was not straight on, but in the left wall. The light appeared to be emanating from behind it. I tugged it open.

On the other side was a room, quite remarkably large and fitted with six beds, washing facilities, a cold box and various other amenities such as towels, sheets, a couple of chairs and a tallboy. Also inside were Connie, a pot of coffee, a small jug of whiskey, a lamp, several candles and . . . my suitcase.

"Sit down, James. Connie, could you pour us both a tot and a cup? Have the same yourself. You've had quite the afternoon, my girl."

I practically fell onto one of the beds, exhaustion and fear making my legs tremble.

"Auntie, where . . ." I began.

"Hush, James. Have a sip first. I have much to tell you. And I will have to leave you when the police arrive. Connie will go up to await them and ring the bell for me to come. Are you hungry?"

"Not . . . not yet."

"No, I can imagine. There's food in that box. Dried meat, hard breads, some sweets. Help yourself. I'll bring you a proper dinner later. All right, Connie. Best go up now."

"Yes, ma'am." Connie gave something like a curtsy and left through another door.

"Do you know where you are, James?"

"The basement, Auntie."

"Yes, sort of. We're actually under the back yard, not the house. Don't worry; this room has been reinforced and won't fall in on you," she said to my worried expression.

I nodded, appreciatively I hoped, and waited for her to continue.

She drained her whiskey glass with a practiced toss of the head, put it down, and sat on the bed across from me, legs apart and elbows braced on her knees.

"James, what happened yesterday?"

It was far too late to hold anything back. I told her, detail by detail, how Alice Garrison had awaited me on the street, dragged me into the alley and kissed me, then begged me to marry her and take her away.

"Did you kiss her back?"

"For a few seconds, Auntie. It seemed horribly rude not to."

She laughed at that.

"And then?"

"I told her it was impossible. And I ran. Literally. I ran home."

"No wonder you looked so wild last night. You poor thing." She sighed sympathetically and shook her head at me. "You've had some bad luck, James, being chosen by Alice Garrison."

A bell rang.

"Damn. There they are. All right. Wait here — I mean it, James Sinclair, do not move — and I'll be back as soon as I deal with them."

It did not take long, thank God. Being alone in that claustrophobic cave gave me the chills. There was nowhere to prowl, but I did pace, taking the occasional sip of whiskey to calm my nerves.

She returned five minutes later.

"I'm afraid it's worse than I'd hoped, James. No point in sugar-coating this. They've charged you with rape."

I sat down again, hard. I could not take it in. Shaking, I dropped my now-empty glass on the floor, and my head fell into my hands. The potential court case, based on what I had read in the papers, reeled through my brain. "Do you deny, Mr. Sinclair, that you met poor, fragile Miss Garrison on such-and-such a date, and kissed her in the alley? No? Is it so far a leap to suggest that you took advantage of this delicate, beautiful, innocent girl?"

And so on. Oh my God. How could I defend myself?

"But it isn't true," I whispered. "It isn't."

"It doesn't matter, I'm afraid. Garrison has Toronto in his pocket. You'll be convicted. Or killed."

"What am I going to do, Auntie?"

"Call me Hannah now. We're officially partners in crime. Not the one you're accused of, mind you."

"What crime, then?"

"Fleeing justice."

"I don't . . . I don't understand."

"George Garrison was right about part of what he said. Your life is over in Toronto. We have to make sure your life is not over elsewhere."

"I'm leaving Toronto?"

"Yes. The day after tomorrow, at night. You will stay here until then. Connie and I will take care of you. But I need a day to make arrangements."

I blinked at her like a fish wondering why he was out of water. And after a moment, I understood.

"You've done this before. Haven't you? This room. The beds, the hatch, the lamp."

"Excellent deduction, James." Her voice dripped with sarcasm. "Have you ever heard of the Underground Railroad?"

Chapter Twelve

When Hannah Vogel was a young woman, she detected something strange and unusual happening in her home.

The daughter of a German immigrant — a massive man of unshakeable conviction — she grew up discussing politics, the consequences of bad government, and the clear differences between good and evil. A happy child just the same, Hannah enjoyed remarkable freedom for a girl in a growing city. Toronto thirty-five years ago was a much smaller place — less than half its current size — and much safer. Her father, raised in a small town nestled between rolling farmland hills, wanted her to discover, learn, run and fly.

At the age of fifteen, the curtains of childhood fell away from her eyes. Curious, independent and willful, and having sensed quiet comings and goings in the middle of many nights, she searched for — and found — the sanctuary below the grasses and flowers of the back yard.

Papa Vogel had done his best to hide the nocturnal traffic from his daughter; despite the danger it presented, his ethics would not allow him to stop. When Hannah asked him point blank why there was a room under the dirt with a dark man in it, he told her.

"The man was a slave," he said, in still slightly accented English. "Now he is free. As you are, my beautiful girl."

Hannah became a sergeant-at-arms. She helped cook for and tend to the people in their care. They largely protected men or families, since their quarters were inappropriate for unmarried men and women. As the years went by, she became part of the secret group transporting Americans from

Toronto to less-populated parts of Canada. Bounty hunters were a serious and constant threat, and they tended to begin their searches in the border cities and bigger towns. Therefore, the further north or west the people went, the better.

Through this network, she met her husband, Peter. When Helmut Vogel died — Hannah's mother having passed two years earlier — the young couple continued the practice with conviction and secrecy.

Until Peter was caught and murdered by a bounty hunter, along with a young African American considered particularly valuable to his "owner." The hunter, given a massive purse to conduct his search, found the two men hiding in a farm building not far from the city. They ran, of course, once they detected someone approaching; but they were too late.

The hunter was a bad shot. He was not supposed to kill the young slave and paid for it dearly. But Peter and his charge were dead, just the same.

Hannah plunged into a grief so profound that she could no longer operate her stop on the railroad, nor do much else. Six months pregnant at the time, she did not leave her bed except for dire necessity until the child was born. She bore a son and named him for his father. He was now a farmer, like his grandfather had once been, somewhere out past Fort William. There had been enough money to buy a little land, and he had since grown his holdings.

Eventually, she started to take in boarders again, quickly changing back to her maiden name since the house had long been known as Vogel's, and for safety, to distance herself from her dead husband.

Fat tears fell down my cheeks as she told her story. I wanted to comfort the woman I now called Hannah, but wondered if physical demonstrativeness would be welcome.

"Two years later," she went on, "there was still need. The Railroad had helped a hundred thousand slaves escape, and we were proud of that, of being part of that. But the Civil War loomed; we knew it, we could feel it. It was no time to shut down. I forced myself to return to the cause.

"One night, a man came to me. A particular man. He was, I am so sorry to say, a mess. He had been beaten; he had escaped a bounty hunter, but barely, after a brutal fight; he had been on the road alone for a long time. He was horribly scarred, hungry and weak. It was clear he could not go on, not for quite some time. I agreed to take him in, to nurse him and feed him. My heart broke when I saw him; I could not have refused.

"He began to heal, and to regain his strength. Light came back to his eyes. And I realized what a beautiful, beautiful man he was. Physically and emotionally."

Her voice cracked and she stopped speaking. I had not taken a real breath in several minutes. Now I inhaled deeply, with a shudder.

"What happened, Hannah? What happened next?" I asked, in my softest tone.

She cleared her throat, gave her head a shake and recovered a hint of her humour.

"Well, what do you think, James? I fell into him as if I had been starving for years. Which I had been, after Peter was killed. I loved my husband. Madly. But I also loved this man. And he loved me with a passion I cannot describe. Night after night, I would slip downstairs after everyone was asleep. I had already taken in boarders; I needed the money. It was difficult to keep this place a secret. It was dangerous to come here every night, but I did it anyway. Oh, God," she said, clearly remembering. Her body shook, and I saw the erotic longing Hannah kept locked inside.

"We made love every night. Sometimes all night. But I knew I would have to let him go, once it was safe and he was completely healthy. He could not stay here. They were looking for him. We both knew it.

"Then, of course, the bounty hunters appeared. They had been through before, but we managed to keep him safe. But there were more of them, and now they were specifically looking for him. We were terrified. And so, we arranged for him to leave. I thought I'd die."

The hell with it, I thought. I took Hannah's hand in both of mine.

"God, I'm so sorry, Hannah."

"Yes. So am I. To this day. We slipped him out and away. Officially, if he is still alive, he remains a fugitive from justice in the United States."

"What was his name, Hannah?"

She gave me a crooked smile. "He had a beautiful African name. But I would not call him by it. It was too dangerous. What if I let it slip one day? It was never a problem when people stayed for just a night or two, but he was here for months. And my lover.

"And so, I asked him if I could address him by another name. Chosen by myself. He understood, in the name of safety and secrecy. And I called him James."

My eyes flew open.

"So you see, James, you have much in common with this man. Your name. Your circumstance of being a fugitive. And you remind me of him. Handsome, gentle, tall, strong, kind. I will be damned if you'll be jailed, or worse, on a trumped-up charge. I am going to get you out of here," she said, passion and anger sparking off every word.

What was about to happen hit me then, like a fist in the stomach. What about my mother? Oh God, what about Meg? What would she think when she heard I stood accused of assaulting another woman?

"I can't go, Hannah. My mum. My Meg. My job. My name! I can't!"

"You must, James. You may be able to return one day, although I doubt it. I know it's terrible and terrifying, but you cannot stay here. Go west. Stay low. I can send you a message if your case is thrown out of court. And I'm sorry about Meg. But you will find love again. I know it. If I did, if I could, you will too. I promise you."

"Can you get a message to Mum? Or can I see her before I go?"

"I can, but no, you can't see her. They will be watching your parents' place. But I'll find her and tell her what's really happened."

"What has really happened, Hannah? I don't understand. I just don't."

"Really? Come now, apply that brain of yours."

"She — Alice — she's angry that I spurned her? This is her revenge?"

"Yes. Well, possibly. But what else?"

"There's more? I don't know. I have no idea."

"For the love of God, James. Obviously, she's pregnant. Someone needs to be blamed. They've chosen you."

Chapter Thirteen

The lamp burned late into the night. Hannah explained in minute detail how and when I would emerge from the underground sanctuary under early morning darkness. An escort would direct me to a spot along the railway, which with any luck would not be under surveillance.

The train would take me as far as Fort William, where Peter, her son, would meet me. It would be impossible to pack enough food and belongings for the trip, so Peter would outfit me to the best of his ability before sending me on my way.

The next part of the journey would also be by train to the Manitoba village of Winnipeg, situated at the confluence of the Red and Assiniboine Rivers.

"You could try to settle there," Hannah said. "But it's suddenly become quite accessible. The railroad reached Winnipeg a couple of months ago now. I wonder if you should go further west, to the southern part of the North-West Territories."

"If so, I'll need a horse."

"Yes. It would be a long ride, but you might be safer further away. Peter can help you locate a horse."

"What about going north?"

"I doubt you'd enjoy the weather, James — not that it will be warm in winter on the southern plains. But I hear it's brutal up by Hudson Bay, and not just in January. I also wonder if the opportunities for work would be as good if you headed north. It's hard to say. I've never been out west, of course."

Terror filled my heart and soul as we discussed my upcoming displacement from family, society, employment and everything else I knew and loved. I had never been on a train, much less hopped one; nor had I ever ridden a horse. My pockets were not filled with cash. Would cash even be of much use in the middle of nowhere?

"Hannah, can I not just stay and try to clear my name? I didn't do anything to Alice. Nor to any other woman, apart from kissing Meg. Please, isn't there a way?"

She rose from the chair and came across the room, sat on the bed and gathered me into her arms.

"No, my poor boy. You don't understand the power George Garrison has. Even if you don't go to jail, or aren't shot in the alley, your name will be ruined. Do you understand? I'm so sorry, James. So sorry."

I wept, desperate tears flowing from my eyes and my entire body shaking in my surrogate mother's arms.

Finally, the storm subsided. Hannah left me for a few moments and returned with food, tea, and a little more whiskey. She had slipped something into that tea, because an hour later I was out. Sleeping like the dead. When I awakened, twelve hours later, I almost wished I was. Dead.

• • •

It was time. My small bag was packed; Hannah had given me a few extra dollars and as much dried food as she could stuff into another, smaller bag, which we tied to the larger one. On a scrap of paper were written addresses, names and basic directions. Even with these items prepared for my flight, I felt as though I was headed for the executioner's block.

Hannah led me through the dark tunnel, but instead of emerging from the hatch, we took a sharp turn toward yet another tunnel. Another set of rickety steps. Another invisible opening in the earth.

We stood below the flat door, silent and waiting. A quiet, single knock came moments later, followed by the sight of a starry sky.

"There's no moon," said a low voice, belonging to the man who had opened the hatch.

"Thank God," whispered Hannah. "Up you go, James. Quickly, now. Follow Joseph, stay low, do everything he says."

She grabbed me and held me tightly, so closely that I could feel her sobs against my chest. I hugged her back wildly, as if I would never again have contact with anyone I loved.

"Thank you, Hannah," I said in her ear. "I will never forget you."

"Nor I you, James Sinclair." She released me and gave me a small push toward the ladder. "Now go."

Hoisting my bare and precious possessions, I clambered up the ladder and emerged to meet Joseph, realizing with a shock that the man was of African descent. Was he risking his own life to lead fugitives out of the city? I started to thank him, but he put a finger to his lips and clamped his other hand over my mouth. He jerked his head to the right, and we were off.

I realized I had come up at the foot of the garden, in an area surrounded by dense bushes and tall trees. We did not run but walked rapidly and quietly down the alleys and paths toward the edge of town. It took at least an hour, but it could have been two; my perception of time was abstract, disjointed, unstuck. I had already spent thirty-six hours in near darkness underground.

Close to our destination, Joseph slowed his pace, peered into the night and finally took my arm. We slipped down into a damp ditch and waited.

Joseph exhaled and finally spoke.

"This is where you will jump on the train," he said. "It won't be going full speed yet; we're not that far from the yards, so it shouldn't be too bad. You run alongside and look for something to grab onto; maybe a ladder. Hope you find a railcar that's not full of goods, right? Look for a partially open door. Sling your arm into a rung and hold on tight, then ease over into the car.

"This load is going to Winnipeg, but it will stop in Fort William. Try to stay on until then. If someone finds you, you've got to jump off, you hear? At Fort William, get off the train, run like hell into the trees directly to your right. North. Got that? Peter Vogel will find you."

"Yes, got it. I think. But Joseph, why are you doing this? Isn't it dangerous for you?"

"I would sell my soul for Hannah Vogel. All the people she saved." Joseph shook his head in awe. "And the bounty hunting stopped, mostly, after the

Civil War. I'm all right now, young man. But you're not. Are you ready? Here it comes."

I did not see anything, but clearly Joseph knew or felt something. A moment later, so did I — a heavy shaking, a rumble reverberating through my feet. My heart hammered, my legs felt like lead; I could not believe I was about to jump onto a moving train, like the hobos I had heard about.

Me. A hobo. I was, in fact, a hobo.

"All right, go!" Joseph shouted above the sudden din. He gave me a powerful boost to the railbed, yelled "ladder on your left" at the top of his lungs, and I lurched and sprung for it.

I grabbed at the third rung, not wanting my legs to dangle among the churning wheels, and pulled myself up, by now feeling the drag of extra weight from the bags swinging from my shoulders. I made it. But the door to the railcar was not open. Now what?

The only option was climbing to the roof and praying for access further down the train. I hoisted my body up and flattened myself for a moment, breathing like a steam engine. All I could think was, there better not be a tunnel up ahead anytime soon.

But the thought galvanized me into action, even as the train gathered speed. I crawled along the roof, came down between the cars and went back up again. No joy on the next car, either. I crawled, came down, went back up, peered over the side and found the door ajar, just a sliver of an opening. Would I fit through it?

I could not tell, but I had to try. Carefully, I gripped grooves on the roof, swung over the side and tried to slide my feet into that sliver. That worked, but getting the rest of my body in would be a trick, if it fit at all.

A second later, the door swung open, and two sets of big hands reached out and grabbed me by my thighs and waist. I froze, certain I had been captured by large lawmen, but what could I do? If I had fallen or jumped then, I would have been dead. Sliced and mangled. I allowed myself to be dragged inside.

They were not police officers. They were, of course, hobos, who had likely gained access to the train near the railyards where security was lax during the strike. I could not have risked it, on pain of imprisonment, but they may have been willing to take the chance.

"Thank you," I said, once able to breathe. "Very much."

"Don't thank us yet," growled the larger one. "Who th'hell are you? Haven't seen you on a train before. Or anywhere, come to that. Yer not a copper, are you?"

Managing not to roll my eyes — police officers did not jump trains just for fun — I shook my head violently. "No."

"So? What're you doin' here?"

I did not see much point in lying. I decided to tell the truth, if not all of it.

"I'm on my way to Fort William to . . . to meet someone. Can't afford the fare. Name's James. Yours?"

"Jones. This here's Clancy." The second man nodded but remained silent. "Got a knife?"

Oh hell.

"Yes sir. Just a small one, for cutting food."

"You have food?"

"Not much. You?"

"No, but we caught ourselves a rabbit. Need a knife to cut it. Lost mine on the fly, goddammit."

"How will you cook it?"

"You are a new one, aren't you? We'll set a fire, right here. Give me the damn knife."

There was a poser, as Mum sometimes said. Did he mean to kill me with it, for my meagre possessions? Or did I seriously have a chance at roasted rabbit? I considered offering to butcher the little beast myself, but never having done such a thing, I would likely make a mess of it. And then my life would not be worth a cent.

"Where's the rabbit?" I asked, buying time.

"Over there." He jerked his head, which I could barely see in the darkness, much less the rabbit. "Don't trust me, eh?"

"Well, just met you, didn't I," I answered, trying to pick up the rhythm of his speech.

He laughed at that, a wheezy sort of howl that made me worry about both his sanity and the condition of his lungs.

"Right. And we just met you, too. Tellya what. We'll try to trust each other long enough to fill our bellies. Then we'll see what's what. What d'you have for food?"

"Hard biscuit, some jerky, apples."

"Sounds good to me, alongside our hare."

There really did not seem to be an option. Nervous just the same, I dug out my pocketknife and handed it over, leaning toward him at the waist to keep my distance. He simply nodded in thanks, turned to retrieve the small furry body, and began to skin it with expert speed. Clancy, meanwhile, gathered burnable bits into a heap and placed them in a metal container.

Before long, the rabbit spat its juices into the small fire. Jones duly returned the knife, which I cleaned to the best of my ability before slicing two apples and placing the pieces near the heat. In my view, there were few things as delicious as sweet, broiled apple. I took out a large piece of the bread and broke it into three even pieces.

What a feast. The men had a few drops of whiskey, and we dined gloriously on meat and fruit and bread. We joked around a bit — well, Jones and I did; Clancy was silent as a rock and mostly ate as if starving. I wondered how to assure them that I was neither killer nor thief. More importantly, how could I assure myself the same of them? It was two against one in this railcar.

Should I tell them about my circumstances? Would they tell me theirs?

"So you're on the fly. D'you know the hobo's code, youngster?" Jones suddenly asked.

"No, sir. I'm afraid I'm new to this."

"D'you consider yourself a hobo?"

"I do. I'm off west, not sure where, but looking for work."

"Well, then. Listen and learn."

With a great amount of pride, Jones launched into an explanation of the code apparently adhered to by hobos.

Do not take the work of others. Be respectful when in towns and cities. Do not attract the notice of law enforcement, and if you do, be polite. Honour nature. Behave like a gentleman. Ride the trains considerately.

"Got paper?" he asked.

I handed over the scrap of paper Hannah had given me. He produced a pencil stub and began to draw symbols, warning me to watch for them when I hit towns. A top hat, signifying a gentleman. A circle with two arrows, meaning get out now. A wavy line with an X on top, suggesting clean water and a camping area. A caduceus, indicating a doctor in the house willing to treat hobos.

"Most important," Jones said, and stopped for emphasis. He handed me the paper, looked me in the eye, and said, "Never take advantage of someone in a bad situation. Not hobos, not locals. Get me?"

"I do, sir."

"Call me Jones. Get some sleep."

And I did.

Chapter Fourteen

I awakened to bright sunshine, bones and muscles aching from the hard floor and the constant jarring of the train's chug. Jones or Clancy had opened the door a crack to let air flow into our stuffy space. I realized, as I never had before, that I was still alive.

True to the code, they had not taken advantage. My food and my things lay beside me. My body seemed intact. While I could not say life was good, it could have been worse under the circumstances. Or possibly nonexistent.

"Awake, youngster?"

"Yes. Good morning, Jones. Good morning, Clancy."

"Sleep well?"

"Actually, I did. You?"

"Yep. Let's get us some breakfast."

I unearthed more apples and they dug into their sacks, producing a hard lump of cheese and some scavenged roots unrecognizable to me. A little more bread from my stores completed our small, rustic meal.

"How much longer will it be to Fort William?" I asked.

"Well, let's see. You came aboard twelve hours ago, more or less. I'd say another sixteen should about do it."

I looked at my watch, still a tad worried about displaying it. It was nine; that meant we would arrive at about one in the morning, hopefully in moonless dark. It also meant we had an entire day to kill in this confined space.

"We'll stop to take on coal and water," Jones informed me. "When the train starts to slow down, hide. Over there. I'll close the door."

"And if they find us?"

"If they find 'us' there won't be a problem, more'n likely. I'm not so sure about you." He turned, braced himself against the open door, and cocked an eyebrow. "On the run from something?"

Heat rushed to my face. Consternation overwhelmed me. If I told them the truth, would they believe me, kick me out, or simply bash my head in? Raping a woman would definitely not fit into the hobo's code. Besides, my simple existence in the same railcar would put them both at risk if the police tracked me down.

"I know a good man when I see one," he said quietly.

I bowed my head, gritted my teeth, made a decision and looked up at him.

"I'm sorry," I said. "I am on the run. I've been accused of hurting a young woman. I did not do it. I am so sorry. I didn't know you'd be on the train; I didn't mean to risk your freedom. Do you want me to jump?"

"Now, youngster, let's not get ahead of ourselves. Tell us what happened."

I did. Briefly, but I did not leave out any of the vital details. My story still killed half an hour.

"Lemme guess," Jones said when I finally stopped talking. "This girl has a big, bad daddy, or husband."

"Yes."

"Damn, young James. That's a hell of a story. I see. Well . . ." he stopped speaking as the train began to slow. "We'll talk more later. Now hide. Don't worry. No one will find you. Go."

I wriggled my way behind a small tower of boxes and dragged burlap bags around the sides and over my head; Jones tucked me in. A mile or two later, the train screeched and shuddered and stopped, and I could hear the crew hollering to one another. Coal and water being loaded.

Our door being opened.

Damn, damn, damn. I stopped breathing and stood frozen in my corner. Jones and Clancy had also concealed themselves, possibly because it was rote, possibly because of me. Someone — I could not see anything —

stepped into the car, and, I assumed, looked around. Feet stomped to the left, then to the right.

"Jones. You better not be in here." The voice was big, but not nasty. Then it laughed. "I'd better not see you at Fort William."

The footsteps retreated. I heard the man jump to the railbed and close the door behind him. A second later, I sneezed.

"Dusty in here," I heard Jones say from his corner. "Don't move yet, James. Just in case."

No way in hell would I budge until the train began to move again. Twenty minutes or so later it finally did, and I removed the filthy burlap bag from my face. Coughing, eyes streaming, it became clear in that moment that finding and transporting clean water would likely be my biggest challenge on this journey.

Sliding the door open again just a crack, Jones took an enormous breath of fresh air and indicated for me to do the same. For the next few hours, we sat down, stood up, sat down again and talked. I explained that I needed to travel beyond the end of the railroad, out of easy reach of George Garrison and the eastern police. Jones and Clancy nodded and considered my plight.

"Y'might go out Pile O'Bones way," Jones said. "Railway won't get there for a while yet. You'd have a few months or so to get yourself settled."

"Have you been there, Jones?"

"Not me. No train, probably not much work."

"Might be some as the track gets built," I suggested.

"Maybe. I'll think on it. So from Winnipeg . . ."

Jones went on to describe the journey west of the Manitoba town, to the best of his knowledge. It sounded terrifying, but it was also an option. I resolved to ask Peter Vogel what he knew about this Pile of Bones. Even the name was daunting.

Darkness finally fell, and I dozed fitfully, fearing that I would sleep through the arrival at Fort William. Jones said there was no hope in hell of that, but I still worried.

No need. The hoot of the train's horn startled me out of sleep. I came out of a dream with a small shout, to Jones's amusement.

"I told you," he said, laughing. "Y'have five minutes, James. Get your things together."

I scrambled to my feet, shaking the dust and straw from my clothing, and did as he suggested. We stood at the door, we three, gazing out at the trees sliding by, the stars in the sky, the occasional bright eyes of a frightened deer.

The train slowed, and slowed, and finally stopped.

"Good luck, youngster. I wish you all the best."

"Thank you for everything, Jones. I'm truly grateful. Will I see you again one day?"

"Count on it. Now. Ready? Go. Jump, jump far, and run like hell. Go!"

But I did not, just yet. I turned to him and offered him my hand, knowing I had made a friend whom I would miss, even after just twenty-nine hours' acquaintanceship. He took it, gave it a mighty shake, and nodded.

"Goodbye, Clancy. Goodbye, Jones. Be well and safe."

I turned to the door, jumped off the train and leapt off the railbed into the forbidding beyond.

• • •

Strange rustlings, howls and cries disturbed the quiet of the small wilderness at the edge of town. My city ears perked in all directions, trying to distinguish large animals likely to attack from smaller, less frightening beasts.

Hunkered among bushes below the soaring pines, I had never felt so alone nor so invisible. I wondered how Peter would find me. I could not very well call out nor start a fire.

A twig snapped. Something, or someone, was right behind me; I felt hot breath on my neck, an instant before a large, rough hand clamped itself over my mouth.

God Almighty.

Chapter Fifteen

"Sinclair?"

Since I could not speak, I nodded in agreement — an idiotic thing to do, but it was an instinctive response. I prayed this person was Peter Vogel and not an officer of the law. Or worse.

"You're going to have to learn a few things while you're on the run. Like not letting people sneak up on you," said the voice, right in my ear. "I'm releasing you now. Not a word. Follow me. Put a hand on my back so you don't get lost."

I rose from my crouch and did as I was told. The floor of the forest, dense with fallen branches, old leaves and brush, crackled under our feet. No moon shone, although faint light from the stars allowed for slight visibility. Shadows danced, animals growled and early insects buzzed.

Half an hour later, we came to a clearing. Peter pointed ahead and to the left, and whispered, "Stay low."

Across the fields we went, grateful for darkness. Finally, vague shapes of small buildings came into view, and a moment later we walked into a farmhouse, large and clean and warm. Something smelled heavenly.

"Have a chair, James. You must be exhausted. I'm Peter, obviously." A woman walked into the room. "This is my wife, Ellen."

"Hello, James. I've put by some of the chicken we had for dinner. Would you like some?"

"More than I can say, Mrs. Vogel. Thank you."

She brought a covered plate out of the oven and set it before me. I am embarrassed to admit I ate the food as if I were one of the animals of the forest we had recently left behind.

"First things first," Peter said, after I had devoured the delicious chicken, potatoes and carrots. "You'll stay here tonight, catch your breath, get some sleep. We have a false wall in the basement with a bed behind it. The train will come tomorrow at about the same time, and we'll sneak you on. Hopefully you won't be on the fly."

"What is 'on the fly?' One of the hobos on the train used that expression."

"Jumping the train. Clearly a dangerous activity. You obviously managed it out of Toronto, though. Do you know where you're going yet?"

"Winnipeg first. Jones — the hobo — suggested Pile of Bones as a final destination. It's not on the railway yet."

"Not a bad idea. It's a long way from Winnipeg, though. It will take you at least twelve days, but that's under perfect conditions on a very strong horse. I'd say more like fourteen to sixteen. Before you leave, we'll kit you out with some gear. The rest of it you'll pick up in Winnipeg with your mount. Sound all right?"

"Yes. Thank you. Very much. I appreciate everything you've done, and what Hannah has done."

"How is she? My mother?"

"I think she's well. She certainly seemed to be in great health. Very strong, very . . . kind."

Peter gave a monstrous exhale of relief. "Glad to hear it. Let's get some sleep. If I don't see you by ten in the morning, I'll come down and shake you up."

He led me down to a room remarkably like the one in Hannah's basement, although much smaller. I knew this would be the last night of relative safety and peace for a long, long time. Despite that harrowing knowledge, I slept like the just and righteous.

• • •

Peter did have to awaken me. Even the arousing aroma of bacon frying had not done the trick. After breakfast, he offered some pointers on being more aware of potential danger; described the flatlands awaiting me further west; added some kit and food to my scanty luggage; and explained how to find my next contact in Winnipeg.

The day dragged on. I slept again in the afternoon, waking for dinner. Then at midnight, it was time to leave.

We retraced our path back to the train siding and awaited its arrival. When it stopped, I shook Peter's hand, found an open car and slipped inside. Beat the hell out of jumping on.

There was no one in the railcar this time. I was entirely alone and missed the company of Jones and Clancy — despite the latter's stoic silence. It made the trip long, quiet, depressing and uneventful.

Ten hours later, under a hard, bright blue sky, the train chugged into Winnipeg. The town was beginning to see the growth and bustle that had taken over Toronto years earlier. The second the train stopped, I was on the move, hopping onto the railbed and running hellbent for cover. It wasn't easy; this was bald prairie compared to the densely-treed and rocky landscape of Fort William. I finally spied a vacant, decrepit shed and dove inside to catch my breath.

Peter had drawn a map indicating the location of the horse stable, north and east of the train station. It was not far; nothing was. Winnipeg's population of about nine thousand was a fraction of Toronto's eighty thousand.

Poking my head tentatively out of the little shelter, I saw no one and nothing but muddy paths and scrub. Judging by the map, roads extended at strange and confusing angles from my location, so I ducked down to the Red River and followed its flow north, feeling some protection amid the foliage along its banks. I passed an encampment of Cree people (I knew they were Cree from Peter's explanations) and attracted a few questioning looks, but they let me be.

The river suddenly took a sharp eastern turn, telling me it was time to head inland. No roads here — just rutted cart paths and other indications of horse traffic. The stable had to be nearby. I emerged from the brush and a few minutes later, I saw it.

A man stood in the middle of the corral, tall, grizzled and dressed in full cowboy gear. He fed the beautiful beasts from a bucket of what appeared to be oats; they nickered and nuzzled him in appreciation.

"Mr. Acton?"

His head snapped around. "Yes?"

"I'm James Sinclair."

"Right. Get in here. Quick. Gate's over there."

I hurried over and let myself into the corral as the animals stared me down. Flecks of horse dung and bits of straw hung in the air, and the aromas were intense; yet I found them pleasant, almost soothing.

"Ever ridden a horse before?" Acton asked, clearly disinterested in exchanging pleasantries.

"No," I admitted. "Couldn't afford one."

"Right." He looked me up and down. "Hungry?"

"Yes, sir. Always."

"We'll grab some food and get down to it."

The meal was hardscrabble, but I was grateful for it just the same. Once we had swallowed the last bites, he grabbed a pair of chaps from a hook in the porch of the house, instructed me to put them on, and out we went for my first lesson.

"This," he said, "is your horse. Bucephalus." Named for Alexander the Great's steed. He pronounced it "buck-eh-phaloos," so he had clearly read the name but never heard it said. I did not smile, nor did I correct him. That might have been fatal to the relationship — and besides, the man was obviously a reader. No shame there.

"He's a buckskin, as you can see, so there be two reasons to call him Buck." Made sense, I thought. "Good strong horse, but young. Has spirit. Might take a while for you to get on and stay on."

Buck. Named for a historical creature and his cinnamon hide and not, I hoped, for his method of unseating a rider.

"Now walk on up to him, real easy-like. Say his name, nice and low, and give him this." Acton handed me an apple. "Let him nip it up with his lips. Go on, now."

Following his advice to the letter, I muttered, "Here, Buck, you beauty. Good Buck. Nice Buck." It sounded ridiculous to my ears; I had never spoken to a horse before.

He regarded me with suspicion, but slowly walked toward me and his apple. A moment later, we were almost nose to nose, staring into each other's eyes. Then he snorted, tossed his black mane and protruded his lips, taking the treat into his mouth and crunching it with huge teeth.

"Pat him," Acton said.

I reached out with as much confidence as I could muster and gently patted his silky, powerful neck, still quietly saying his name.

"Good. Right. Let's get you up there."

Buck already wore his saddle. Acton directed me to put a foot in the stirrup, then swing the other leg over Buck's back. Harder than it seemed, but after two tries I managed it.

The second my backside landed in the saddle, Buck lived up to his name. Before I could blink, I was lying winded among the horseshit, dirt and straw on the corral ground, which luckily provided a fairly soft landing.

"Oof," I said, expelling all the air in my lungs. Acton came over in a hurry and bent to peer into my face.

"Are y'all right?"

"I . . . think so," I said, testing my back and shoulders, then my legs. "Yes. Nothing broken, anyway."

"You have to learn to hang on, man, 'til he gets used to you. Let's try again."

I swore under my breath as I scrambled up. No bones were busted, but I could feel bruises forming. This time, I approached my horse with further murmurs, explaining that we were about to become good friends. I swung into the saddle on the first go, as gently as I could, then hung on to reins and pommel like grim death.

Whinnying, Buck bucked again, front hooves rising in the air and pounding the dust below as they fell; but it was a slightly less violent event, and although I slid precariously in the saddle, I stayed on.

I grinned at Acton.

"Better," he said. "Give me the reins but hang on to that pommel."

For an hour, Acton led Buck with me aloft around the corral. We walked, then trotted, then cantered. He explained how to post, how to grip the horse's body with my thighs, how to create that small click with my tongue and teeth to encourage speed.

Finally, he threw back the reins and with a nod indicated that I was on my own. Buck did not like that too much. He tossed and snorted and bucked a little, but seemed to be adjusting to my weight and presence.

By nightfall, both of us had been thoroughly put through our paces. I dismounted, sore as hell in every muscle. My legs nearly did not support me when my feet landed on Mother Earth.

"Not too bad, son," Acton judged. "Not too bad. We'll call it a night. Be back out here in the morning. Then we'll be seeing you off."

As we walked back to the house, he seemed to have another thought.

"Can you shoot at all?"

"No, sir."

"What in hell did they teach you out east?"

"Nothing of much use in the west, apparently. I'm a machinist and a goldsmith."

"That might help you in the future, but we have to get you there first. Alive. You'll have to stay another day. Tomorrow, target practice. How do you expect to eat in the next fortnight without being able to shoot?"

• • •

The gun proved to be an oft-used Winchester carbine, although it worked well enough.

Acton presented it unloaded, a wise move since I might easily have discharged my first bullet into his body.

Why it had not occurred to me that I would need a weapon I could not explain. Obviously, packing enough food for twelve to sixteen days was impossible, and where would one find a grocer in the middle of the wild, open prairie? And what if I encountered, as Acton ominously suggested, an "unfriendly?"

After a wakeful night and an early breakfast, he led me out well beyond the corral into a copse of trees set up with cans on stumps and various other makeshift targets. He showed me how to line up my sights, peer down the barrel and focus on the tip. Not until I'd mastered holding the carbine did he teach me how to load it.

Longer than a revolver and shorter than a rifle, it felt natural and easy in my hands. What I was unprepared for was the recoil. I would not say it kicked like a horse, but the impact on my shoulder was guaranteed to leave a bruise, adding to the black-and-blue marks inflicted by Buck the day before.

"Steady there, James," Acton said. "You'll get used to it. You've got to take more of the impact in your muscles, in your arms. Try again."

I snicked the lever to drop another cartridge, braced myself and tautened my arm muscles. Inhale, exhale, fire. It still kicked, but the sudden slam into my shoulder was less shocking and not quite as aggressive.

Five or six attempts later, I finally hit something — a can perched some distance away. It flew into the air, bearing a big hole inflicted by my bullet. I could practically feel Acton's surprise, and turned to see an approving smirk on his weathered face.

"You'll be all right," he said. "We'll practice for a while, then you'll get back on the horse. He'll have to get used to you shooting while mounted."

Hell, I thought. Yet another great way to get bucked off Buck.

Yet, while he startled and ran madly off into the bush, I stayed on and he eventually stopped, snorting and stamping amid long and apparently succulent grasses. Which he immediately began to crop. Not a bad outcome; he had his treat after the shock of the gun's report.

The rest of the day was spent shooting, riding, and doing both simultaneously. Acton finally called a halt to my training in the late afternoon, fed me and sent me off to bed. I would be leaving early the next day.

•   •   •

In the deep dark of four in the morning, Acton roused me from heavy slumber. I had never been so intensely, physically, painfully active in my life, and exhaustion led to an uninterrupted night.

Another breakfast, and we were out packing my saddlebags, the carbine attached alongside the saddle itself, a bedroll and groundsheet tucked atop Buck's ample backside. Acton still had a long list of advice to give.

"Always watch for water. Never pass up a chance to drink, not for yourself nor for the horse. Fill your bottles. Keep your gun loaded with the safety on. If you see game, stop and kill it, then clean it immediately. Dry it if you can. Preserve your matches. Put out your fires and use dirt, not water. And for the love of God, keep your eyes open. You never know who you'll run into out there."

He gave me a map, illustrating to the best of his knowledge a potential route to Pile of Bones.

"I don't know how to thank you," I said.

"Don't worry about that. Thank me by surviving. I have a reputation to uphold, you know. Now up you go."

Once astride Buck, I looked down at my mentor with a new and shocking thought.

"Who will pay you for all of this? I'm taking your horse, your gun, your food and your time. And I have no money. Well, very little."

"Hannah will sort things out. Down the road, young James, pay her back if you can. Right?"

"I will. I swear I will. Although no money could ever repay her for all she's done for me, nor Peter, nor you."

He reached up with a gnarled hand, gave me an inscrutable look and nodded sharply, once.

"I know you will. Now get."

Acton slapped Buck's rump and I was off into the wilderness, alone except for my gun and my horse.

Chapter Sixteen

It is hard to describe how daunting nothingness can be.

In my youth, I had often gone down to the monstrous lake abutting Toronto to stare over the blue-grey waves swelling to the horizon, wondering where they ended — if, indeed, they did. I would gaze at the night sky, musing about how far the glittering stars reached into the heavens.

Mere minutes out of Winnipeg, I mentally added the vast expanse of endless prairie to my list of unfathomable wonders. Dotted only with small clumps of scraggly trees, the scrubland reached as far as the eye could see, regardless of my progress. It went on, and on, and on.

Dust billowed into my nostrils, kicked up from Buck's hooves as they relentlessly contacted the dry earth. He seemed content to trot, not walk, for which I was grateful. Wherever the hell I was going, I wanted to get there as quickly as possible. But a full canter or gallop would wear him out, and we would need his reserves of power if we encountered danger.

As utterly, bleakly terrifying as it was, at least it was spring, not winter. A hint of green decorated the occasional budding leaf and blade of grass, and the warming weather would not outright kill a man. I could not imagine this plain covered in stark white snow, cold and brutal and blinding in the sun.

Because Acton had warned me to watch for water, I constantly scanned the horizon for potential potholes and sloughs. I saw none. Hours after leaving the small city behind, even as the sun began to sink, I spied for the first time a little hollow up ahead. Clicking my tongue at Buck, I encouraged him with a slap of the reins to head south at a faster clip.

He knew something was up. I could tell. Unerringly, he headed directly for the tiny valley; he had obviously seen such a thing before and knew what it suggested. Tired and thirsty, we mutually (I felt) and desperately wanted to find a pond or stream and somewhere to rest.

Having been without human company for an entire day, I began to speak to Buck. Whether he understood me or not did not matter a great deal. I craved a semblance of interaction with another living being.

"What do you think, Buck? Is there water over there? We should go see. Let's go see. I know I could use a drink. I bet you could too."

More drivel of a similar nature poured out of my mouth. I may have imagined it, but I could have sworn Buck nodded his massive head in agreement.

Finally, we met the crest of the small hollow, deeper and wider than it had seemed from a mile away. A rushing brook flowed down from a faraway hill and into the dell, the most welcome sight of my life not including the beautiful and alluring Meg.

A narrow, shallow little stream it was, but more than adequate for Buck and me. It occurred to me that we were incredibly lucky to be travelling after the spring snowmelt. I would put money on it that by deep summer this spring would be gone, leaving the dry bed behind.

We were not the first to arrive, I realized after a moment of pure, joyous relief. Two deer stood at the water's edge, drinking deeply from the clean, sparkling brook. I noted three things: they were very thirsty, ergo they also had trouble finding water . . . and they were also food on the hoof.

Alarmed by Buck's snorting, the larger of the beasts looked up with wild, wide eyes, flinched and skittered away, followed by the smaller one. I would have to be fast. Water would have to wait.

Grabbing the carbine, I flicked the safety off and snapped the reins on Buck's neck. We careened down the hill as I scrambled to swing the gun toward the deer.

Killing one of the animals too near the water source would be a very bad idea; it would sully the brook with blood and God knew what else. But deer are fleet, and I doubted we would catch them in full flight; more likely they would be far from the stream by the time I got a shot off. I slowed Buck's gait back down to a trot and then pulled him to a stop, watching the deer closely. They danced into a small stand of trees, but as we halted our progress, so did they. If we came any closer, they would run. I would have to shoot from here, and hope my aim was true enough to miss the trees and hit the prospective venison.

Besides, after just one day of learning to use the damned gun, could I actually hit something while galloping? Probably not.

Slowly, I raised the carbine to my shoulder, squinted down the barrel and fired.

The smaller deer squealed and fell to the ground, as the larger leapt and ran, dodging through the trees. My God. I could not believe that I had hit one of them.

I swung off Buck's back and advanced on the fallen beast, gun still aimed in its direction. It lay bleeding from the haunch and breathing heavily — sadly alive and in great pain if its rolling eyes were any indication.

Shooting an animal at a distance is one thing. Watching it pant in agony right at your feet is another. I had never done either before, but I tell you the former is a much easier thing requiring little bravery or compassion.

I shot the deer in the forehead. It died instantly.

Buck reared behind me as I fell to my knees and vomited profusely into the bushes. Self-hatred, even more than gore, will churn your stomach.

Once I had retched up everything inside me, I rose, sweating and woozy, and staggered down to the brook. There, I flattened my body on the ground, stuck my head in the water and drank. Seconds later, Buck appeared right beside me, his long, thick tongue lapping thirstily at impossible speed.

For some minutes, I did not move. I was not sure I could. I lay limply with my face half in the young waterweeds and the rest of me in the foliage along the bank. Buck, however, was not having any of my sloth. Once finished drinking, he ambled over and nudged me with his nose. He did not have to speak English. Get up, he said.

Grabbing the bridle, I pulled myself to my feet and tried to get my brain around what needed to be done: skinning and eviscerating the deer before dark.

Never having done such a thing, I squeezed my eyes shut and focused on the memory of Jones dealing with the rabbit on the train. Rabbits are not deer, but I had little else to go by.

The hideous process took hours. I do not know how many. I butchered the poor beast to the best of my ability and dug a hole for the remains. Some of the meat I cut into strips and hung them to dry on a piece of rope; the remainder I prepared to cook over my evening fire.

Thank God I had found this hollow. On top of the water and the wildlife, there were sufficient sticks, twigs and fallen branches, along with dry leaves from the previous fall, to start and maintain a small fire. In my kit were two Y-shaped steel bars, which I pushed into the earth and fitted with a spit. Even so, cooking all the meat within the time available appeared to be impossible. The deer provided an incredible amount of food.

Complete darkness, apart from the light of the fire, surrounded me by the time I had cooked the meat. I led Buck into the wood, tied him loosely to a tree and let him graze as I ate my lonely meal off the end of my knife.

A strange and disquieting howl occasionally broke the silence. As the night wore on, the single plaintiff was joined by others, until an eerie choir sang around me. I had never heard such a sound, and so I tried to remember the advice I had been given and the books I had read.

Too far south and too exposed for wolves, it had to be coyotes. Not much I could do about that. I only prayed they would not come to investigate the tantalizing smell of cooked deer. The only other annoyances were small voles and early spring insects.

Somehow, I would have to attempt sleep in this wild, unfamiliar place.

I laid out the ground sheet and bedroll in the most sheltered part of the little wood, covered myself as fully as possible, and closed my aching eyes.

Chapter Seventeen

Apparently I had slept, because I awakened with the dawn in a state of significant shock. Where the hell was I? And why did my head pound like a drum being beaten?

Tentatively, I opened one eye, only to slam it shut again. Bloody hell, that hurt. I began to vaguely remember that I was nowhere, with no one, and with nothing ahead of me but more open prairie.

Damn. There had been a horse. Buck. Where was Buck? I reopened the offending eye and saw him quietly cropping a few metres away. Relieved, I crept out of my bed to relieve myself in the trees, lurching from trunk to trunk. I thought I would never stop urinating, but even that hurt. And I was thirsty.

Water. The brook. Right.

I plunged toward the stream, legs wobbling, sank to my knees and drank heavily. It was then that I realized I was sweating profusely, so I dunked my head in the water and came up gasping from its icy assault on my senses.

Buck whinnied just then, and I understood he too was thirsty and still confined by reins to a tree. I stood up, intending to release him, and instantly found myself sprawled in the dirt.

No doubt about it. I was sick.

Feverish and aching, I crawled over to Buck and untied him, then wondered what the hell I could manage to do next. Riding a horse in bright sunlight over a dusty plain did not sound appealing, to say the least — if I could even get into the saddle.

Clinging to Buck's mane, I dragged myself to a standing position and felt the world whirl around me. I hung on for dear life, then sidled over to the stirrup, stuck my foot in and somehow crawled onto his back. Once I was aloft, Buck started a slow plod toward the stream. As he lowered his head to the water, I lurched to the side, fell to the ground and passed out.

• • •

"Is he dead?" someone said.

I was not, since I heard the words, but I thought I would rather be. Pouring sweat, head ready to explode, I could not open my encrusted eyes. How long had I been lying there? And who was speaking? Was I about to die anyway, at the hands of roving villains?

"No," said another voice. I felt a finger on my throat. "But he's plenty sick." Another light touch. "Burning up. Here, Miranda, douse this in the stream. And bring a cup, too. We'll try to get his fever down."

That sounded promising. At least they did not intend to murder me outright.

"Grog," I croaked.

"Ah. He speaks. Try not to, mister. Conserve your strength. We'll bring you some water."

I tried to nod, but movement was excruciating and I gave it up. Moments later, Miranda apparently returned with a soaked handkerchief. She, or the other speaker, squeezed the icy water on my face and gently dabbed at my gluey eyelids.

Women. There were women out here.

The non-Miranda voice said, "Gently, now. I'm going to lift your head so you can drink. All right?"

"Murp," I answered.

She clearly took that for a yes because she slipped an arm around my neck and carefully tipped a cup toward my parched lips. I sipped, spluttered, swallowed, and sipped again. The water slipped down my throat like heaven's rain.

"What'll we do with him, Beth?" Miranda's voice said breathlessly.

"Well, we can't leave him here. I don't know if he's sick enough to die, but we can't take the chance. Run back and get Father. He'll know what to do. We might have to take him with us. But Father will have to say. Now go."

I dimly heard Miranda's feet pounding the dust as she ran off, presumably to a camp or some such thing. I supposed there might be a settlement nearby, but I had not seen nor heard one.

Beth began to unbutton my shirt, which made me a bit nervous. I succumbed to her ministrations, though, since I really had no choice. She used the damp bandana to cool my chest; as she did, I heard a small intake of breath but had no idea what that meant. Maybe I had been bitten by insects or burned by the sun, and she was shocked or troubled by the sight of injury.

Another sip of water, then.

"Don't move, now," Beth said. "I'm going back to the creek. I'll be right back."

I hardly needed to be told. I could barely twitch a muscle. If these people were not friendly, I was in deep trouble, but there was nothing I could do about it. So far, so good, at the hands of this kind woman.

Beth returned as promised, applied the wet cloth to my steaming forehead and shuttered eyes, and again brought the cup to my mouth.

"You're dehydrated," she said. "Now drink, but slowly. A sip at a time."

More cool water soothed my naked chest.

"I'll get that fever down, damn it," she muttered.

Amazed, I realized it was working. I felt a molecule better. I tested my tongue against my teeth, then tentatively licked my cracked lips, wondering again how long I had been lying out in the sun.

"Thank you," I managed to say. "Very kind."

"Hush, now. You're welcome. Here. Take another wee sip."

Obediently, I swallowed again. Nothing had ever tasted better than that fresh spring water. It revived me enough that questions began to spill into my brain.

"What day is it?" I asked. "What time is it?"

"Tuesday. Mid-afternoon, I'd say."

Holy God. I had been lying here for at least a day, if not longer. Time swirled around me. Had I left Winnipeg on Sunday morning? Eaten the deer, awakened Monday morning, climbed onto Buck and fainted . . . Buck. Where was my horse?

"You've been here a while," Beth noted. "Stay quiet, now. My father is on his way."

"Have you seen my horse?"

"No."

For the next half hour, she continued to murmur soothingly and apply the cold, wet compresses as I worried about my best, and out here my only, friend.

Finally, more voices. Miranda's bright, breathless, fluting little one; two deep, masculine baritones. I opened my eyes and beheld the two sisters, for they were so alike they could not have been otherwise. Miranda and Beth, perhaps fourteen and eighteen. Behind them loomed an older man of forty or so, and a younger one, clearly his son.

"Beth, what are you doing?" asked her father. "Are you all right?"

"Of course, Father. This man is sick. Fever. I've given him some water. He can't really move."

Thank God the man simply nodded, then bent from his six feet to stare into my face.

"Who are you, young man? Can you talk?"

"James Davidson," I said, deciding in that second not to reveal too much. I was a wanted man, after all. My second name would have to do.

"What in hell are you doing out here alone?" he asked. A very good question, I had to admit.

"I'm moving west," I said, then began to cough uncontrollably. My lungs felt like stones covered in prairie dust.

"Father, he can't really talk much right now," Beth pleaded on my behalf.

"West, eh," said the man, ignoring his daughter. "How far west?"

"Pile of Bones," I said. "I think."

"Trying to outrun the railway?"

"Something like that, yes."

"Where are you from, James Davidson?"

"Out east. Near Toronto."

"Are you a good man, James?"

"Yes, sir. I am." What else could I say, really?

"Right. Well, Beth, I suppose we can't leave him here. Where's your beast, Davidson?"

"I don't know. His name is Buck."

The father took it upon himself to holler my horse's name. It hurt my ears, but a few seconds later, I heard a rustling, then a gentle sort of clop on the dusty earth. An enormous nose ducked from the sky to nuzzle my face.

"That would be him then," said the father. "I am John Parsons. These are my daughters, Miranda and Beth; this is my son, Martin. Can you ride?"

"I . . . I don't know, sir." I tried to sit up and failed, but managed to prop myself on my elbows.

"Well, we have to get you out of here."

Some conversation ensued between John and Martin, and they finally decided to prop me up in front of John on his horse, while Martin would lead Buck behind him. Grabbing me by the arms, they led me to a big chestnut and heaved me aboard. John swung up behind me and off we went in a little parade.

I had no idea where we were going but was in no position to ask or object. After a mere ten or fifteen minutes, we arrived at a small camp, populated by perhaps eight tents of one kind or another, and at least four other families. A large fire had been set alight at the centre of the grouping. At first, I wondered why they were so far from the stream, but then realized there was more shelter here for a larger group of people.

They helped me down from the horse and sequestered me in a separate tent that held various provisions, none of them food. Beth and Martin took down my scanty possessions, including my bed roll, from Buck's back and led him away for — I hoped — some oats and water.

Exhorted to rest, I did my best, but having apparently slept for something like thirty hours, I lay awake and mused about my new circumstances. Who were these people, what were they doing here, and why were they being so kind? I had a fever, for heaven's sake. Were they not afraid of contagion?

The answer to that came two hours later, when Beth appeared with a plate of stew and hard bread.

"How are you feeling, James?" she asked, putting the plate down beside me. "Do you think you can eat?"

"Yes," I said, suddenly ravenous. "Thank you very much."

"That fever," she said, shaking her head. "Some of us have had it too. Mother was very ill with it."

"I'm sorry. Is she all right now?"

"Not too bad. Very weak. We decided to make camp for a few days. Too hard to travel with sick people."

Odd. If this illness had made the rounds with these people, where did it originate? Maybe they had also been in contact with hobos. It was my only and best guess.

"Where are you going, then?" I asked.

"Brandon House. Papa thinks he and Martin can get some railway work. He hopes he can stay put, find some farmland."

I nodded. That was my story, more or less.

"You too, then?" she asked, a quick light in her eyes.

"Yes, but I'm heading further out west."

"Oh."

"I feel much better, thanks to you. Maybe I can help out when I can stand again. I'm incredibly grateful, Beth."

She blushed and made a vague gesture with her hand. "It was nothing."

"No, it wasn't. You may have saved my life."

Her eyes widened; she stared at me, caught in the thought, then shook her head.

"You're strong and young and . . ." she stopped. "You'd have been fine."

"Maybe, maybe not. Thank you."

Blushing again, she scrambled up off her knees and said, "I must go. Mother will need me. I'll be back later to check on you." She rushed out in a blur of faded skirts and flying hair.

Chapter Eighteen

I must have passed out again. The next thing I knew it was morning, judging by the light. Carefully, I opened one eye — successfully — then tried the other. No diamond-splinter headache, and the world remained on its normal axis. Looking around, I realized Beth had returned at some point during the night; the plate and utensils had been removed, but she had left me a fresh cup of water.

Drinking it thirstily, I contemplated what to do next. The fever had broken and I desperately had to empty my bladder. Time to stand up and face the day.

I eased myself to my knees, then onto my feet and went to the flap covering the tent's opening. Peering through the door, I saw a few of the women preparing breakfast some distance away, and quickly ducked around to the back of my little temporary home to relieve myself.

God, I was filthy. Covered in dust and dried mud, twigs and leaves stuck to my clothing and hair; I itched and stank. My chest, however, seemed fine, apart from a few insect bites. Why, I wondered, did Beth react as she did? I put the thought aside. I was starving. And worried about Buck.

Not knowing what else to do, I brushed myself off to the extent possible and approached the small group of women cooking at the fire. An older woman dug an elbow into Beth's side when she saw me.

"Good morning," said my saviour, standing and rubbing her hands on a wide apron. "How do you feel?"

"Better, thanks to you. I was wondering about my horse."

"He's over there," she said, pointing, "along with the other horses. Don't worry, he has had water and food."

Food. I salivated at the aromas of beans, meat and fried bread coming from the pans. Coffee, too. Beth noticed my gaze and gave a small laugh.

"Breakfast will be ready in a few minutes, if you want to check on your friend."

I nodded with a wide smile and took myself off to visit Buck. He did appear fine, and nickered as I neared. He needed a good grooming himself, and I wondered where I could find water to clean us both up. Not the stream, since it seemed to be a pristine source of drinking water. Assuring Buck I'd be back later, I returned to the camp when I heard a bell ring, followed by a loud shout declaring breakfast was ready.

Despite the group's hospitality, I felt like a burden and an intruder, but Beth took my situation in hand and gestured to a rough log that served as a bench. She filled a plate with the steaming food and brought it over, along with a cup of strong black coffee.

"Get this into you," she said. "You'll need your strength."

I thanked her profusely and asked if there was any nearby water, clean enough for washing but not potable. A small slough not far away, a few minutes to the north, would suit, she said.

The men began to filter into the eating area from wherever they had been — gathering wood, perhaps, or hunting. Halfway through my meal, John Parsons joined me with his own full plate.

"Are you all right then, James Davidson?" he inquired.

"Much better, sir, thank you."

"You'd best stay with us another day or so. Don't want you fainting out there."

"I appreciate that, sir. Is there anything I can do to help around here, to repay you for all this kindness?"

"We can always use wood if you're up to scavenging for some. God knows it's not plentiful out here." He took a monstrous bite of bacon. "You're headed for Pile of Bones, are you."

What was he getting at? Making conversation, or trying to figure me out?

"Yes, sir."

"Now why would a nice Toronto boy be heading so far west?" It was the latter, then.

"Well, as I said, heading out to where the railway's going."

"Brandon House would be much closer."

I did not know how to answer that question. The truth was that I wanted to get as far away as possible from Garrison, to give myself at least a few months before he could easily reach me. I pretended to chew as I mulled a convincing lie.

"Pile of Bones was suggested to me by someone I trust," I finally answered, lamely. "I suppose I could stop somewhere nearer. I haven't heard of Brandon House."

"Ah. Well, keep it in mind, young man. You could do worse. And what do you do?"

"I'm a goldsmith and a machinist." I did not have a lie prepared for that question.

"I see. Not much use for goldsmiths out here."

"No. I'm hoping to find work with a blacksmith or at a machine shop. Always carts and wheels and things to fix."

"True, James. Very true." He finished up his food and stood. "Well. Think about the wood, if you're feeling well enough."

Thus released, I returned my plate and muttered something about heading out to the slough before searching for wood. Some of my things were in the tent, but my personal kit and Buck's comb were still tucked into the saddlebags. I returned to my horse, untied him and led him in the direction of the pothole.

Five minutes later, I came upon the small body of water, lying shallow but cool and free of weeds and slime. I thanked my not-entirely-lucky stars again that it was spring and not summer, when the heat would sully the ponds and creeks of the bald prairie.

It was not entirely bald. A few trees, just coming into leaf, edged the slough. I shucked my clothing and hung everything but my underwear from the scanty branches. Digging out a sliver of soap from the saddlebag along with Buck's brush, I removed everything but the bridle from his big body and led him into the water.

Once up to my waist, I removed the offending underwear and scrubbed it with soap, rinsed it and tucked it into Buck's bridle. I then rubbed him down and let him drink his fill before soaping myself from torso to hair. The water was cold but not icy; even so, I thought with intense nostalgia of Hannah Vogel's hot baths. Being naked for the first time in days, not to mention relatively clean, dispelled the ache of the memory. Sluiced of the fever sweat, the dust and nature's detritus, I felt almost renewed and definitely refreshed.

A rustle came from behind me. Just the wind, I told myself. Smarten up, my brain added. I had a lot to learn about being alone in the middle of nothingness and braced myself to look around — just in case beast or man approached. I was naked, after all. Making a run for it would be tricky, to say the least.

I crouched behind Buck, who snorted but raised no particular alarm. Likely not a large animal, then. Peering over his back, I saw nothing, but heard a second faint noise, as of something scrabbling in grasses and dry leaves. A rabbit, perhaps?

Either way, the being knew I was there. I splashed noisily in the water and said loudly, "Time to go back, Buck. Are you ready?"

He whinnied in assent, and just as I came around him, I heard a little squeak. Another rustle. And saw just the shadow of a figure darting away.

Someone had been spying on me.

●　　●　　●

Disconcerting, being spied on. I listened for any further evidence of nearby animals or humans, but detecting nothing, I led Buck out of the water and dragged my dirty clothes onto my clean body. I had two extra pairs of underwear in the saddle, so at least there was that.

We spent the rest of the morning searching for wood. Parsons was right; dry branches were hard to come by, but we managed to scrabble together a decent bundle, tied up with a long piece of leather I had packed for this sort of purpose. Riding back to camp, I resolved to leave the next morning. The small event at the slough had unnerved me.

When I arrived, lunch was already being served. It seemed the entire community had gathered for the noon meal; there must have been forty people surrounding the cooking fire. The food included some roasted meat, a root vegetable, more bread and more beans.

Once I had dropped the bundle of twigs by the fire, I became slowly but completely surrounded by the curious members of the group. Questions flew furiously: Where was I from? Where was I going, and why? What did I do for a living? How old was I?

Clearly, John Parsons had not shared all my details with his bunch, and I did my best to answer politely but briefly. I did not want to lie. I could not tell the truth. And I wondered which one of them had seen most of me in the water. Or was it some other interloper?

Curiosity somewhat slaked, and with the sun soaring in the sky, most of the people headed for shelter after an hour of chatter. It seemed the best thing for me to hide, as well, so I returned to my tent. I was not fully recovered, I realized, and fell asleep immediately.

For a long time, as it turned out. Beth came to fetch me for dinner, as the afternoon began its slow turn into evening.

"Are you feeling all right?" she asked, anxiety in her voice.

"Yes, I'm quite fine, thanks. Just tired from the fever. I'll be right as rain by tomorrow, I'm sure."

"Does that mean you're leaving in the morning?"

"Yes, I think so. I don't want to be a burden, Beth."

"You're no burden, James. Come and have some supper."

I learned a bit more about these people over the final meal. They had come from southern Ontario searching for a place to settle where they could, as Beth had mentioned, buy land. But railway work was crucial to the plan; they needed the money to cover the farm purchase, not to mention buy the beasts and equipment.

Land was cheaper in Western Canada than it was in Ontario, and hard to come by in the United States. They wanted a larger holding, more than they could afford at home. Therefore, they had sold up and began the trip to Brandon House.

At some point along the way, they had purchased provisions in railway towns, where I thought they had likely contracted the fever.

"How long will you stay here?" I asked Beth, as an aside to the conversation.

"Two or three more days. As soon as Mother and two of the other women are well enough. You could wait for us, James. Travel is safer in numbers."

"I could, but I really need to get going. It's a long trip and I only have so much food and so on."

She nodded, a bit sadly, and looked down.

"What's wrong, Beth?"

"Oh, nothing. It's just . . . it would be nice to have someone new to talk to. That's all. I'd better go and check on Mother."

As I watched her hurry away, I thought it was indeed nice to have someone to talk to. This land made a man — and I am sure a woman — feel lonely as hell.

CHAPTER NINETEEN

In the utter blackness of a moonless prairie night, far from any light apart from the small, distant flicker of the fire, I awakened with a start to realize I was not alone.

A quiet presence lay a foot or two away. I sensed breathing and smelled sweetness.

"Beth," I said, suddenly knowing and propping myself on my elbows. "What's wrong? What are you doing here?"

She emitted a small sob. "I'm sorry," she said.

"For what? Are you all right?"

"Y-y-yes. I think so. I feel very . . . strange."

"Are you catching the fever?" I sat upright, carefully wrapping my blanket around my hips.

"No." She seemed to pull herself together but did not change her position. "I saw you today, James."

Ah. The spy.

"How, er, much of me did you see?"

"Enough."

Then she did sit up, and as my eyes adjusted to the gloom, I saw she wore only a thin shift. The bulk of skirts and blouses did not surround her shadowy, slim body. She reached for the hem and in one swift, sure movement removed the skimpy garment.

"Can you see me, James? I want you to see me."

I could not see much, but the swells of perfect breast and slender flank were faintly illuminated by starlight. I tried to breathe and for a moment could not speak.

"Beth," I finally said hoarsely. "What are you doing?"

"I want you to love me," she whispered. "My body . . . I can't bear it. It aches so. I saw your muscles, James. I want to feel them."

She reached out with a tentative hand and touched me on the shoulder, drew her hand along my arm and entwined her fingers with mine. Sliding closer, she lifted my hand to her mouth and kissed the second finger, before placing it on the side of her warm breast. Her other hand reached out and landed on my chest.

I had never heard a woman breathe like that, and never felt a woman's hands on my bare skin. The sensations burned through me like lightning through a pine; I pulled away, my own breath coming hot and gasping.

I did not know what to say or do. How could I push away this beautiful, aching, desirable and very naked girl? I recovered my powers of speech at the thought of her innocence. Not to mention my own.

"Beth, stop. Just wait a moment. How old are you?"

"I'm eighteen, James. I am a woman. And you are clearly a man."

Thoughts of the pregnant Alice Garrison sent a wave of nausea through my body. I knew better than anyone that I was not at fault, but I had been exiled from Toronto on merely the suspicion of wrongdoing. Yet I also knew more about physical love, at least intellectually, than many young men, thanks to Mum. Sexual education was important to her, and she had delivered the information without a single blush, euphemism or prevarication.

"And my moon is waning," added Beth quietly. "I want you, James. Please."

Full, soft lips were suddenly caressing my mouth, and desire threatened to drown me. So intense was the feeling, I felt as if I was flailing in deep water, unable to find the surface of control. I gripped her shoulders and kissed her back madly, wildly. The blanket fell away from my hips, and we were on our knees, pressed against one another, exchanging fire for fire.

I thought I might lose my mind. My hands slipped from her shoulders and down her back to cup her smooth, rounded buttocks as she moaned into my mouth. I lifted her then, and carefully placed her on my thin bedroll, her hair spread gloriously on the coat I used for a pillow.

Seeing a woman in the throes of intense desire for the first time is impossible to forget. She panted and begged and cried out, thrusting her breasts toward me and pushing my head down to her nipples. I kissed and sucked them both; her hips bucked and twitched, and I hoped I could release her. I knew how, in theory, but had no experience of it.

Beth smelled like fresh air and ancient musk, luring me into a state of awed absorption. I drew my tongue down her breastbone and belly, marveling at the slightly salty sweet skin, and finally reached the silk I sought.

I was surprised at how slippery she was; how did erotic passion create this wet warmth? Not in the least put off, I gently touched her with my lips and tongue, and after a delicate search discovered the spot Mum had told me about. There was no doubt, based on Beth's reaction. She gasped, then choked a scream by covering her face with my coat. I clasped her backside, held her in place, and only moments later her entire body convulsed. She thrashed and shuddered under me for a minute or more, then seemed to melt into a state of exhaustion.

I crawled up her body and held her in my arms, wondering just what I was going to do to manage my own extreme arousal. Finally, she turned, kissed me deeply and said, "Will you not enter me, James?"

"I want to, Beth. I don't . . . know if it's right."

"I won't get pregnant. As I said."

"That's not the point."

"It is to me."

"Beth, we may never see each other again. I'd feel like a bounder."

"You haven't changed your mind, then."

"No. I must leave tomorrow. There's no help for it." I could not tell her why.

She sighed deeply but seemed to accept my answer. Her hand touched my face, then my chest, and she gently drew it down my body, finally clasping me firmly.

"I won't let you go like this," she said.

Just as it was with her, the release came hard, fast, and so powerfully I wondered if I had fainted. For a moment afterward, I was unsure whether to be horrified, embarrassed or simply grateful. But Beth sighed again, this time with something like contentment, or perhaps self-congratulation, and I decided to simply be happy. For once.

"Is it stupid to say thank you?" I muttered into her hair.

"No. Thank you, too, James."

She turned and curled herself into me, and after some nonsensical murmurings, we fell asleep. Until she awakened two hours later, and we started the entire process all over again.

Before dawn, she slipped out of our cocoon and out the door, but not before I saw the tears trickle down her cheeks in the early half-light.

"I'm so sorry, Beth," I whispered.

Then I dressed, gathered my things, found my horse and rode away.

Chapter Twenty

The blinding sun beat down on the dusty plain, and before long my stomach rumbled. I also longed for another round of physical love with Beth.

My thoughts churned around the events of the night before. I felt utterly baffled by Beth's desire for me; perhaps I had been the only man she had encountered in some time, outside her group. She must have found me somewhat desirable, though. What woman begs to make love with a man she does not want?

At my next stop for water, I stripped to the waist and peered into the glassy pond. I saw someone I did not recognize. Long brown hair curled almost to my collarbone, and a scruffy growth of beard obscured my chin. Sunburned cheeks glowed beneath my eyes. I looked years older than I had a week ago.

Returning to the saddle, I pulled out an aging piece of hard bread and a chunk of the deer meat I had dried into jerky. The food tasted awful, but my spirit needed nourishment more than my stomach.

Beth had shown me, like no one else — apart from Meg, although on a different level — what having a woman in your arms and in your bed could do to a man. It could make him crave that warmth, that companionship. That incredible release. How long would it be before I found a woman who would complete my life?

Were there any women, wherever I settled?

The day dragged on, uneventful and dreadful. As did the next day, and the next, and the next.

The upside to this boredom and loneliness was that I was making considerable progress toward my new home; I estimated that I might be halfway there. I was, however, also running out of food. I had not passed any sizeable settlement for days, nor had I encountered game apart from one small rabbit. I would soon have to find food for Buck, as well — something more substantial than the grasses he had been grazing.

I found something resembling a trail on the fourth day; not much of one, but there were distinct tracks cutting through the scanty bits of brush. I hoped that if I followed the vague, shallow ruts, I might encounter human beings. Soon. Friendly ones, preferably.

The next morning, I awakened to an unearthly noise. It shocked me out of sleep; thank God I had tucked myself into the side of a small hill. Buck, standing nearby, reared and snorted. Right. Not a nightmare, then.

I scrambled out of my bedroll, pulled on my jacket and braced myself, gun at the ready. What the hell could possibly make that strange screeching noise? It did not sound like any animal I had ever heard or heard of. Some kind of futuristic machine? What would it be doing out here?

It grew louder. The squealing sounded like an enormous animal in great pain, yet I was sure it was not a bison — few of them still roamed the plains — nor a horse. Panic made me think of elephants shrieking into the morning air, and I laughed wildly at the idea.

There be monsters out west, I had always thought in my younger days. I hoped my imagination would not prove accurate.

Buck's eyes rolled and he stamped the ground, huffing. Time to investigate before he lost his mind and ran away. I muttered soothing words in his ear and he calmed slightly; but I still tied his reins to a bush before crawling up the hillock to see what I could see.

There were at least twenty of them. Dust billowed from the wheels as the noise reached discomfiting proportions. I lay on my belly, mouth agape in wonder at the carts coming toward me at remarkable speed. Each drawn by an ox or a horse, most were covered with tarps of hide or canvas. Those that were open, I discerned, overflowed with goods: barrels of things, crates of stuff, more hides stacked high.

Traders. Obviously. Potential friends or foes, I could not guess; but there was one of me, and many of them. The need for food and feed crept into my decision-making process, layered over the fear that gripped my gut. My ears protested, begging me not to approach. Just let them go by; hide in the hollow and carry on, they said.

What I had not counted on were the sharp eyes of the people bearing down on me.

"Arrêt!" cried a voice. Its owner lifted a musket into the air. "Naki!"

He had seen me. I assumed these words meant stop, or come out of there, or show yourself. Judging by the tone of the voice, he was not greeting me with hello. I put the carbine down, hiding it at arm's length, and slowly got to my feet, hands high in the air.

The large man on the horse, whom I assumed was the lookout because he rode alongside the screeching vehicles, thundered toward me and moments later glared down into my face.

"Arrêt," he repeated, then gave me a quizzical look. "Stop right there. Levez vos mains. Keep your hands up."

He swung down in a smooth movement demonstrating his expert horsemanship; even quaking with terror, I could not help but admire his elegance.

"French? English?" he demanded, clearly realizing I was not Cree.

"English."

"Are you alone?"

I decided to simply nod.

"What are you doing here?"

"I'm heading for Pile of Bones. Just moving west. Sir."

He laughed at that. "Je m'appelle . . . I am Dumas. Your name?"

"Sinclair. James Sinclair."

"St. Clair? French? But you speak English."

"Scots. Sinclair," I repeated.

"Sinclair. Ah. And are you clear of sin?"

That comment jolted me. I was, but someone in Toronto hoped to prove otherwise.

"I am," I said.

He cocked his head at me and lowered his gun. "Are you mounted?"

"Yes."

"Perhaps you should ride along with us. Tell me your story. Safer that way. Where is your horse?"

"Down the hill. I hope."

"And do you also have a gun?"

"Yes."

"But you are not armed."

"No. I put it down when you called to me."

"Very smart. And very brave."

"Hardly," I said with a small laugh. "You have me at a disadvantage."

He gave me a smile, showing strong teeth. "Let's find your horse and gun."

He dismounted, and I led the way down the slope. Dumas simply watched me as I gathered my bedroll, strapped it to Buck's back and reclaimed my carbine. I did not think I had much of a choice but to attach myself to this wagon train. Would he shoot me if I declined? I doubted it; he could have done so already. But he was also right. If his people were friendly, it would be safer to travel with them than alone.

I felt a little weak from taut nerves and lack of proper nutrition. I climbed, relieved, onto Buck's back. Dumas turned and we followed him back to the now-slowed collection of carts, beasts and humans. When the driver of the lead wagon saw Dumas returning, he clicked his tongue against his teeth and the train began to move again. We rode alongside.

Dumas said nothing for the first mile or so, peering at me from under his hat as if sizing me up.

"Tell me, now," he finally said.

"What do you want to know?"

"What are you doing out here all alone?"

"It's a long story."

"I have a lot of time."

I gave him the sanitized and not entirely accurate version. I was from Toronto; I was coming out west to seek my fortune; I was hoping to get ahead of the railroad, maybe get established before the boom. He asked me if I had a profession, and I answered him truthfully. His eyebrows lifted.

"Could you help us fix these carts, if needed? We can do it ourselves, but you could hurry up the process."

"I've never worked on carts like these, but I'm sure I could."

He sank back into silence, mulling over what I had told him.

"That's not all of it, I think. With your skills, you should have done well in Toronto."

"No. Not quite all." I was a terrible liar, and I knew it.

"A fugitive, then. From something. The law? Love? Disaster?"

"Close enough."

"Maybe you will tell me later."

"Maybe." My own curiosity overcame me. "May I ask who you are? Where you're going?"

"We are Red River Métis. We are traders. We make this trip every year, from St. Paul through the Winnipeg region and up to Lac La Biche."

"Where is that? I've never heard of it."

"High in the North-West Territories. A very long way. But trading is good. These lands have few people, compared to your Toronto, but there are enough. And they need goods."

"Why," I asked tentatively, "do the carts squeal so loudly?"

"They are made entirely of wood, with a little leather here and there. And so, they screech."

"Can't you oil them?"

"No. The dust gathers in the oil and clogs the axles."

That made sense. I had hoped I was onto something that might reduce the ear-splitting noise, but obviously they had thought of that.

We trotted along for another hour until I realized I might fall, weak with hunger, off my horse. There had been no time for breakfast. I reached over into the saddle and brought out my last chunk of slightly mouldy and very hard bread.

Dumas contemplated me as I chewed.

"You need food," he said.

"Yes," I agreed. "Badly. Do you have any that I could buy?"

"Of course. But I have an idea. We will stop to eat soon; you will join us as a guest. But then tonight at the fire, you will tell me your real story. Agreed?"

My face must have been a study in internal argument. It would be a relief to talk about it. But would he believe me? Would he consider me a danger to the women in the caravan? What would happen then?

"Agreed," I said.

That night, settled with full stomachs around a roaring fire, with Buck happily chomping his oats and slurping his water, Dumas handed me a small tin cup of whiskey. This was no moonshine. It was the real thing, and it tasted like heaven and hellfire. It also opened my mouth, as I am sure he knew it would.

"All right, Sinclair. The whole story."

As it spilled from my lips, even I felt amazement at what had happened over the past few weeks and months. I explained, with a sharp pang of sorrow over my mother's likely grief, how I had left my parents' home. How I had become a goldsmith, which led to meeting Alice Garrison, which led to her father's accusation. I told Dumas about my escape from Hannah Vogel's boarding house, which had been connected to the Underground Railroad, and about hopping the trains and finding my horse and gun. I told him about meeting the hobos, Jones and Clancy. I even told him about Hannah's former lover, something I should have kept to myself; but the whiskey was having its intended effect.

I must have talked for two hours. The sun, by then, was well down and we sat in black velvet darkness, staring into the flames. I did not protest too much about the allegations, however. I did not go on about how I did not do it; how I had never touched the girl, apart from that one wild kiss she bestowed upon me. He would either believe me or he would not.

I finally stopped talking and waited.

"*Incroyable*," he finally said. "That bastard."

My chest released a gust of held breath.

"I know this Garrison," Dumas said next to my extreme amazement.

"You do?"

"I've heard of him. His long arms are reaching out onto the plains. He is buying land, speculating on selling it to the railway. Some of these lands are Métis lands; some belong to the Nations. He is a brutal man. If you do not agree to sell to him, he will force you."

"How does he do that, Dumas?"

"Burns buildings and tents. Frightens and hurts the women, and worse. Threatens gunfire. He has men out here. They are not good men."

If they were anything like Garrison, they would not be. I suddenly realized what this meant for me.

"He's already here, then. At least his henchmen are."

"Yes. You may have to go further west, James, and then take stock. Or you could come with us to Lac La Biche."

I thought about that for a moment, but then shook my head. "Thank you, but no. I'd like to settle down as soon as possible."

He nodded, staring into the leaping flames. "There is a tiny settlement west of Pile of Bones. They say it might be the next major stop on the railroad. You might consider that, at least for a while. There is another settlement coming up north of there, on the river, if you have to move on. No railway there yet."

I considered his profile: a powerful man with a sharp jaw, and large brown eyes set over strong slanting cheekbones. Over dinner, the women had fussed over him, and I could see why. He was not a scout. He was a leader.

"Would you have believed my story if you hadn't heard of Garrison?" I asked.

"Yes. I would have. You are guileless, James. I will try to beat that out of you in the next few days. But I admit it gave you more credibility."

Chapter Twenty-one

The camp fell quiet; even the beasts, exhausted, made little noise. Surrounded by humans, warmed by the fire, I passed out from the sheer relief of sharing my woes, and a little whiskey.

At the dawn, a great bustle awakened me. The women set fires and began to cook food as the men saw to the oxen and horses. Hides and blankets were gathered and returned to the carts. Rising, I went searching for Buck, only to find that he had already been fed and watered.

A sweet girl of perhaps fourteen shyly presented me with a plate heaped with fresh flatbread, hot salted meat and dried fruit. I thanked her with a smile and a nod; she gravely nodded back.

Dumas came to tell me about the day ahead. We would continue west toward the verdant Qu'Appelle Valley, formed by ancient melting glaciers. A river by the same name split the hills and provided a reliable water supply.

"We should make it there by tomorrow sometime," he mused. I could not wait to see it; I envisioned a green oasis in the middle of the plain. "We will stop there for a while, rest and replenish our water barrels."

Moments later, the carts were loaded, the fires extinguished and the beasts bridled. In no time, we were squealing down the trail ahead of the sun. I was already adjusting to the din.

We travelled for hours, stopped for a cold lunch, and travelled some more. In the late afternoon, we reached a small settlement of people, identified by Dumas as a Plains Cree Nation. I helped unload the goods from the carts as Dumas spoke fluently to the chief, as he described him later, and accepted something in a pouch as payment.

At one point, I heard him use the word "naki" again, which he had yelled at me the day before. A Cree word, then. Stop. I stuffed that into my brain for future use.

A few miles later, Dumas raised his arm and signalled to the people behind us: the carts slowed, and I realized we would now stop for the night. A little bluff offered shelter from the wind, and a small hollow nearby held the promise of water.

We chatted again that night, had another drop of whiskey, and slept soundly by the fire.

I could get used to this, I thought. Humans, food, direction, knowledge, conversation. Other than sleeping rough, it was a return to civilization.

• • •

The crack of a rifle shot sang through the air. I lurched up, only to be instantly pressed down by Dumas' large hand.

"Idiot," he hissed. "Stay down."

Another crack.

"What's happening?" I asked, flat on my stomach.

"Raiders."

The dawn had just begun to creep over the eastern horizon; whoever wielded the rifle had hoped to catch my new Métis friends by surprise. The shooter was certainly not alone.

"How many, do you think?"

"Don't know," said Dumas, checking his weapon. "Get your gun. Is it fully loaded?"

"Yes. I haven't shot it for two days."

At the first shot, the camp jumped and churned into full resistance mode. They had been through this before — likely many times. The little ones hid behind the carts, shuttled there by their mothers. Every man seized his gun and flopped on his belly.

"I hope you can shoot," Dumas said.

We slithered like snakes toward one of the carts and took cover. Dumas raised his head above the planks and scanned for the interlopers, then ducked back down.

"They're coming from the south," he said. "We have maybe a minute. Looks like at least twenty of them, judging by the dust. Are you ready?"

No. I was terrified. But I nodded just the same.

We heard the galloping hooves strike the earth. Peering through the wheel spokes, I saw the horses' legs, thundering toward us in a terrifying line of force. If Dumas had a battle plan, I did not know it.

"Tell me what to do," I gasped.

"Wait until they're closer. Watch what I do. Then shoot. That is all. And try not to get hit."

Dumas poked the barrel of his rifled musket through the wheel and breathed, steadying himself for accuracy. I copied his actions and thrust my carbine forward.

"Not yet . . . not yet . . ." he muttered.

Another shot, then another came from the attackers, followed by whoops and yee-haws that carried like war cries in the cool morning air.

"Now," Dumas said. "Aim for the legs."

The thought of hobbling and likely murdering a horse made me nauseous, but there was nothing for it. The protection of these families was all that mattered.

I fired.

The horse fell, screaming, mere feet from the wagon that divided us from the raiders. The rider came down hard under his mount's heavy body: one down. In the few seconds it took for me to find another target, I heard volleys of shots all around me. The Métis gave as good as they got, but the raiders were mounted and upon us from on high. They had us at a powerful disadvantage.

Dumas fired in the same moment I did, bringing a second horse and rider to the ground. At least we were diminishing the ranks, but I knew, as Dumas certainly did, that the others would be in the camp in seconds. And they would be furious about their fallen comrades, as well as ruthless and greedy.

They came around the west side, horses pounding and men yelling. Dumas scrambled to the east side of the cart and I followed, breath coming short and fast. Fuck this, my brain said, surprising me even in that moment. I stood, braced my carbine on the cart, and emitted a yell of my own.

A raider's narrowed eyes focused on me as his head spun around; they were all I could see above a black bandana tied over nose and mouth. As his body turned in the saddle, he swung his rifle in my direction. I fired again, twice, as quickly as the gun would allow. A bullet flew over his head, but the second found its mark. The dark eyes registered shock and amazement as blood began to spread inexorably over his chest.

The other raiders now surrounded the camp and the small war was in full cry. Dumas' men traded fire as we left our position and plunged into the fray, unshielded by the cart. I ran toward one of the men, moving diagonally to make his shot more difficult, screaming at the top of my lungs with bloodlust in my heart. I could not shoot him, but I could shoot the horse and did so. The poor beast fell to its forelegs and threw his rider over his head.

I fell too, onto my stomach, and crawled behind another cart, looking for the next possible target. As I did, I witnessed Dumas standing tall in the middle of the camp, firing his weapon at one, then another, then another rider. The scene was horrifying and magnificent at the same time.

Yet another raider emerged from the north, riding like a demon toward Dumas. My friend stood his ground and shot again; the horse lurched and whinnied, but the man held on and fired. Dumas sank to the ground, clutching his thigh.

"Bastard!" I screamed, and burst from my hiding place, aiming directly at the raider as I ran. Much better by now at shooting while mounted, I drilled my bullet into his hip.

Then I dove at Dumas, who bled copiously from his wound. He was a sitting duck and I couldn't leave him there, injured and unprotected. Flat on the ground, I dragged him away as two of the Métis men did their best to cover us. They were excellent marksmen. Two more enemies pitched off their horses as I pulled Dumas under the nearest cart.

"So you can shoot," he gasped. Sweat ran down his face in rivers.

"Apparently. Be quiet, Dumas."

The fight continued around us, and I saw one, then two, then three of the camp's men fall; but I focused on Dumas and his leg. Ripping away the heavy fabric of his pant, I saw the blood pulsing from the bullet hole. No time to remove the lead slug. I tore the tail of my own shirt off and pressed it against the wound, then tied the improvised bandage with the shreds of his pantleg.

"Don't move, my friend. I'll be back."

I emerged from under the cart, dragged down some blankets to hide Dumas, and grabbed his rifle. Three bullets left.

Looking up to survey the scene, it seemed that the raiders had been reduced to a rump; but one rode hellbent through the tent area. He reached down from his horse, but I could not understand why . . . until he straightened, with one arm tightly curled under the slender arms of the girl who had served me breakfast. He swung her into the saddle as she kicked and screamed; but of course he was too strong. She could not break his grasp.

Nor could I shoot him from my angle; I would more than likely hit the girl. No doubt in my mind about his intention. She would never be seen again.

He pulled on the reins; the horse reared, turned and sped away with its double burden. I had to chase him, and not on foot. I ducked behind the tents and raced to the horses, finding Buck in a lather but otherwise unharmed.

"Ready for a race, Buck?" I asked him, panting as I jumped aboard. "Let's go."

Buck was more than ready for a gallop; fury widened his eyes. I tugged him about and let him fly. Please, God, let him be faster than the other horse, I begged. Please.

The evil bastard who had kidnapped the girl was riding south; we followed his dusty trail. I urged Buck on, and before long he gained on the other horse; I imagined he took it as a challenge. But what the hell should I do? Shoot the man in the back? Shoot the horse in the rump? What would happen to the girl if I did?

My brain tried to deal with the various trajectories and outcomes as I let Buck surge ahead. I highly doubted that negotiation would be an option.

Suddenly, the horse ahead of me slowed. Did he not sense he was being chased? Or did the man simply plan to turn around and shoot me — or, God forbid, Buck — protected by the girl's body?

I pulled Buck back, hoping the kidnapper had not detected us. A little grove of trees provided some cover, and I quickly led Buck under some branches. He breathed heavily, but so did the other horse.

It had come to a full stop. The man jumped down, dragged the girl out of the saddle and hauled her, weeping and squirming, to the ground. If I knew anything about men, they were easily distracted by desire, if that was what this was. He could not wait any longer to have this girl and had let his guard down.

In a flash, he rucked up her skirts while rapidly dealing with himself. She screamed again and he slapped her, hard. I thought my head would explode with rage. I raced out of the trees, yelling at the top of my lungs for him to stop; he stood and turned in shock, britches already falling.

I stopped running and shot the bastard in the balls.

And then in the heart.

CHAPTER TWENTY-TWO

He was definitely dead.

And I, milksop and Mama's boy from an eastern city, who had never done more than squash a spider and clench my father's fist before this mad journey . . . I was glad. I had done murder, more than once today. So it had to be.

Thank God he did not fall on her; he toppled toward me, missing her feet by inches. Cautiously, I approached the terrified and weeping child, for she was little more than that. It did not take much imagination to consider that she might also be terrified of me; after all, I had just shot the man looming over her slight body. But she had also given me food and a nod yesterday, and I would have to persuade her to trust me.

I wished I had been more courteous that morning and asked for her name. I did not even know if she spoke English, as well as French and Michif, but I had to try. Damn it, I really had to learn some more French. I cast about in my brain for the few words I remembered from the school of Mum.

"Chérie," I finally dragged out of my brain. I bent at the waist as far as possible to reduce my considerable height and walked very slowly toward her. "Sweetheart. Are you all right? You're safe now. I know that was very frightening, but I will take you back to the camp. Okay? Retournez? Bien?"

She brought herself up to her knees and sat staring at the lifeless form of her attacker. Finally, she turned her gaze up at me, as if finally realizing I had spoken; but she did not reply.

"What is your name, little one?" I asked. "Votre nom?"

She continued to stare for another moment and tipped her head to one side, perhaps considering my request.

"Isabelle," she said, in no more than a whisper.

I crouched before her, three or four feet away. "Isabelle. That is so beautiful."

She ducked her head and looked away.

I tried again. "Did you know that many great queens in history had your name? They were very strong and brave. Like you."

Her head snapped back toward me, her lips parting in surprise. So yes, she could speak English, and I had her full attention.

"Do you think you can ride back with me? Back to the camp? It's not safe out here."

"It's not safe at the camp either," she pointed out. A fresh tear coursed down her cheek.

Hell. That was true. Well, we would have to return at some juncture, so . . .

"What if we go most of the way, hide in the trees and see?" I suggested.

She hesitated, chewing a knuckle.

"I will not hurt you. I promise." I crossed my heart. I had to convince her, somehow. I could not leave her out here alone.

"Promise?"

Oh God. "Yes, I do." How could I make her feel safe? "Here. Take my knife," I said, dragging it out of my boot. It was not much of a knife, but it was better than nothing. I could hardly give her my gun. "If I do anything wrong, you can stab me with it."

Isabelle blinked, then held out her hand for the small weapon.

"If we find any more bad men, I can stab them too."

Not the worst idea I had heard, actually. Maybe the girls should be armed for just such a situation. Or maybe the "bad men" would simply wrest the weapon away. What a terrible dilemma.

"That's a good plan. Are you ready to go?"

"Yes."

Buck sidled his way up behind me, and I helped Isabelle mount first, hoping it would not feel like being grabbed by a kidnapper and would-be rapist. I very slowly swung up behind her and clicked Buck into a trot. A gallop might spook her.

This being accomplished — she sat quietly before me, watching the plain ahead — I began to worry about what we would find at the camp. Would Dumas be all right? How many were dead? Had the last raider been run off or killed?

I slowed Buck to a walk as we neared and directed him into a clump of high bushes. I could not see much, but I also could not hear anything. No shots, no agitated whinnies, no yells or screams. Loath to leave Isabelle unprotected, I debated my options: let Buck look after her and go in alone, or risk another devastating event if the raiders were still about.

Neither course of action seemed remotely sane. I decided to let Isabelle choose. She likely had more experience with this sort of thing than I.

"Do you want to stay here with Buck, Isabelle? Just while I check things out? Or do you want to come along? We'd have to be very, very quiet."

"I am quiet," she objected. "I'm coming with you."

I slid out of the saddle and reached up for her; she demurred briefly but then allowed me to help her down. Leading Buck, we walked a few more yards, and then I told my stalwart horse to wait. He snorted but held up, and we crept along on foot.

The scene that met our eyes was horrific. The battle had been won, but the casualties were significant. Seeing no sign of the attackers, I sprinted the last little way into the heart of the camp. Blood ran, men lay dead, women keened and wept.

Isabelle screamed at the sight and flew into the middle of the madness, crying for her mother. A woman lifted her head, saw her daughter, and ran toward her, weeping. She caught Isabelle up in her arms and hugged her tightly, saying, "Mon Dieu, merci, merci." At least her mother was alive and apparently well.

Dumas. Where was Dumas? Had they found him under the blankets I had used to cover him?

"Madame," I said, approaching Isabelle's mother. "Where is Dumas?"

"I don't know! I don't know!"

"I'll find him. Wait here."

I dashed to the cart under which I had left him and made out the shape of a large body, still lying under blankets and hides. It occurred to me that the entire rescue of Isabelle had taken no more than half an hour, and the people were so busy triaging the wounded, they likely had not had time to seek a missing member.

Throwing myself to my knees, I skidded slightly in the bloodied dust to Dumas' side and threw back the coverings.

"Dumas! Are you awake? Are you all right? Speak to me."

Not a word. I felt his head; it was clammy, and his clothing was soaked with blood and sweat. Damn. I shook him slightly, but it was no use.

I ran back to Isabelle and asked her for my knife; she handed it to me without protest.

"I need alcohol," I told her mother. "Quickly. Where can I get some? The whiskey. Something."

"Dumas?" she asked.

"Yes. Please. Hurry."

"I will help you. Come."

"Madame, what is your name?" I asked, again horrified at my discourtesy, as we strode toward a cart containing barrels of alcohol.

"Je m'appelle . . . I am Jeanne."

"I am James."

"I know."

At the cart, she reached for a bottle and decanted the alcohol, then followed me to where Dumas lay.

"Oh!" she cried, darting at him. "Michel! Michel! Wake up! Réveillez!"

"We have to get this bullet out of him, and stop the bleeding," I said.

She looked at me as if I were mad. "Of course."

Of course. She had been through this before; I was the greenhorn.

"I'm sorry," I said, and she nodded. "Let's do it."

I poured the alcohol liberally over my knife and then into Michel Dumas' gory wound. He twitched, thank God. That got his brain's attention, at least.

"Have you done this before?" I asked Jeanne.

"Yes. Not often; we have a healer in our family." She took the knife, but her hands shook. "I cannot. I cannot cut open my husband's leg."

"Your husband?" I gasped. She was his wife, and therefore Isabelle was Dumas' daughter. He was a dark horse. I could not understand why he had not told me. "All right. I will try. No time to waste."

Under Jeanne's instruction, I used the knife to open the wound further, splashing alcohol as I did, and peered inside for the bullet. He bled less profusely, which helped, but I saw no sign of a slug. I went further in. Finally, I detected a slight gleam, which could have been metal or human sinew.

"Do you have a tool to pull the bullet out?" I asked hopefully. "What could I use?"

"Ah," she said, steadying up now that we were making progress. She stood to reach into the cart, burrowed about for a brief while, and knelt again, extending a small pair of tongs. More alcohol sanitized them as much as possible, and I dove into Dumas' leg.

I grasped the gleaming thing, but it slipped away from me in the blood. I tried again, and again, and slowly, carefully, drew it out. More blood spurted, but the offending bullet no longer resided in his leg.

"Quickly, now," Jeanne said. "Pressure. Here." She gave me a cloth drawn from a pocket of her dress and I plastered it onto Dumas' thigh.

"Can we move him?"

"In a moment. I will find a travois and one of the men. Wait with him."

Two minutes later, she was back with a helper and we gently transferred Dumas from the blood red earth to the travois before dragging him to his tent.

Jeanne shooed me away and dove in after him to put a poultice on his leg and dose him with medicine. He remained unconscious, but his breathing had improved. I took a deep breath of my own and collapsed in the dust.

I sat with my elbows braced on my knees, hands clasped together and my head down, trying to fathom what I had done that day. Murder, of horses and men. A strange surgery. A race across the plain to reclaim Isabelle. This was life on the Prairies? What was I doing here?

A small sound caught my attention, and I looked up to see Isabelle standing before me with a chunk of bread on a plate and a cup of whiskey. These she placed beside me, then knelt and threw her little arms around my neck.

I burst into tears as she whispered in my ear. "Mercee, m'sieur. Thank you."

Chapter Twenty-three

Dumas made it through the night. Jeanne would not leave his side, but two of the other women finally persuaded her to sleep for a few hours as they kept watch. I slept restlessly, worrying about my new friend. I could not stop myself from heading over to his tent from time to time, hoping for some news about his condition.

When one of the women popped out for water and more whiskey, I stopped her and begged for information.

"He's alive," she said. "He is a strong man. We will see in the morning. Now you must sleep. Go."

I supposed that was the best possible news and I would not get much more. I returned to my bedroll and drifted away until dawn.

As the sun rose and my eyelids could no longer resist the light, I crawled out of my tent and realized that the men of the camp had been up all night, taking shifts at guard duty. I felt terribly guilty that I had not participated and approached one of the men.

"Can I take a shift? I'm sorry, I didn't realize . . ."

He shook his head, then jerked it over toward the fire. "Eat," he said. "Later we will see."

I gathered that perhaps I was not trustworthy enough to stand guard. They may have had a point. I had never done it before and keeping watch at night was likely a learned skill. But breakfast, as alluring as the thought was, had to wait. I limped over to Dumas' tent again, sore muscles reminding me of the rigours they had endured the previous day.

"Hello," I called quietly.

"Come in, James," Jeanne answered.

I pushed aside the flap and ducked inside. Dumas lay on a cot covered in a blanket to ward off the early morning chill; he looked like hell, but his eyes were open.

"Dumas," I said. "How are you? I'm glad to see you awake."

"I'm fine, James," he said, which was greeted by a snort from his wife.

"He is not, but he is alive," Jeanne said. "Thanks in the largest part to you."

I waved away the comment before asking my next question.

"I'm sorry, Dumas. That was insane. I — hate to ask, but how many men did you lose?"

"Four," he said quietly. "We will bury them today. We will then continue our journey tomorrow."

"Tomorrow? Can you travel?"

"I must. We cannot stay here for long. The raiders will have friends, and they will find us. We can't risk another battle."

"No. I can help with the . . . the graves."

"Thank you, James. That would be very kind. But first. I can't find the words to tell you . . ." his voice broke. "My beautiful Isabelle. Gratitude overwhelms me. What can I do? How can I ever thank you for that? And for my, ah, surgery. I don't know what to say."

I had no words either. I approached Dumas and took his hand. He grasped mine with all the considerable strength he still had and stared into my eyes. In that moment, I felt a bond of friendship like never before, born of shared experience, of a shared hell, and a chance encounter in the middle of nowhere.

• • •

We dug six feet into the dusty earth four times. Once the graves were prepared, Dumas was again loaded onto the travois and dragged to the site beside a small hill to provide shelter and eternal protection for the dead.

The families followed, heads bowed in grief. Dumas could not stand, but his words rang with all the power he could muster. He was their leader, and he would not let them down in this moment of tragic loss. I knew this of him, even after a few days' acquaintance.

Most of the ceremony was conducted in Michif, the Métis traditional language, but he added a few sentences in English for my benefit.

"Our warriors were strong and brave. Death does not change that. They fought for us; they protected their families. We will remember them, honour them, and hold their spirits in our hearts, even as we must leave their bodies behind."

He nodded, then, and we slowly filled the graves with earth as the women and children wept. So did Dumas. So did I.

The men were laid to rest in black fabric shrouds; those who had carried their bodies to the gravesite wore black ribbons tied around their arms, and these were placed in the graves along with tobacco and sweetgrass. No bells tolled. Finally, a procession formed and moved slowly back toward the camp without a backward glance.

At dinner, plates were set out for the dead, the food upon them subsequently burned in a roaring fire. I watched these ceremonies with fascination, and at the end of the night, asked Dumas about the rituals. He explained that under normal conditions, the dead would be honoured with a four-day wake, but that was impossible now.

"We must leave in the morning," he said. "Even that might be too late. Be ready at dawn."

I slept little, nerves twitching me awake at regular intervals. Would there be a night raid, I wondered? I thought it was likely, but it never came. When the sun eased over the eastern horizon, I packed my bedroll and other bits of things and struck the tent. All around me, the people did the same in a quiet, organized, deft ballet they had clearly performed hundreds of times. Sentries stood, guns cocked, at strategic positions, scanning the plain in every direction.

Breakfast was cold that morning. While the raiders knew our position, Dumas did not want to add smoke as a signal that we were still there. By full light, we were on the move again, squealing our way toward the verdant valley that we hoped would bring sustenance, water and peace.

•　•　•

The Qu'Appelle Valley dipped below us, river gleaming under moonlight, as we arrived well after sunset. One of Dumas' men led the way down the bank, and I suddenly realized with considerable shock that we neared a small settlement. I could see fires dancing and smoke rising, smell food cooking, hear voices raised in chatter.

We were expected, apparently. With Dumas sidelined, Clément Pelletier, the lead scout, rode first into the tiny town, where he was greeted by cheers and whoops. Men walked out to clap him on the back once he had dismounted; they spoke in rapid Michif, and I gathered only from their nods and bowed heads that Clément was telling them about the raid and the loss of life.

Two men approached our wagon train and lifted Dumas out of his cart, so gently he might have been a child. A third person with a large leather bag on her shoulder came running; she stopped at Dumas' side and peered into his face, illuminated slightly by firelight. I gathered this person was a healer, a theory supported by her actions. She felt Dumas' head, ran hands down his arms and legs, and nodded to the two men.

They had not noticed me yet. Dumas said a few words to the healer, whose head snapped around in my direction.

"Welcome," she said. "I am Marie Beauchesne. You removed Dumas' bullet?"

"Yes. I'm pleased to meet you, Madame."

"We will see what kind of a job you did, Mr. Sinclair. Adequate, at least, since Michel is still alive. Come. You must be hungry."

She disappeared at a trot, followed by the men carrying Dumas with Jeanne close behind. The rest of us made our way into the village square, where Clément began barking orders and pointing in various directions. The horses we led to the edge of the square, where a large trough awaited them. Carts were parked in a small clearing to the east. We set up a few of the tents and went in for dinner. I scarfed down my meal as raucous greetings were shared among the travellers and the townspeople.

For the first time since leaving Toronto, I felt relatively safe. Dumas had cleared me with the settlers as a reasonable human being, and we were a large group. A raid might cause another small war, but we would be sure to win handily.

Still, despite the relief washing over me, I was anxious to be on my way. As I watched the revelry, it occurred to me that if the raiders were Garrison's men, and they had made note of a white man's association with the Métis traders, they might come searching for me. Therefore, my presence held danger for my new friends, not to mention myself. I wanted to reach my destination as quickly as possible.

I rose and went to find the healer's hut, which was easy enough. It stood near the tiny town square, possibly to be near the massive community fire, and was brightly painted with a serpent decorating the door. A caduceus.

The settlement was far from the railway; was this a signal to hobos who had strayed from the line? Or a common symbol for Métis healers?

"Come in," said Marie Beauchesne to my knock.

I ducked inside to see Dumas lying directly ahead of me, apparently awake and seemingly comfortable. He did not squirm in pain nor was he sweating. Good signs, I hoped.

"How do you feel, Dumas?" I asked, as I knelt on the floor beside him.

"All things considered, I'm all right," he said. "Have you had something to eat?"

"I have. They've been very kind. Will you stay here for a while, until you heal?"

"Yes, at least a few days. Marie tells me I have you to thank for my leg. You must have used something to keep the infection away."

"I did. Whiskey. And a hell of a lot of it."

He laughed. "I thought so. I wondered why I smelled like alcohol when I woke up. Thank you, James. You probably saved my leg. Maybe my life. But enough of that. You have something to say, I think."

"Yes. I must leave in the morning. I'll be sorry to go. But I can't help but wonder if Garrison is on your heels in part because of me. And he may find me wherever I am; but I must get farther out, away from the raiders."

Dumas nodded. "I understand. I will miss you, James. Have you decided where you're headed?"

"I think I will go to Pile of Bones, then over to the new settlement you call Moose Jaw. How long will it take me from here?"

"Another few days. Pile of Bones is maybe three, four days out, and Moose Jaw another two or three. We're at the southern end of the valley; this area is known as Katepwa. There are trails, but you may want to stay off them. Still, they will help lead you south and west."

He paused for a moment. "I will send Clément with you for the first few miles. He will point you in the right direction."

"I can't let you do that, my friend."

"You can, and you will. No good getting lost now, and I owe you so much. Clem will be fine; best scout I have ever seen. And I will feel better knowing you have had a good start. James, we will see each other again. I will know where you are, and once we have completed our journey north, I will find you on the way back. Depend on it."

"I'll never forget you, Dumas."

"Nor I you."

I held out my hand, and he grasped it firmly. "Goodbye, James. For now."

Chapter Twenty-four

At first light, Clément Pelletier and I rode out of the settlement and along the river until we were forced to head south. Our bellies were full, our horses were rested, and the morning gleamed with the promise of a perfect day.

He accompanied me, silent and watchful, for three hours. Then he pointed down, and I noticed the faint markings of a wagon trail.

"Follow," said the man of few words. "If you see dust, get off. Here." He handed me a sack. "Now go. Ride hard. When you get to Pile of Bones, do not use your real name. Rest. There is an inn. Then go due west. You will find your new home."

"Thank you, Clément."

He clapped me on the shoulder, looked into my eyes for a moment, nodded and reined his horse around. He rode away in a small whirlwind.

I was alone again, except for Buck. No time to peer inside my bag; the man said to ride hard. I clicked my teeth, gave Buck a gentle prod with my heel, and we cantered down the dusty trail.

Trees and hills became sparse as we rode along. The countryside spread, flat and uninhabited, to each horizon. All very well to say get off the trail should trouble arise, I thought; where the hell would I hide? Tricky, too, to keep a stable eye on the distance as Buck flew, snorting and thundering, over the hard ground. I began to wonder if we would find a sheltered camping spot. It did not look good.

Hours later, I spied a small hill up ahead and slowed Buck to a walk. It would have to do; at least it would provide a break from the wind. I swung off Buck's back and hit the dirt on shaky legs that had been clamping the saddle for ten hours.

I started a small fire, gave Buck as much water as I could, and let him nose the scanty grasses while I pitched my small tent. Finally, I opened the sack: tucked inside were a skin of water, a bottle of whiskey, a large piece of the flatbread they called bannock, dried apples and cured, salted meat. I bit into the bread, still fresh and delicious, took a huge gulp of the whiskey, and fell asleep.

The next day rolled along much like the previous one; I saw no human and pushed poor Buck to go like hell. A hunk of bread, a piece of meat, a swallow of whiskey, another night on the rock-hard ground. But on the third day, early in the afternoon, I reached Pile of Bones.

The settlement rose ahead of me to the south, just a few wooden-frame buildings and a cluster of tents. Fire smoke rose lazily in the still, hot air. A trickle of a creek ran past the buildings, hardly a sufficient water supply for a growing town.

I craved a bath, a hot meal and a bed, but wondered if stopping would be a good idea.

Craving overcame worry. Besides, Buck needed a rest and a long drink of water. I made my way into Pile of Bones, hat low on my brow, peering stealthily out from under its brim in every direction. The few people on the street did look my way — I was a stranger, after all, in a town that could not have been populated with more than five hundred souls — but none appeared sinister.

Feeling slightly braver, I rode up to the tiny hotel and tied Buck to its hitching post. He was the only horse outside, a fact that gave me hope of a room.

A neatly dressed middle-aged man with pomaded hair stood behind the counter, eyeing my dusty self with something close to disapproval.

"May I help you?"

"Yes. I'm hoping for a room, just for tonight."

"Mmphm. Well, I have one. Will you, ah, be needing hot water?"

"I definitely will. How much?"

He pointed to a scribbled sign behind the desk. The room was one dollar; hot water went for twenty-five cents, which I thought was rather high considering my experience at Hannah Vogel's.

"Thank you. I'll take it. And about my horse. Where can I stable him?"

"Across the street," he said, handing me a key. "Room's down the hall on your left. When do you want the hot water?"

"Half an hour?"

"Okay," he said, ungraciously. "Bathroom is across from you and to the left as you come out."

"Anywhere to eat in this town?"

"The missus can rustle up some dinner. Soup and beef tonight. Fifteen cents. All right?"

"Yes, thanks. I'll be back as soon as I deal with the horse."

"Just a minute, mister. You have to sign the register first."

Damn. I had not come up with an alias yet; you would think I could have managed that over almost three solitary days on the trail. I searched my brain for a reasonable moniker as I reached for the pen and dipped it in the inkwell.

Clancy Jones is what emerged from its tip. Apparently, I had had the hobos on my mind after seeing the serpent on the healer's door. Well, it would have to do. It was only one night, but I would have to remember to answer to Mr. Jones.

As I returned to Buck, I checked the side wall of the little inn for hobo's marks. There were none.

I led him across the street to the stable, again checking inside before going in. The youngster in attendance, perhaps three or four years shy of my own age, was accommodating and reassuring: yes, he would give Buck all the water he wanted and a big bucket of oats. He would sleep undisturbed and be supervised throughout the night. All would be well. I hoped I could trust him. He seemed anxious to please. Just to be on the safe side, I flipped him a coin.

I untied my gear, slung it along with Dumas' bag of treats over my shoulder, and returned to the hotel, almost unable to wait for bath, food and bed. I shook with fatigue and hunger.

I walked quickly to my room, unlocked the door and closed it behind me. The room was less than remarkable and not sparkling with cleanliness, but there were a bed, a basin and a small dresser. Throwing my gear on the bed, I sat down and rubbed every sore muscle I could reach. Fifteen minutes later,

I was immersed in hot water, and I stayed in the bath until it turned stone cold.

Dinner proved to be adequate, and I ate in the company of my host, his wife and another guest. It could have been my imagination, but I thought the woman was casting a great many glances my way. Did I make her nervous?

The conversation was all about the railway. As it turned out, it was getting close. Closer than I had thought.

"Shouldn't be more than a few months, if that," the guest, who had been introduced as Mr. Riley, said. "Maybe even a few weeks. Were you hoping for work on the line, Mr. Jones?"

It took me a second. When it clicked that he had addressed me, I pretended to swallow hard, as if I had had food in my mouth and could not answer.

"Uh, well, I've been thinking about it. If they need more hands."

"Always looking, Mr. Jones. Always looking."

This man was with the railway. Buck and I would be on the road before dawn, galloping hellbent toward Moose Jaw.

• • •

An ear-shattering bang awakened me several hours later. It was dead dark, apart from frequent ghastly blue-white streaks of light. The deafening thunder had sent my body into full alert; I lurched into a sitting position gasping for breath and turned to the window, which vibrated with a most alarming rattle.

A pale, streaming face peered in from the other side. Without a second's thought, I hit the floor, trying not to yell in shock. Scrabbling for my gun, I tried to wriggle under the bed but quickly realized it was hopeless; not enough room for a man under there, and I was a sizeable one. My eyes flicked back at the window, where hands associated with the face were waving frantically. I could not make out the face's features, but another bolt of lightning revealed them. It was the stable boy.

Terror pierced my heart. Was something wrong with Buck? Or had he fled in fear of the noise and light? I had to talk to the youth, even if he was armed and dangerous.

Scrambling to my feet, I held the gun at my side and approached the window; the youngster held up his hands and shook his head violently. I took that to mean he was unarmed. Or a liar.

The window screeched open in its warped wooden frame.

"Is something wrong with my horse?" I panted at him. "Are you unarmed?"

"Yes! I mean, I'm unarmed," he said in a stage whisper. "No, your horse is fine. Can I come in? It's a little wet out here. And we have to be quiet."

I stood aside and let him hoist himself over the sill and into the room, where he immediately formed a puddle under his dripping self. Dripping did not cover it. He was soaked; a small waterfall poured from his oilskin-clad shoulders.

"Listen," he said. "You have to get out of here. Right away."

"Why? What are you talking about?" This did not sound good, but maybe the kid was excitable.

"They know who you are. I heard the man from down the hall talking with the innkeeper; they were on the porch late this evening, and I was just coming out to . . . well, you know. Head to the biffy. Anyway. They say you're wanted, and your name isn't Jones. Is that true, mister?"

My eyes betrayed me. I could feel them growing wide in panic; not a lot of point in denying that I was on the run. Still, I did not want to give away the entire game. Not just yet.

"Who am I supposed to be, then?"

"Some bad guy from down east."

"Hmm. And who is this man? He was introduced as Trevor Riley. Is that right?"

"Yes, as far as I know. At least, that's the name he gave me. Says he's a mucky-muck with the railroad."

Riley had been vague when I had asked him about his work. With the railway? Ha. He was with Garrison. And my plan to ride at dawn had been a good one. Just not good enough.

I took a couple of steps and reached over to the washstand to grab the kid a towel. As I handed it over, he said, "Thanks, mister, but you really have to get going. Now."

"Why are you here, telling me this? I'm grateful . . . what's your name?"

"Tom."

"I'm very grateful, Tom. But why?"

"Well, you don't seem like a bad guy from down east. Plus Mr. Riley never gives me a tip. You did. And he . . . well, I don't like the way he treats his horse. Always has sores on the flanks. Poor thing flinches while I'm currying him." Tom shook his head, first in sorrow, and then to shut himself up. "Sorry. Here I am talking. You gots to go."

The weather posed some issues with that idea. I had not been through a storm quite like this one with Buck, and I wondered how he would respond to the cataclysm occurring outside. To be honest, I was not sure how I was going to deal with it. I peered out the window; to say it was raining would have been an unfair description of Mother Nature's power. It poured as if God was spilling buckets on the dry earth. I realized, then, that it was already May. Thunderstorms were rare in a prairie spring, I had been told, but it had been surprisingly hot.

My few seconds of musing were interrupted by Tom violently shaking my arm. I came to my senses and gave him a shaky grin, then clapped him on the shoulder.

"Thank God I'm on the first floor. Okay, Tom. I'll be at the stable in five minutes. And thank you. I hope to repay the favour someday."

"Make it three minutes. I'll let you in the back door." With that, he spun around and threw himself out the window into the drenching madness.

I stared after him for a moment. I knew that had it not been for the wild weather, I might already have been a dead man. Dragged from my bed and slaughtered where no one would ever find my body.

CHAPTER TWENTY-FIVE

I packed up the few items I had removed from my bag, mopped the floor with the towel to eradicate evidence of a visitor, pulled on my coat and slipped out the window, closing it as quietly as possible behind me. Once on the ground, I looked wildly around me but knew I would not be able to see anyone lurking around a corner. Or even someone right in front of me. I had to take my chances.

I ran desperately across the street, which was by now a muddy river deep enough in the ruts to cover my shins. Tom was watching for me; the man-door at the back was open a crack, and he pushed it open slightly as I arrived, soaked and panting.

Slipping inside, I waited a moment for the water to stop sluicing down my face and for my eyes to adjust to a different gloom. Buck, two stalls away, turned his massive head toward me and grunted. Probably asking where the hell I had been. Another crash from the heavens made him snort and waggle a bit, but he did not flinch or rear. Maybe we would make it.

Maybe we would not.

"He'll be okay," Tom said, as if reading my mind. "He's been the calmest one in the stable all night. Great horse there, if you ask me."

"I appreciate that, Tom."

"Are you going to tell me your name, mister?"

"It's James," I said, instantly deciding to tell him and holding out my hand. He deserved my trust. "James Sinclair. And I am from down east, but I am not a bad guy. I promise."

"I know. Buck seems to like you. Good sign."

"I like him. He's my best friend right now."

I approached Buck then, and he nuzzled me as I ran my hand down his silky neck.

"Are you okay, boy?" I asked him. "Do you think we can ride?"

I could have sworn that he nodded.

Voices. Outside. At the moment, no thunder clapped and I could hear men talking, coming nearer. Tom's eyes met mine as he put a finger to his lips; he gestured with the other hand to get down. I threw myself into the straw bedding and burrowed into the heap, which smelled simultaneously like sweet heaven and manure. Buck stood over me, motionless, like the guardian he was.

Seconds later, the man door opened and Riley stepped inside, followed by two other men whose voices I didn't recognize.

"Hey, boy," Riley addressed Tom. I peered through the straw and the slats of the stable to see Tom straighten his shoulders.

"Yes, sir?"

"Have you seen Mr. Jones?"

"No, sir." Short and sweet. Good tactics, I thought.

"I see his horse is still here."

"Yes, sir."

"Couldn't have gone far without him. Okay, boys, let's go have a look around." Not another word to Tom. No thanks, no tip. What an asshole. Fortunately, Riley could not have known that Tom had taken a shine to me and hidden me in the stable. He left, banging the door behind him.

Stuck for the time being, I stayed in my smelly bed for several minutes; neither of us spoke, and Buck remained frozen in place. God, I loved that horse. Finally, Tom whispered, "I think they've really gone."

A rumble followed this statement, a big improvement from the earlier deafening roars and crashes. The storm was moving on. I unearthed myself from the straw, bits of it sticking out from my hair in a strange halo, and tied my belongings to Buck's saddle.

"Tom, which way do you think I should go?"

"South," he said, without hesitation. "They'll expect you to take the trail west. Go south a few miles, then due west, then come back north to meet the trail again. Won't be easy in the dark, but by full light you should be okay."

I had no idea what time it was and checked; apparently about three in the morning. At least an hour of darkness remained. Sunrise came at about five-thirty, but the dawn would begin well before. Time to leave, and in a hurry.

Tom slipped out to do some rapid surveillance before returning and waving me on. I led Buck to the man-door, wondering if he would fit through, and he did — just barely.

"I don't know how to thank you," I told Tom, "but if you ever need help, you can count on me. I'll be just three days down the road, to the west."

"Thanks, Mister. I might have to take you up on that one day."

"I hope you do. Goodbye, Tom."

With that, I mounted my horse and turned his head to the south. Buck and I were once again alone and on the run.

• • •

The pouring rain turned to drizzle and then abated as the thunder rolled to the east. Two hours later, we plodded over the wet plain in thin sunshine, having travelled a few miles south before turning west. Anxious to find the western trail, I turned north again by late morning. Getting lost at this point would be seriously perilous.

Some quick mental arithmetic brought me to the conclusion that Riley and his men were likely long since on my trail. It would not have taken more than half an hour for them to check my room, double back to see that my horse was gone and ride out after me. I prayed that Tom was all right.

Buck would not let me click his gait down. He sensed danger and galloped along, ignoring me entirely. I finally gave up, let him have his head and tried not to worry about exhausting him.

This went on for miles. And miles. Finally, as the sun burned off the last lingering mist and began to slide toward the western horizon, he slowed to a canter. We saw no one, heard no one, and I began to relax a little. I realized not long afterward that we had been riding for nearly twelve hours. If Buck was not beat, I sure as hell was.

"For the love of God, Buck. Slow down. We have to find a place to rest, and soon."

He snorted in reply and slowed again, this time to a walk. The air was heavy with moisture; I had no idea the prairie could be so humid. Sweat mixed with the airborne water and rolled down both our bodies. I would have killed for another bath.

Buck turned north. His nose was unerring. With a gasp, I realized we had reconnected with the river — or found a new one. A sigh of relief escaped me. We plunged into the valley and splashed into the water. I paused only to remove my shirt before dousing myself from head to waist as Buck gulped his fill.

I could not start a fire. There was precious little wood anyway, and the smoke would surely be a beacon if the men were hot on my heels. Best to eat cold and find a hiding spot.

The light still lingered, but I was so exhausted I knew I would sleep regardless of sun, moon or star light. We tucked into the side of the river, ate our oats and dried meat and bread, and collapsed. I could only hope that they were following the trail and would not find us tonight.

They did not. Another day and a half and we rode into the tiny but — incredibly — bustling town of Moose Jaw. I was under no delusions. They would find me eventually. But I had made it to my new home.

CHAPTER TWENTY-SIX

Moose Jaw perched near a river far more promising than the trickling creek serving the larger Pile of Bones. Clearly, this community anticipated the imminent arrival of the railway. Shacks, tents and a couple of shops lined a few short streets. A small industrial area appeared to be popping up, awaiting the needs of the railroad itself and the associated business it would bring.

I would later learn that perhaps three or four hundred souls populated the little town, but people were practically streaming in — on a per capita basis, at least. I liked it. A lot.

I profoundly did not want to stay in the single small hotel, due to ease of discovery, but I was extremely tired of sleeping rough. Besides, there must have been twelve horses hitched to the hotel's post. Would they even have a room? But what were my options?

Buck clopped slowly through town, allowing me to look around and consider the situation. Nothing looked promising on the main street. At the end of it, I turned south on a short and evidently newer street, home to a few wooden structures and several tents.

I almost missed it. It was not big, but it was clear. On the side of one of the wood frames, someone had drawn a wavy line with a sketch of a little house beneath it. Clean water. A place to stay. And welcoming to hobos.

Slipping off Buck's back, I approached the little building, cautiously peering around to make sure I was not being followed. In the window was a scrawled sign: room to let. Hesitantly, I knocked lightly on the door. Someone threw it open a second later. They must have seen me coming.

A burly man stood before me, muscular and wide although no more than five-foot-six, with greying hair and kind but vague eyes. He looked directly into my chest at first, but quickly turned his gaze up to my face.

"Yes?" he said. "Who is it?"

I cleared my throat.

"My name is . . ." I paused. There was likely no point in lying. Riley knew who I was, so it really did not matter anymore. "James Sinclair. I'm new in town, and I saw your sign. I was wondering about your room, sir. Is it available?"

He nodded. "Just a minute. Sarah!" he yelled, turning his head toward the inside of the house. "Possible customer!"

He turned back to me. "It's up to her. The wife. Can't have just anyone in the house, you know. She'll have to give you the ol' once-over."

He did not quite meet my eyes, and I realized with one of those flashes of understanding that he was blind. At least functionally blind.

I removed my hat and, turning it in my hands, stood as still as possible as I awaited "the wife." Nerves were getting the better of me. If these people thought I was unsuitable . . .

The patter of feet and the clucking of a tongue heralded Sarah's arrival.

"Bert. You should let me answer the door. Hello, young man."

"I heard him coming. No point in letting people wait. I can still take care of myself, Sarah. This is James Sinclair."

"Pleased to meet you," she said, giving me a short but friendly nod. "Have a seat here on the porch. I'll see if I have some lemonade left."

She scuttled back inside, and Bert indicated a grouping of rather elegant chairs at the side of the porch.

"Pleasant day," he offered, as we sat down. "Quite the storm the other night."

"Yes, it was."

"You're on horseback."

"Yes."

"Is he all right?"

"I think so. He won't wander off."

Sarah returned carrying three glasses streaming with condensation and brimming with pale liquid, which looked to me like sunshine mixed with happiness. It was delicious — tangy and not too sweet. I downed mine in four gulps. She smiled at me, her pretty, slightly plump face crinkling, and poured more lemonade into my glass from the pitcher.

"So, young man. What brings you to Moose Jaw?" she asked, sitting down with a soft sigh that sounded like relief.

"This is delicious," I said. "Thank you so much. And, ah, I suppose you could say I've come to seek my fortune." I added a laugh. "Ha. Well, at least a place to settle and start a business."

"And what do you do?"

"I'm a goldsmith," I said, unable to keep the usual note of pride out of my voice. "I'm also a machinist, though. I was trained in the same shop where my father worked. And I have some experience with trains. I thought the end of the line, at least for now, would be a good place to be. More opportunity."

Sarah's eyebrows shot up as I spoke, and she glanced at Bert, who looked back at her despite his vision problems.

"I see. Where are you from?"

Gah. It had to happen.

"Toronto."

Bert spit out his sip of lemonade and coughed hard enough that Sarah leaned over and beat him on the back.

"Y'what, youngster?" he finally croaked. "Why in hell would you want to come all this way from the big city?"

"Adventure," I said firmly.

Bert's face told me that he did not believe me.

"You wanted to ride for weeks all the way from Toronto, across the endless plain, all alone, to end up here."

"I wasn't entirely alone. Not always. I met some people along the way. And I had Buck." I sounded defensive even to my own ears. I had little doubt that this man, with his exceptional hearing, detected it too.

"And you need a room," Sarah put in, placing a hand on Bert's arm. She seemed to have a better impression of me.

"Yes."

"For how long?"

"Until I can find or build a home, ma'am. I saw the hobo's code markings on your house, and hoped you'd have me."

"But you're not really a hobo."

"No."

"How did you know about the code, then?"

"I met some hobos on the train out of Toronto. They kindly explained about it."

She narrowed her eyes at me. "You have a story to tell. I know you do. I can feel it." Bert nodded at this. "Can you assure me, can you promise me, James, that you are a good and kind man? That you will respect our home and our rules?"

"I do. I will. I promise."

"And that you will tell us your story?"

Weakly, I said, "Yes."

She stood up. "Get your things. And bring your horse. There's a stable out back."

Relief made my legs turn to jelly. "Thank you. I know you're taking a chance on me, but I promise you, I will be the best tenant ever." I shook their hands and went to retrieve Buck.

I should have asked their price and looked at the room first, but I did not care. I likely had no other option, and anyone who would serve me lemonade before asking questions had my vote for best person of the year. I led Buck to the back and ensconced him in the stable, where water and hay were waiting. I whispered to him, promising a good curry in the evening, and asked him to be a good boy.

Grabbing my sacks of things, I returned to the house where Sarah awaited me at the back door. Up the stairs, then, to a large room with lace curtains, a patchwork quilt on a soft bed, a washstand with porcelain basin, a dresser and a small wardrobe. All of it spotless. Homey.

"What do you think, James? Is it all right?" she asked.

"It's more than all right, ma'am," I breathed. "It's magnificent."

"Well, that's very kind. Have a bit of a wash, then, and come downstairs when you're ready. Dinner is at six."

"What will I owe you, ma'am?"

"Please call me Sarah. And we'll discuss that over dinner. All right?"

"Yes, thank you."

She left, closing the door behind her, and I sank onto the bed. It was odd, I thought, that she would not just propose a price for room and board. Well, I would find out why later.

Almost too tired to stand, I forced myself to approach the basin and got a good look at my head and shoulders in the mirror. A few bits of straw still stuck out of my hair. My face was covered in a thin layer of dust, sticking to a sheen of sweat. It suddenly all struck me as ridiculous — not just my appearance, but the experiences of the last few weeks — and I began to laugh like a madman. Until I began to hiccup, and a tear rolled down my face, leaving a streak in the dust.

· · ·

Five minutes before the appointed time, I quietly crept down the stairs, not entirely sure where I was going and hoping not to disturb my new landlords. By the time I made the hallway, Bert came out from a door at the side and welcomed me.

"This way, young James," he said, leading the way to the kitchen. "Dinner's almost ready."

The aroma of what I thought was beef stew and homemade bread made my stomach flip and rumble. I had not had a proper meal for a while, and certainly not indoors in what felt like a safe environment.

"Sit down, James," Sarah said in greeting. "Would you like a drop of beer with your meal?"

"Beer!" I exclaimed, before I could stop myself. "Yes, please."

She moved around the kitchen with dexterous precision, pouring beer, spooning stew into wide bowls, cutting bread. It all landed on the table in three minutes, and we tucked in.

"So," said Sarah after a few bites. "You say you're a machinist."

"Yes, ma'am. Ah, Sarah."

"Ever done any blacksmithing?"

"Yes, a little."

Again that meaningful look between them.

"Did . . . did you need some work done?" I asked. "I'd be happy to help out. I've never shoed a horse, but I can fix wagons and things."

Sarah pursed her lips and laid a hand on Bert's arm. "What do you think, dear?"

"Worth a try, is what I think. You?"

"Yes. Go on, then."

"Son," he began. "As you've likely realized, I've gone mostly blind. Began noticing it a few years back; became worse and worse as I got older."

"I'm sorry," I stammered, wondering where this was going.

"Not anything you should be sorry for. Life brings what it will. I am a blacksmith, but I can do precious little work now. I've been looking for someone to help, maybe take over the business at some point. Not a lot of people to choose from, here, and those there be, well . . . either I don't like 'em, or Sarah doesn't much." He paused for a glug of beer. "I'd have to put you through your paces, you hear? But first things first. Would you be interested in such a thing?"

I should have thought about this for at least thirty seconds, but I did not even take a breath.

"Yes, I am. Very interested."

A grin spread slowly across Bert's face. He must have been handsome and dashing at some time in his life; I could imagine Sarah being swept away by such a smile.

"All right then. That's good. Very good. Tomorrow, if that's not too soon for you, we'll wander over to the shop and you can take a look. We'll check on your horse's shoon while we're at it. He's been through his paces, I'm sure."

Right. Horseshoes. I was suddenly both horrified and happy that the state of Buck's hoof wear had not occurred to me earlier. I would have worried about him even more as we rode across the wide-open, blacksmith-free plain.

After dinner, I leaned across the table and I told Bert and Sarah Thompson everything. All of it. Well, almost. How I had met Alice Garrison, and how she had confronted me in the alley, begging me to take her away. How her father had come to Hannah Vogel's house and accused me of rape. How Hannah had spirited me out of Toronto via the remnants of the Underground Railroad, and I had come to meet Buck. The hobos. Dumas and his wagon train. I left out a few details I was less proud of, like the encounter in the dark tent with a passionate Beth, and how I had made her scream. And she me. The memory was hard to bear, intensely arousing, and may have made my tale a little less believable. Besides, it was private.

I finished my story with a plea. I could feel my eyes widening with desperation.

"You have to believe me. I never touched Alice Garrison, apart from that kiss. In fact, I've never . . . you know. I don't know why her father came after me. All I know is that Hannah said my life was over if I stayed, and I believed her. I still do."

"That seems clear," Sarah agreed, "since this Riley person is obviously after you. You don't have any proof of any of this, I suppose."

"Is there a telegraph line yet?" I asked in hope.

"Yep," Bert said. "Just installed a short while ago, for the railway."

"That means it's close, doesn't it?"

"Very. Few more months, tops. Maybe less. Did you need to send a telegram?"

"Yes. I'm hoping to get the proof you need."

CHAPTER TWENTY-SEVEN

They obviously believed me. I suppose, in retrospect, it made sense: a man accused of rape would not share that information if it were at all possible to avoid. After currying a half-awake Buck, I slept like an exhausted child for ten solid hours on my soft bed, sprawled half under the homemade patchwork quilt.

A knock at the door awakened me at eight, and I lurched up, wondering for a second where the hell I was.

"James," Sarah's voice called quietly. "Are you awake? Breakfast is ready. Has been for a while."

"I'm sorry, Sarah," I answered through the door. "I don't normally sleep so late. I'll be right there."

I splashed my face with water and combed down my hair, finally getting the last bits of broken straw out of it. A quick stop at the biffy and I felt almost human. Sarah had kept eggs, bacon and toast warm for me; she added dried tomatoes and apples to the plate and set it before me, along with a steaming mug of coffee. Milk and sugar, butter and jam were on the table. Wolfing down the food, I was surprised the aromas from the kitchen had not awakened me earlier.

Bert, on his third cup of caffeine, asked, "How did you sleep, James?"

"Unbelievably well," I said around a mouthful of toast. "And this is manna from heaven."

"Do you still want to visit the telegraph office first? Then we'll go to the shop?"

"I'd like to, yes, if you don't mind."

"All righty, then. You needn't do so on our account, but if you still want to . . . finish up and when you're ready we'll go into town."

I hid a smile at that comment. "Going into town" meant a block's walk up the short street and around the corner. It remained hot, so Bert and I struck out without jackets over our shirtsleeves. He managed incredibly well on the rutted streets due, I assumed, to making this trip daily. Unerringly, he turned onto Main Street and led me to the telegraph office.

Dark and dusty, it was nonetheless helmed by a tidy looking young man with garters on his arms, black hair thickly greased and scraped away from his slim face. Only one other customer was inside, a man about my age gazing at the posters and notices on the wall. I glanced over, relieved to see none of the notices bore my likeness.

"Hello, Bert," the telegraph employee greeted my landlord. "How're things today?"

"Just fine, Henry, just fine. And you?"

"I'm fine too. What can I do for you?"

"This is my . . . ah . . . nephew, James," Bert said, with a quick sidelong glance that suggested I should shut up about our new erroneous relationship. "Needs to send a note to his mam or some such."

"Of course, of course," said Henry, slipping eyeglasses from the top of his head over his face. "Which city, please?"

"Toronto."

"Name?"

"Hannah Vogel." I spelled it.

"Telegraphic address?"

Damn. I did not know it and told him so, although he raised an eyebrow.

"Not to worry. If you have a street address, we'll find her, but it'll cost you more," he warned.

"That's okay," I said. "I'm willing to pay." I had little money left, but this was important. "We're not accustomed to getting many telegrams," I added lamely in explanation. "Actually, I'd like to send two. This is my aunt. I'll send Mum's afterward."

He nodded. "Okay, shoot."

Damn, again. How could I word this missive without revealing the entire mess? I sputtered for a moment, then grabbed hold of myself. He clicked as I spoke.

"Dear Auntie Hannah. Alive and well. Hope this finds you same. Could you please send reference to Moose Jaw, North-West Territories. Have found place to live and work. Love James. Stop." I wanted to add so much more but could not — not without giving the game away to anyone who might see the telegram. I hoped Hannah could read between these short lines.

Then, barely able to keep from weeping, I sent a second one to my mother.

"Mum. I love you and I miss you. I am alive and well, and sorry for . . ." I paused. "Uh. Not sending message earlier. Will be in touch again. Hugs to sisters. Love James. Stop."

There. That was the best I could do under the circumstances. I paid Henry and whirled toward the door, trying to stop my shoulders from heaving. The other man turned to me, an expression of concern on his face. He clapped me on the shoulder and gave me a sympathetic nod.

I nodded back with gratitude and lurched outside to wait for Bert.

When he emerged, he patted me awkwardly on the back. "There, there, son. There now. It will be all right. I'm sure you miss your people."

I gulped and snorted out some vague answer. "How long do these things usually take?" I asked when I could speak without blubbering.

"You mean replies? Shouldn't be too long. And don't worry, son. We're in your corner. I can see you."

• • •

Surreptitiously, I wiped my eyes as we walked side by side toward the blacksmith's shop. It stood at the end of Main Street, in the small but blooming industrial area I had noted the day before. Bert handed me a monstrous key and nodded toward the lock.

"Be easier if you open up," he admitted.

I took the key from him, unlocked the door and swung it open. Revealed immediately were the forge, an incredible number of tools hanging neatly on the walls, a monstrous scuttle of coal and another of wood, and a slack tub. This last was filled with water for quenching hot metals. Most of the trappings were familiar to me. I found myself wondering in the same second how I could make myself goldsmithing tools but shook the thought from my head. That would have to wait.

"What do you think?" Bert asked. "Seem familiar?"

"Yes," I said. "Most of it. I'm easy with fixing wheels and wagons and things, as I said. What do you mostly do?"

"Well, quite a bit of all that. A lot of horseshoeing, of course. And I've made a ring or two."

"You have? Do you mean wedding rings?"

"Yep. No goldsmith hereabouts, although the occasional trader comes through with jewellery. But we have one now." He smiled.

"What metals did you use? Gold or silver or something else?"

"Mostly silver. Bit of gold. People will trade their bits of nice things if they need a horse or ox shod. They have financial priorities, James. But then some wee girl and her beau will appear, dying to be married . . . or to get between the sheets, most like." Bert grinned. "Ah, well. Love will have its way. I can teach you the shoeing, James. The rest, I think, you may be just fine with."

There was a light knock on the door. Someone obviously had seen it flung wide and taken the opportunity to pop by. Still, I whirled around in a brief panic. Had Riley found me already?

No. The man standing in the doorway nearly filled it with his considerable bulk, all of it muscle and bone. He must have been six-foot-three, at the very least; I was over six feet and he was certainly taller than I. He towered over Bert, grinning, and I realized with a shock, as my eyes adjusted to the bright sun, that he was African by descent. I had not seen a Black man since I left Toronto, and few enough of them there.

"Hello, Bert," he said in a deep, rumbling voice, almost devoid of accent.

"Hello, Jim," Bert answered. "How the hell are you? Haven't seen you in a while."

"You haven't been around for a while," Jim said mildly. "Where've you been?"

"The wife and I went over to Pile of Bones, hoping to find a doctor. You know Doc Arlington's been unwell. I haven't opened the shop since we got back."

Jim nodded, his gaze dropping to the floor as if in sorrow. More for Bert's failing vision and associated lack of service, I perceived, than for the ailing Doc Arlington.

"I'm glad to see you back, Bert. Who is this, if you don't mind me asking?"

Bert gave an apologetic grunt. "I'm sorry. Jim, this is my new . . . partner. James Sinclair. James, meet Jim Baker. He owns the hardware down the street. Good customer. Good friend."

I held out my hand at the same time Jim did. He gave me a big smile as his warm, strong grip met my own.

"Nice to meet you," he said. "I'm thinking this means you're reopening, Bert. I surely do hope so."

"You bet, Jim. Got something for us?"

"I surely do. Pile of stuff. I'll bring it all over tomorrow. Give your new partner a moment to get settled. When did this all happen?"

"Just yesterday," Bert answered. "First time I've shown him the shop. Maybe give us two days, get the youngster up to speed."

"For sure. Where are you from, James?"

"Down east, sir."

"Come all this way to seek your fortune, then."

"I have. I'm very lucky to have met Bert."

"You are. Best man in these parts."

Bert squirmed a bit at the compliment. "Jim, why don't you pop over for dinner tomorrow? We'll get caught up."

"Well, now. That's a very kind invitation, if you don't think I'll be imposing."

"Not at all. It'd be great to have you, and you and James here can get acquainted."

"Thank you, Bert, and thank Sarah for me ahead of time. See you tomorrow. I'll bring you a drop of something." He waggled his eyebrows, grinned again, gave a small salute and was off.

Bert bowed his head and shook it as the big man left.

"What's wrong, Bert?"

"Just thinking about Jim. Tough life. Had a wife for a short time who up and died on him; terrible sad. Good man. Always has a kind word, pays up front, works hard. Keeps a smile on his face despite it all. Right, then. Let's take a look at what we've got here."

We spent the next few hours examining all the tools, sharpening things as we went, and Bert took me through the creation of a horseshoe. If I do say so myself, I mastered it pretty quickly. It was certainly easier than setting a diamond in a ring without breaking a claw or chipping a facet.

After a quick and late lunch devoured at home, we retrieved Buck from his stall behind the house and gave his shoes a once-over.

"See here?" Bert said, even though he could not. But he could feel. "This shoe needs attention. You're lucky he didn't throw it."

"Can we walk him to the shop?" I asked in some alarm; I had no idea if that would be safe for Buck.

"Of course. Just don't gallop him over. We'll lead him and he'll be fine. Let's go."

Buck nuzzled my neck. I thought he may have missed me, or possibly the imperfect shoe was giving him some grief. I patted his neck in return, slipped the halter over his head and took the reins, muttering to him.

"We'll get you fixed up good as new, Buck. And then you can have a good rest. You deserve it, my friend."

It took an hour or so for me to fashion a new horseshoe and figure out how to put it in place without hurting Buck or damaging his hoof. Bert was an excellent teacher and guide, and between us, we had it sorted by dinnertime. As we came up to the house — a mere five minutes away on foot — Henry came running down the street, blowing like a steam engine.

"Sirs! Bert! James! I have a telegra-ham," he puffed. "Just came as I was locking up. Looks important, so I thought I'd ru-hun over."

He thrust the missive into my hands and stood there sweating and beaming at me. I quickly gathered a tip was in order and fished in my pocket for a coin. This duly delivered, he nodded, beamed some more, and took himself off.

My legs turned to water. What could be 'important,' as Henry had said? I sat down hard on the stoop and forced myself to read.

"DELIVER IMMEDIATELY," screamed the first two words.

"Alice Garrison dead. Miscarriage. Father on warpath. Take care. More news and reference to come. Love Hannah. Stop."

Chapter Twenty-eight

Dead. How could she be dead? That gossamer girl, flighty but full of life, stealing kisses in alleyways, encouraging peeks down her bodice.

But also desperate. Clearly, she really had been pregnant. Who in the name of God would have had intercourse with such a young woman — barely more than a girl? A wave of sorrow crashed over me, followed by panic. She had begged me to take her away. And now she was dead and George Garrison was "on the warpath." Hannah would not have mentioned it if I did not represent the spoils of that war.

"What is it, James?" I dimly heard Bert asking. "Is it bad news?"

I must have made some kind of noise, an indrawn breath of shock.

"Yes. The young woman I told you about last night has died."

"Dear God. That's terrible. Come inside. Sarah will be waiting and I'll pour you a whiskey. Steady you up some."

"I'll stable Buck and be right in."

I needed a moment to think as much as Buck needed his dinner. I led him around the back, filled his trough with food and water, and sat on a bale in the corner of his stall.

Garrison was hunting me down. He already had his raiders on my trail, and now they would redouble their efforts to find me and either kill me or have me arrested. The question of "why me" re-entered my thoughts. What had Alice told her father? I would likely never know.

I had travelled something like sixteen hundred miles to get away from that bastard, and all for naught. Riley knew who I was, and probably knew where I was — more or less. It was only a matter of time before he showed up in Moose Jaw, likely before the railway arrived.

I stood and drove a fist through a rotting plank on the side of the stable wall. Fury infused me like it never had before. I walked back to the house with my knuckles bruised and bleeding and determination in my thumping, angry heart.

I was through with running. I would stay in Moose Jaw and face George Garrison.

Then I would see him in hell.

•   •   •

"What on Earth, James," Sarah said, immediately spying my bleeding hand when I entered the kitchen. "Come here. What happened? Did you have a wee tussle with Buck?"

"No," I said, sinking into a chair.

Sarah brought clean cloths, water and whiskey to the table. Her kind, wide brown eyes gazed into mine for a moment, and then she set herself to cleaning my self-inflicted wounds.

Neither of us spoke until the process was over, although I did flinch and grunt several times.

"Are you going to tell me?" she finally asked.

"I punched a board. I promise to fix it. I'm sorry, Sarah."

"Why did you do that?"

"I lost my temper."

"Ah. Something to do with your telegram?"

"Yes. Sarah . . . actually, where is Bert? I should really say what I have to say to both of you."

"He's just washing up."

Moments later, Bert appeared and poured us all two ounces of his best.

"All right, James. What's up?" he asked.

"I'm in deep trouble," I began. "The telegram was from Hannah. As you know, she is not my aunt; she was my landlady, the woman who got me out of Toronto. I told you the young woman died. Her father is looking for me. He already was, but he's even more determined now."

"What does that mean? What will you do now?"

"I've decided. I'm not running anymore. I'm going to stay here and confront him and his men. But I can't put you in danger. I have to find my own place. And I don't think I can work for you either, Bert. What would happen if they found me at the shop?"

"Now, now," Bert said soothingly. "I've encountered my share of trouble and bad men in my time. Don't be saying that. We'll figure it out."

"I don't know. I'll have to think about that. But I need a place no matter what. I'll start looking for a spot tomorrow."

"Well, there's plenty of open land. Shouldn't be a problem there. But you're going to need some money, and that means you have to work. Not to pressure you, James, but frankly we need the money too. I can't run the shop without you. Why do you think we're letting a room?"

That put things in a slightly different light. I stared at Bert, then at Sarah, who nodded her head.

"We need you, James," she said simply. "Stay with us until you can find a home, but please, please don't leave the business."

They were right. I needed the work and the money, and apparently, so did they. What we would all need now was allies.

"All right," I said, with lingering reluctance. "I don't know how to thank you."

"It will all come out fine in the end," Sarah said.

I wished I shared her confidence.

•   •   •

The following day, Bert and Sarah accompanied me on my search for a good place to build a home. I had spent most of the night thinking about where to live and decided a tent in the middle of town was out. I wanted a proper house, both as fortress and future. As soon as possible. I had never built anything before, but I thought I could do it.

We wandered along the little street and the industrial area, both Sarah and I pointing at possible locations. After a good two hours of prospecting, we came to a wide-open uninhabited area. A stream ran below a small hill; leafy trees rustled in the breeze; fragrant wildflowers dotted the plain. The land was situated outside the town but was still close enough to the smithy.

"This is it," I said. "How do I go about trying to buy it?"

"We'll go to the town office. They'll know," Bert said.

Two hours later, I owned two acres of land on the outskirts of Moose Jaw. I handed over every cent I had and signed a piece of paper declaring that I was good for the remainder. Bert signed it too, attesting that I worked for him. I was dizzy with the excitement of becoming a property owner.

The rest of the day we spent at the shop. Bert had a significant backlog of work to be done, and we repaired wagons and wheels until six. It took a solid hour before my hands stopped shaking from the thrill of buying land.

Bert could still do some of the work himself, but only because he had done it for decades and knew his shop like a mother knows her child. I'd occasionally ask him to check my work, and he finally said, "You've got it, James. Besides, I know if it's right just by listening to you work. I don't have to see it."

Exactly what Graham Tattersall had said when I was banging away on golden rings.

We made it back to the house by six-fifteen. Dinner was ready, Sarah told us, and Jim awaited our arrival in the living room. I had forgotten in all the excitement that he was joining us for the evening meal.

"Be right there, Jim," Bert called. "Sorry to be late. Busy day."

"No problem, Bert. Just arrived, and Sarah has been keeping me company."

Washed and starving, I clattered down the stairs five minutes later. Jim had indeed brought some rather excellent whiskey; after a sip, I asked him where he got it.

"The traders," he said. "Always have the best stuff."

"You mean the Métis traders? Or someone else?"

"Yes, the Métis. They bring it up from the States, or from down east. We'll have to start our own still one day." He laughed. "Wouldn't that be something?"

Talk turned to my new housing adventure. Jim immediately offered to help; besides, I would need his wares, such as tools and nails, to complete the project. I demurred on the offer of help, but Jim insisted.

"You can't raise a house alone," he said, and I accepted gratefully.

"There's also the question of building materials," I added. "Not a hell of a lot of trees or bricks around here. How is that done?"

"Jim's added a lumber yard behind the hardware," Bert informed me. "Good idea, with all the building going on."

"I guess I'm set."

We chatted until late, and I was feeling the whiskey when I asked Jim where he was originally from. I did not mean Africa; I doubted he was a direct immigrant because his speaking voice was only slightly accented. I asked because everyone in Moose Jaw was from somewhere else.

He did not answer right away. He turned his gaze on Sarah, eyebrows slightly raised. Jim obviously held his own secrets, and Sarah and Bert knew them. As they knew mine. She shrugged a little, suggesting it was his own decision whether to trust me. The room became still as Jim wrestled with what to tell me, if anything. Big hands turned the almost-empty tumbler of whiskey around and around, and he stared into the last amber drops.

He looked up at me after a long time and spoke one word.

"Georgia."

All three of them let that sink in for a moment.

"You know what that means, James?" he asked, finally.

"I think so. You came up to Canada on the Underground Railroad."

"I did. Officially, I am still a wanted man. They sent bounty hunters after me; found me the first time, dragged me back. I escaped a few months later for the second time. Damn near found me again."

He swigged back the last of his booze in a powerful gulp. I could see the cords of his neck tauten with emotion.

"Are you worried about the railway coming in?" I asked. "More people, more possibility of being found? Or do you think they'd just leave you alone now?"

"I don't know. I've been gone for so long. More than twenty years. Spent a long time hiding until I decided I couldn't stand it anymore. So I came out to Moose Jaw. Like you."

The question in his eyes and elevated brow was unmistakable. Tit for tat, story for story, his expression said. But I wanted to learn more and pretended not to understand his silent query.

"How did you get here?" I asked.

"Once I got over the border, I was smuggled into Toronto. The people who helped me thought I should go to a bigger place, where I could get some doctoring and maybe just fade into the background." He snorted. "Me. Ha. I was the biggest and the darkest man probably in the whole goddamn city. But I was plenty sick. Festering wounds and some nasty stripes on my back.

"I was plenty lucky. Ended up in a rooming house where the lady was kind and nursed me a bit. A doctor came to see me, a good man. Both silent as the grave. But then word began to spread that bounty hunters were back in town, looking for me and another man. They found him. I hid for weeks but finally I had to go. They probably would not have killed me. I was worth a lot more alive. But who knows? They almost beat me to death the first time."

He took a shuddering breath. "I'd rather have died than go back. No way in hell was I going back. No way."

I had two words for Jim. My insides churned and my hands shook. I had never been so sure of anything in my life, bizarre and improbable as it was.

I leaned across the coffee table, looked into his eyes and said, "Hannah Vogel."

CHAPTER TWENTY-NINE

Jim dropped his glass and leapt to his feet as if he had been jolted by lightning.

"How do you know that name?" he roared. "Who the hell are you?"

I had not expected that reaction, although of course I should have. He probably thought I was a spy, which made a certain amount of sense. How terrifying was it that a stranger of only two days' acquaintance knew the identity of his former nurse, saviour and lover?

Jim's fist hovered in the air, ready to strike. "Talk!" he yelled. "Now!"

Sarah also rose, galvanized by the fear of a donnybrook in her living room.

"Can we please calm down?" she asked. "James. Explain, please. Is this the Hannah you received the telegram from?"

"Yes. The Hannah who hid me in a basement room, took me out the dark hallway that felt as if it would go on forever, released me into the garden where Joseph was waiting, sent me along to a horse breeder in Winnipeg and saved my life. Does that sound familiar?" I asked Jim, my gaze never leaving his face.

Frozen in place, Jim stared back, his fist still poised.

"Could I have made that up?" I asked in challenge.

He dropped his arm and fell back onto the sofa. I watched as his shoulders dropped and his expression changed from fury and fear to wonder and sorrow.

"So she's alive," he whispered.

"Very much so." I pulled the telegram out of my shirt pocket and handed it over.

His hand trembled as he took it; his eyes misted as he read it.

"Hannah. My beautiful Hannah." His head fell heavily into his hands and he wept, shoulders heaving. Sarah went to him and held him in her compassionate arms. I could only imagine what he was thinking, but I came to this: he had lost two beloved women. Now, years after he had left the first, there were telegrams and soon there would be a railway; would he rediscover one of them?

After some time, he quietened. Wiping his eyes, he looked back at me and simply said, "Tell me everything."

I knew all about him. Seemed only fair to share my history. I filled in the blanks, told him about Alice Garrison and her father, and watched his eyes widen in astonishment, narrow in anger, and finally soften in understanding. We were both, after all, wanted men.

With the same first name.

"You are the James she told me about," I said at the end of my story. "She took to me partly because of that. I reminded her of you, just a bit, or so she said."

He laughed. "Not physically, I would think."

"No," I said, laughing too. "She thought we shared some personality traits, though."

He mulled that over, giving me a thorough once-over in light of this new information.

"How is she?" he asked softly.

"She is well. Very well, as far as I could tell. Healthy, strong, still a spitfire."

"Do you . . . do you think she might . . ." he stopped as his voice thickened.

I was not sure exactly what he was reaching for, so I guessed while he got himself under control.

"Want to hear from you?"

A small nod.

"That and . . . might she still, you know . . . care?"

"I can't speak for Hannah. But based on our conversation, I'd say that's a yes. She spoke of you very emotionally."

"Is she married?" That question came out in a strangled whisper.

"No."

The big shoulders dropped another inch.

"What do you want to do, Jim? Do you want me to send her a telegram? We'd have to be careful. Vague. You can't do it; they might twig to your identity. What do you think?"

"Oh God, it's been so long. So long! What will she think?"

"At the very least, she'll be happy you're safe."

He thought about that for a moment, wave after wave of emotion crossing his handsome face. Was it worth reconnecting? Would joy or rejection ensue? Would he enrich or endanger her life? I knew how I would feel. Any decent man — and Jim was nothing if not decent — would ask himself those questions.

"Yes. Yes. Would you? Would you tell her I'm all right, I'm alive? I'd be so grateful. I can't believe this is happening. Hannah." He paused again. "Is she still so beautiful?"

"She is, Jim. She really is."

This man was still in love with Hannah, after all these years, after all the pain, after marrying another woman, after it all. I had no doubt, and neither did Sarah, who reattached herself to Jim, crooning and patting his shoulders.

And I had no doubt Hannah still loved him.

·   ·   ·

My first stop the next morning was the telegraph office. I had spent the rest of the night tossing in my bed, trying to force the right, oblique, but not-too-vague words out of my slightly drunken brain. A few hours' sleep finally came, but I was up with the rooster crowing at the nearby farm. You can hear a rooster on a quiet morning from a long, long distance, I learned that day.

"Henry," I greeted the young man. "Good morning. I'm here to respond to the telegram you brought over."

"Good morning, James. Happy to help. Let me have it when you're ready."

I took a deep breath, not wanting to stumble or give the game away.

"Message received and understood. All well. Have made new friends already. Bert, Sarah, James. Railway almost here. Maybe you could visit and meet them someday. Sending love. James. Stop."

I experience a small tremor at using "James" instead of "Jim," but she would not understand — she still might not — if I used the latter. I could only hope she would realize my telegrams were carefully worded, a sort of code. But considering the strange miracle of finding Jim after all these years, would she?

It was the best I could do. I paid and tipped Henry, who did not appear to notice the name "James," with a few borrowed coins and went off to the shop.

Bert had agreed that I would work from early morning until two in the afternoon at the smithy. The rest of the day would be devoted to building my house. If a big emergency job came in, I would be expected to stay. His generosity and flexibility overwhelmed me.

Two horses required shoeing that morning, and we were almost finished with the second when a tumult outside caught Bert's attention.

"That's odd," he said. "I wonder what's going on? Can you poke your head out, son, and take a look?"

Obediently, I wiped my filthy hands and made my way to the door. Several men were gesticulating wildly and speaking in raised voices down Main Street.

"Bert, they're down the block, yelling and such. Do you want me to go and see what's up?"

"Yes. I'll have to stay with the beast, so off you go. Obviously, something has happened. Quick, now."

I ran down the middle of the dusty street and hopped onto the boardwalk where the men were shouting, agitation evident in their voices and movements. After a couple of polite attempts to get their attention, I finally hollered, "What's going on?"

"It's the doc," one man yelled back. "Doc Arlington."

"What's the problem?"

"I — we — think he's dead."

"What do you mean, think?"

"Well, he looks dead. None of us are doctors, you know."

Could no one in this town take a pulse?

"Where is he?" I asked.

"Up there in his office."

I took the rickety stairs two at a time and found three more men bouncing off the walls in panic and clearly unsure of what to do. I recalled that Bert had mentioned the doctor was unwell — so unwell he could not help him.

I pushed my way past the men — they must have been in shock, because they asked no questions of me, the interloper — and saw the old doctor sprawled in his chair, head cranked over to one side. I approached him a bit cautiously and touched his arm. He seemed stiff and felt cold; I lifted the lid on one eye as I placed two fingers on his neck.

"Is he dead, then?" a man, not much older than I, asked with a distinct tremor in his voice.

"I'm afraid so. I'm sorry; are you related to him?" I wondered why he was quite so upset.

"No." The large young man's eyes registered terror. "It's just . . . he's the only doc in town."

"Oh, yes, I see . . ."

Another man chimed in. "Maybe you don't. We came to get him for Charlie's wife. She's going to have her baby and having a hard time. Charlie, here, well he was shaking so hard I traipsed up here with him."

Now I really did see. Moose Jaw had relied on the old man. He made them feel safe — well, safer, anyway. I knew nothing about childbirth, apart from what Mum had told me, but someone had to calm these men down. And someone had to help Charlie's wife. But who?

"Any midwives in these parts?" I asked.

Charlie shook his head rather violently as the other man said, "Not that we know of."

What I did not know about Bert and Sarah, I realized in that moment, was whether they had had a family. They had not mentioned. Sarah struck me as one of the three most caring and competent humans I had ever met; I wondered if she would, or could, help. I knew no other women in town and could not come up with another suggestion.

Being an outsider, I was also beginning to realize, had its limited advantages. These men were not thinking clearly, worried as they were about the doctor's death, what it meant for their community, and in the immediate moment, who would deliver this difficult child. My brain was under less pressure and still working.

"Charlie, you must go home and be with your wife," I told the anxious father-to-be. "Sir . . . what's your name?"

"Angus."

"Right. Fellow Scot?"

"My father's side, yes."

"Angus, will you come with me? And who are you?" I asked the third fellow.

"John."

"John. Could you go to the smithy and tell Bert Thompson what's happened?" John nodded, gave a lopsided grin — I thought he seemed rather pleased at being told what to do — and left.

Charlie remained rooted to the spot as if he had grown there. I took the three steps between us, grasped him by the shoulders and said, "Your wife needs you. Go. Comfort her. Tell her help is on the way. Angus will show me where you live, right, Angus? We'll be there as fast as we can. Now go." I gave him a gentle shove toward the door. He nodded miserably and fled.

The deceased doctor would have to be otherwise dealt with. I hoped Bert and John, and the milling crowd outside, would at least lay him out and cover him. The new life was more important right now than the extinguished one.

A flicker of panic entered my own brain. I looked around a bit wildly for the doctor's bag and wondered what instruments might be needed for a birth. In the end, I simply grabbed the big, worn leather case in the corner and rushed down the stairs, Angus behind me.

Back on the street, we parted the crowd, which now stood in mournful quietude having heard the definite news of the doctor's death. Once through, we raced toward the Thompson home. I prayed with every galloping step that Sarah would be both home and armed with birthing knowledge.

Chapter Thirty

"Sarah!" I yelled, bursting through the door. "Sarah, help!"

By the time we reached the house, I had pulled the mantle of community panic over my own shoulders.

"James!" I heard her cry from the kitchen. "What on Earth is the matter?"

"Charlie . . . what's his last name?" I asked Angus, who was still on my heels.

"Preston."

"Charlie Preston's wife is in labour and needs help. What can we do? Can you . . ." I did not know exactly what to ask her. "Deliver babies, I guess?"

"Oh, dear. Poor Ellie. She's had a rough pregnancy. But hasn't Charlie gone for the doctor?"

"Sarah, I'm sorry. He did go, but . . ."

Realization and sorrow crossed her features. "He's dead then."

"Yes."

She looked down for a moment, then nodded. "Let me get washed and we'll go."

The three of us hurried to the Preston home, unfortunately a considerable distance away. Angus went ahead, finding shortcuts through private yards and shallow ditches. We arrived panting and knocked loudly on the door as we tried to catch our breaths.

"Come in. Hurry!" Charlie yelled from within.

Angus held the door open for Sarah and me, then followed us into the dark little house. A small, combined kitchen and living room gave way to two tiny bedrooms at the back; Ellie Preston lay white, exhausted and writhing on a low bed in one of them. After the moment it took for our eyes to adjust to the dim light, Sarah gave a small cry and plunged toward the striving mother.

"Angus," Sarah said as she placed her hand gently on the heaving stomach. "Water. Heat water and hurry up about it. James, what is in Doc's bag?"

I opened it to see various rather frightening-looking tools, bandages and rags, vials of medicines, clamps and forceps. Or so I assumed. I rattled off the contents to Sarah as I rooted through the case.

"We have to boil those forceps and fast. Is there any antiseptic of any kind?"

"Ummm . . . carbolic acid?"

"Yes. Take the forceps to the sink and douse them in it. Then wash them in soap and water. Be careful."

I did so, as quickly and thoroughly as possible, and returned to the bedroom where Sarah was examining the poor young woman, who howled, screamed and wept as the contractions mercilessly continued. I averted my eyes, considering Ellie Preston's physical privacy, until Sarah turned, straightened and motioned to me.

"Probably breech," she muttered. "I feel his head up by the ribcage. Damn."

"What do we do?" I whispered back.

"We have to try to turn him. It's the only thing we can do." Sarah returned to the bed and said to both parents, "I think the babe is turned the wrong way."

"Is that bad?" Charlie gasped.

"Well, it's not great. As you can see, the child isn't coming. We'll see what we can do."

Who, I wondered, were "we?"

"Right, you two. Turn her onto her left side. Let's see if that helps first."

Of course. We. A shaking Charlie and I approached the bed and carefully slipped our hands under Ellie's back, then rolled her as gently as possible. Sarah moved in and massaged the child as it floundered in the womb.

"How long has she been labouring?" she asked Charlie.

"I — I don't really know. Seems like hours and hours. We didn't realize it was wrong until a couple of hours ago. She said the babe wasn't moving the right way. And I'd gone to find Doc Arlington, but the door was locked; I thought he was out. But he was dead. I guess John broke in. We were so worried. Rightly so, as it turned out." His voice broke, but he choked out, "Please, Sarah. You have to help her."

"Now, now, Charlie, we'll do everything we can. He's not the first breech baby to come into this world."

But it became clear over the next few minutes that the baby was stubborn. He would not turn over. Poor Ellie had to be returned to her prone position and spoke for the first time.

"Sarah," she gasped. "Am I going to die? Is the baby going to die? I feel like . . . I'm going to die. I'm so tired, Sarah."

Sarah pressed her lips together before speaking; I thought she was fighting tears. I certainly was.

"Ellie," she crooned. "We're not going to let any of that happen. Just try to breathe for a moment. Breathe with me. In now. Out now. Nice and deep." This went on for a short while, until Sarah said, "Now take a little rest."

Sarah took me by the arm and led me into the kitchen, where the water had finally come to a boil.

"We have to turn that child. It will be extremely painful for Ellie. You have to help me. I don't think I'm strong enough, and it usually takes two or three people anyway. Are you ready? We're going to save that baby, damn it."

Terrified at the responsibility and the prospect of seeing this woman in even more pain, I nodded mutely.

"We're also going to need those forceps. She's almost certainly too exhausted to push him out on her own. Keep them clean. Angus, give the water two more minutes on the boil, then bring it in."

We returned to the room and Sarah sat next to Ellie on the bed, reaching for her hand. Quietly, she explained what we were about to do, and asked for her consent. Ellie simply nodded and closed her eyes. Sarah then deputized Charlie to hold on to his wife unless asked to do otherwise.

The next half hour was a blur of screams, blood and terror. My hands worked a hard abdomen, feeling things that both horrified and exalted me.

This little life, struggling to join the world, seemed the only thing that mattered. Sarah pushed down while I pushed over and slowly the baby changed its position. Whether it was the right position, though, I had no idea. I prayed he would decide to flip around soon; I doubted my arms would hold out much longer, and Sarah's must have been on fire. Turning this child was unbelievably hard work.

Finally, Sarah took in a sharp breath, ducked her head between the mother's legs and peered inside. Her hand slipped up for a second and came out covered in blood.

"I think he is finally crowning," she said with a tired smile. "Forceps, James. Ellie, can you push at all?"

Ellie could no longer speak, but feebly bore down one last time with the last of her energy. Sarah tried to expand the forceps but shook her head at me.

"You'll have to do it," she said. "I have no strength left."

"I've never done this before, Sarah."

"Neither have I."

I looked at her in horror, but this poor mother had no options. I grasped the forceps and knelt at Ellie's feet, my jaw clenched and muscles straining. What if I hurt the wee thing trying so hard to be born? Moreover, the intimacy of what I was about to do almost made me leap to my feet and run out the door. Blood I did not fear. Gazing upon a woman in such distress was an entirely different thing. Besides, what would her husband think?

Squeezing my eyes shut for a second, I took a deep breath, which had the fortunate effect of steadying my shaking hands. I reopened my eyes to peer at the paddle-shaped, large metal tongs and imagined sliding them in on either side of the baby's head. I looked meaningfully at the distraught father, begging him for permission, and he gave me one, terrified nod.

Another profound inhale, and I parted Ellie's legs to see the gaping birth canal, slippery with the fluids and gore that accompany so many rites of life and death. Suddenly, the incredible beauty of what was occurring right before me replaced the fear; I was determined that this baby would be born alive.

I could just see his, or her, head. I opened the forceps with one hand and felt around the little skull with the other. Ellie barely twitched, although she did moan, which I decided to view as a good sign. She was still with us and could still feel.

I would have killed pretty much anyone for a doctor just then. But she had me.

"All right, here we go," I said. "Ellie, I'm going to bring your baby now. Hold on."

With extreme care, I slipped the instrument inside, trying to avoid the child's eyes. He was still turned sideways, but at least his head was coming first. And I pulled, but he would not come.

"Sarah, he's stuck or something," I said, panic rising again.

"Might be the cord. Can you feel around his head, see if it's tangled around him?"

"I can . . . yes, there it is," I said, my hand sliding over the baby's head and neck. "It seems to be wrapped around him. What do I do now?"

"You must untangle it or he will strangle. Try to slip it over his head."

For the love of God, could anything else go wrong with this babe? Stretching the umbilical cord over the head was incredibly difficult, especially considering I was doing this blind. I pulled hard and Ellie gave a howl, which I assumed resulted from the tug.

Something finally seemed to give way; I felt a sense of relieved pressure and returned to focusing on the forceps. As gently as I could, which was not very, I held tight to that baby and dragged. Finally, he began to emerge: his tiny head, followed by skinny little shoulders . . . and then the rest of him just slipped out onto the bed. Sarah scooped him up, cut the cord and gave him a healthy slap on his rather enormous rump, comparatively speaking. And yes, he was a he.

After making a small choking noise, the baby wailed, a rather dreadful tinny sound that may have been the most beautiful music I had ever heard.

"He's pink," Sarah declared. "Thank God."

I had not even considered the dire possibility that the babe, once delivered, would be blue. Already on my knees, I slumped onto my backside in relief.

"Thank God," I echoed.

Charlie, by now holding his incredibly wee son, simply wept.

•   •   •

The birth was not the end of it, of course. Sarah shooed me out to deal with the afterbirth and the exhausted mother. I worried deeply about Ellie as I stood in the kitchen trembling with fatigue and reverence. Angus, still holding the fort out front, handed me three fingers of liquor, which I was tempted to drink off but decided to sip instead. Collapse threatened and I preferred not to make an ass of myself.

Some time later, Sarah appeared in the doorway, daubed with blood, eyes ringed in blue, almost unable to walk. I reached for her and helped her into a chair, but I could not bear the tension of not knowing.

"How is she? How is the boy?"

"They're going to be fine," she said, her weary voice tinged with triumph. "She's lost a lot of blood, but not too much, I think. And it will take a few weeks before she can manage. But they will both be fine. And James, the baby has been named."

"Already? That was fast."

"Easy decision, they said. Charles Sinclair Preston. Congratulations, James. You're a namesake and, if you want to be, a godfather."

CHAPTER THIRTY-ONE

Sarah and I limped home, Angus trailing along to make sure neither of us fell unconscious in the street. I really, really liked Angus.

Bert, having been apprised of the crisis by John, had come home and managed to heat up a pot of soup on the stove. We ate, the four of us. Angus went home and we tumbled into bed, exhausted beyond the ability to talk.

The following day proved magnificent in its complete lack of dire events. Bert and I worked for a few hours; at two, I went to visit Jim at the hardware store and ordered the lumber and tools and nails and things I would need for the house.

He vibrated slightly during the transaction, and of course I realized why.

"I'm afraid I haven't had a telegram yet," I told him. "But it's only been a day."

"You'll let me know."

"Of course. Immediately."

"When would you like all of this delivered?"

"How soon can you do it?"

"Tomorrow?"

"That would be great. Thanks, Jim. I'll see you tomorrow."

"I hear you helped a babe come into the world yesterday."

"I guess I did. It was amazing. Terrifying, but amazing."

"Good on you, James. Well done. I'm sure it was both."

I left the store glowing from the praise. It really had been both. When I returned to the Thompson home, Sarah told me she had been to see Ellie and the wee one, who would be referred to as Small Charlie for now to distinguish him from his father. And had I decided whether I would be his godfather?

Yes, I certainly would.

Life in Moose Jaw was starting to agree with me.

• • •

Banging away at a metal wheel rim late the following morning, I looked up to see Angus arrive at the blacksmith's shop. Anxiety lined his face, and I was terrified that something had happened to Small Charlie or his mother.

"What's wrong?" I said, dispensing with greetings or small talk. "Is the baby . . ." I could not finish that sentence.

"No, no, the wee one is fine. Good morning, James. Bert."

"Morning, Angus. Well, what then?"

"Well . . . I'm not sure what this means, but I was having my breakfast at the hotel just a little while ago. I went back up to the bar to get another cup of coffee, and I overheard a man saying your name. Didn't recognize him. He's not from around here. Thought you should know."

I felt my face pale under its browned skin. That had not taken long.

"Did you hear anything else he said?"

"Nothing that made sense. Something about a newcomer from down east, and had the barkeep seen him?"

"What did the barkeep say?"

"Just shook his head."

"Who's the barkeep? Do I know him?"

"That would be John. The John you met yesterday at Doc Arlington's."

"Mighty kind of him to do that."

"Mighty kind of you to save a baby's life."

"Wasn't just me."

"It was largely you."

"It was you and Sarah and Charlie, too. What did this man look like?"

"Fairly tall, long dark hair, dressed mostly in black. Bit of a scar on his cheekbone."

"Is this the man looking for you, James?" Bert asked.

"It's his henchman."

"Want to tell me what the hell is going on?" Angus asked.

"Short form of a long story, this man's boss says I . . . ruined his daughter. The daughter is now dead. The man you saw in the bar — name of Riley — does his dirty work for him. He's been chasing me across the prairies. I didn't do it, Angus. I don't know who did. But the boss, George Garrison, is a very powerful man back in Toronto. Innocence didn't matter; I was done for, so I had to light out. And here I am."

"I see. Damn. Well, you can count on me, James. But you have to stay out of sight, as much as possible, until this gets figured out. And don't go near the hotel. We'll see what we can do about running this Riley out of town."

"He's going to find me, Angus. It's just a matter of time. I hope I'll be out of Bert and Sarah's home before that, though."

"I hear you're building a house."

"Yep."

"We'd better get on that, then."

Before I could close my gaping mouth or start to object, Angus had turned on his heel and run out the shop door.

"Good people around here," Bert observed.

"Very good people."

Three hours later, a massive rumbling reached my ears even over the clanging in the shop. I abandoned my post and went to the door to see an enormous flatbed cart drawn by two large and powerful horses. The cart groaned under a stack of cured wood, topped with various tools, trusses, sacks likely filled with nails, and the widely-grinning Jim and Angus, who merely waved as they rattled by. Clearly, that was my cue to join them at the building site.

"That would be your house driving by," Bert said, also grinning.

"I guess it would."

"Off you go, then, James. This can wait 'til morning."

I thanked him profusely and took off running down the street. My little plot of land lay tucked a short way behind the shop, and I was not yet panting when I met Jim jumping off the cart's driver's box. I walked up to him, grabbed his hand and shook it vigorously and speechlessly.

"You're welcome," he said, still smiling. "Let's get at it."

We three began to unload the wood and tools when John appeared followed by Charlie, who really should have remained at home with his wife and baby son. I suggested such a thing, and he said the neighbour had come over to help out. And then three more men, whom I did not know, arrived. Before long, everything was on the ground and the men were starting to organize the trusses.

"Ever seen a barn raising?" Jim asked.

"N-no. A barn raising?"

"In these parts, when a farmer needs some help building a barn, everyone comes on by and pitches in. The walls and roof are literally raised by the men. Can also be done with a house. Just won't take as long, because it's so much smaller and lighter. Here, take a look at these plans, see what you think."

Gobsmacked, I looked down at the paper he had thrust into my hands. The sketch revealed a square building with a lean-to, configured much like Charlie and Ellie's home. A kitchen, living room and dining area dominated the front, with two bedrooms at the back. There was even a tiny outhouse illustrated on the side.

"This," I said, clearing my throat, "is perfect."

"Glad you like it. Okay, boys, let's get going," Jim said more loudly, and everyone gathered around him to view the plans. Minutes later, the men began nailing frames together. Once these were done, they added studs; then they lifted the walls to check the dimensions and ensure they would fit together. Jim nodded happily, giving his seal of approval.

By some magic, Sarah and another woman appeared at six o'clock. They carried massive baskets filled with fried chicken, homemade bread, pickles of all kinds and potato salad. The men roared their approval, dropped their hammers and charged for the food, fervently thanking Sarah and her friend. A third woman arrived in a small wagon bearing beer and water.

I had never felt as much a part of a community as I did in that moment.

"Thank you, Sarah," I said quietly. "This is so kind of you."

She touched my face and smiled at me, rather tremulously. "My pleasure, dear James."

After dinner, we returned to the building for another two hours; the sun was still up, and as Jim said, why waste the light?

"How long will this take?" I asked him. "I can't believe how fast this is going."

He shrugged. "Another day or two. For the outside. Then we have to finish the inside. Depends on everyone's work hours."

"You closed the hardware." Guilt began to creep into my thoughts.

"Nope. Have a kid there. Don't worry. If he needs me, he'll come find me."

At eight, Jim called the day over and everyone placed their tools in a covered box to protect them from rain and dew. Charlie and the other men went home; John returned to his late shift at the bar. Angus and Jim came back to Bert and Sarah's for a beer. All of us dropped like sacks of potatoes onto the living room furniture.

"So," Jim said, plunging straight into the looming problem. "What are we going to do about this Riley?"

"I told him," Angus put in.

"Ah," I said. "I frankly have no idea. But I'm not leaving. I could run to the coast and he'd still find me. I have to confront this here. I'm sorry. I didn't mean to bring trouble to your town. I could move further north, if you think that would help; but I'm not leaving this territory."

"What? And leave your new house behind?" Jim smirked, but then his face settled into a grim mask. "Nothing doing. Besides, you already have friends here. What the hell would happen to you out there, all by yourself? No. We have to see this through. What do you say, Bert? Angus?"

"Well," Bert said slowly, "I finally found myself a blacksmith. Wouldn't be too happy to see him go. Be pretty rough on Sarah and me."

Jim nodded. "Angus?"

"I say he stays. Count me in."

"Sarah?"

"The next time I have to deliver a baby, if we don't get a doctor in here right smartly, I'm going to need James to help me. So. That's settled. What are we going to do, though, Jim?"

He shook his head slowly. "I don't know. But we have to do something. Can't really shoot the man in cold blood. I could try reasoning with him, but I doubt that would work. He has his marching orders, isn't that right, James?"

I nodded.

"I actually have a bit of an idea," Angus said unexpectedly. "It won't be easy, but maybe we could take turns keeping an eye on this bastard? John can watch for him at the hotel; Henry could keep an eye out on Main Street, especially if he comes in to send a telegram; and . . . well, I don't know, but might that work? At least we'd know if he's coming for James."

"What about at night?" Jim asked.

"Don't know about that. Tough one. I could stay here, maybe, if there's another room?" Sarah nodded. "Sending a signal might be tough, though, if something happened. But James and I could take shifts as lookouts."

"We'll have to try to keep this as quiet as possible, but with that many people involved, it'll be tricky," Jim said. "You know what they say about a secret known to more than one."

"The boys will be fine," Angus said reassuringly. "They know when to keep their mouths shut."

As Angus finished speaking, I heard a crash coming from out back; the windows were open to let in the evening breeze. The noise was soon followed by a high whinnying, followed by angry snorting.

"Buck," I cried, and dashed out the back door.

CHAPTER THIRTY-TWO

The stable door swung and creaked in the breeze; someone had obviously opened it and left it ajar. I crept to the side and peered in, but all I could see were Buck's rolling eyes gleaming in the gloom. He snorted some more and pawed the ground. Inhaling deeply while feeling for the knife I now kept holstered on my side, I slowly moved inside.

Someone grabbed my arm and I almost yelled before realizing Jim was restraining me from a rash move. He and Angus had followed me, so quietly I had not heard them come. He showed me his own knife, then nodded.

"Who's there?" I demanded in as authoritative a voice as I could muster.

Buck stomped and whinnied again, but I could hear rustling in the straw over his noises.

"You might as well come out. With your hands up," I added. "You won't get past us. This is the only door."

"James?" said an incredulous voice. I recognized it.

"For the love of God. Jones? Is that you?"

"Yepper. It's me, James. And Clancy's here too. Don't shoot or nothing, will ya?"

Sarah arrived holding a lantern. Her courage never ceased to amaze me. I took the light from her and swung it high; Jones rose into its beam, looking exactly like a bale of hay with all the straw stuck to his clothes, followed by an equally messy Clancy.

"What the hell are you doing here?" I asked. "Scared me half to death. I thought someone was hurting Buck."

"This your horse?" Jones asked. "Nice animal, if a little twitchy. We were just lookin' for somewhere to bed down. Sorry for the trouble, James, ma'am."

"You know these fellows, James?" Jim asked.

"Yes. I met them on the train on my way out here. Jones, Clancy, meet Jim, Angus, and the lady of the house, Sarah."

"If," she said archly, "you'd managed to make it all the way to the house, you would've seen the codes on the wall. No need to hide in the damned stable and scare Buck out of his wits."

"Yes, ma'am. I'm sorry, ma'am," Jones repeated. But he did not look very sorry to me. He looked relieved. Somehow, he had stumbled on a hobo-friendly home.

"Well, come on in and let's have a look at you, then," she said. "I think there's some soup left over from last night, and maybe a piece of that fried chicken. After you apologize to Buck."

I approached Jones, shook his hand and clapped Clancy on the shoulder. I really was happy to see them, although somewhat baffled by their appearance. Then we three turned to my poor frightened horse and gave him apples and oats and neck pats until he calmed down.

"It's okay, Buck," I murmured. "It's okay. Thanks for the warning, though."

As we walked back to the house, I wondered where to put my hobo friends. With Angus deciding to stay over as my guardian angel, there were no more rooms to accommodate Jones and Clancy. Soon enough, after they washed up at Sarah's insistence, she explained this problem.

"You could stay in the stable, though," she mused, ladling soup into bowls. "Until we get James moved out. But only if Buck will have you."

"I think he might, if it's all right with you, Sarah," I said. "Just don't get too close to him," I warned Jones.

"That's settled, then," Sarah said. "Eat up, you two."

I managed to contain myself as they wolfed down the hot soup and cold chicken. I wondered when they had last eaten decent food. Finally, though, I blurted, "What in hell are you two doing here?"

"Well, two things," Jones said. "There's no work out at Pile O' Bones anymore. They've hired enough local men to make up the labour they need on the railway. We figured we'd come out here and be first in line when the line comes closer. And we wondered if we'd find you. You weren't in Pile O' Bones. We looked."

I could feel my eyes opening in alarm. "Did you actually know I was staying here with the Thompsons?" If they knew, everyone did.

Jones shook his head as he gnawed on the last meat-bearing chicken bone.

"Dumb luck." He grinned.

My shoulders came down.

"Right," Jim said. "We have no money for you, but we do have food. What say you come out tomorrow and help us raise James's house? Only be a couple of days, and the work on the railbed won't be started by then. We'll go to the telegraph office and see what's posted there for jobs after that. Deal?"

Jones and Clancy nodded in perfect unison.

"Deal," said Jones, for himself and his silent partner.

Too tired to talk anymore, I led the newcomers back to the stable bearing old blankets unearthed by Sarah and made sure Buck was comfortable with his new bedmates. Back at the house, Angus was taking the first look-out shift from the living room chesterfield. I went to bed for a few hours' sleep, wondering how Jim and Angus and Sarah had arranged a house-raising and food delivery service behind my back in just a few hours.

I would find a way to pay them back.

•　　•　　•

After a hearty breakfast the next morning, Jim, Angus, Jones, Clancy and I returned to the building site at eight. John showed up after his morning shift at the hotel bar, and Charlie appeared by noon, followed by the other three men at two. The speed at which my home rose was completely incredible to me . . . and then I realized I would also need a stable.

"Yes, of course," Jim said when I mentioned this. "The stable will come last, though. Buck will be fine if we don't get it built this week. He has his stall at the Thompsons'."

He had thought of everything. Every day I saw more clearly why Hannah had loved him. Did she still? I thought so, but talk is cheap.

The telegram came at four. Henry pounded on Sarah's door, breathless as always, and was sent over to where we were working. I was not sure which telegram I wanted to see more — Hannah's or Mum's. It worried me that Mum had not responded yet.

Henry wiped the sweat from his brow, gave me his "this looks important" face, and handed over the missive. I trembled a bit as I took it from him.

"Thanks, Henry. I sure appreciate you bringing this over."

"Looks important, James."

I permitted myself a little laugh despite my jangling nerves. "It does, Henry."

I looked down and read.

"James. Thank you for the note. I have sent a letter. Watch for it. Important. Hannah. Stop."

That was it? Damn. How was I going to tell Jim? Why wouldn't she respond by telegram? Bounty hunters could not possibly still be seeking Jim, could they?

Well, there was little I could do about it. I felt Jim's eyes burning into my back, waiting for the news this telegram should have imparted. Good or bad. Love or rejection. Heaven or hell. What I had for him, though, was none of the above.

"Jim," I said to him quietly, once I'd drawn him aside. "I'm sorry. She doesn't say anything, just that she's sent a letter. I hope that's not bad news, aside from not knowing more. Could they still be looking for you? God, I hope not."

"They could. It's unlikely, after all this time, but it's possible. Men do terrible things out of rage and greed."

"Is she just being extra careful, maybe?"

"Maybe. I hope so." Jim's eyes held so much sorrow, I could not hold his gaze. But I did note it was sorrow, not fear.

• • •

The bones of the house went up the next day. A complex system of levers and ropes deposited the roof trusses on the completed frames, and once the entire structure was in place, the walls were quickly hammered on.

Three days later, the rooms were divided, the walls painted, the floor finished and the outhouse in place. I swore to the men in a fit of emotional gratitude that I would repay them somehow, someday. They simply shook my hand, one at a time, and went home. They would be back to help with the stable, Jim assured me.

Meanwhile, Jones and Clancy were helping Angus and me with look-out duty, which allowed everyone to get some sleep and the hobos to rest more comfortably on the sofa every other night. Busy blacksmithing and building, I had not gone into town for the last few days and had heard no further rumblings about Riley seeking to capture or murder me. I knew it could not last. The suspense was killing me, but at least he unintentionally gave me time to finish my home.

A couple of mornings later, another telegram arrived. Henry, by now aware that I was avoiding Main Street, delivered it yet again. Great kid, Henry.

"James. Thank God you're alive. Sorry for delay in responding and so sorry to have to tell you this way but your father is dead. I love you so much. Your Mum. Stop."

Chapter Thirty-three

I do not remember what happened after that. I had gone numb with shock and all the confused emotions that follow the death of a parent you had both loved and hated.

I woke up hungover on the porch in the wee hours of the morning, eyes like sandpaper from weeping and dehydration. I tried to shake some sense into myself but abandoned that activity when my head began to pound and the floor to spin.

All feelings about my father aside, what would now happen to my mother and sisters? They brought in some of the household income, but Da's contribution — despite the strikes and his frequent days off due to drunkenness — made up the lion's share. Making matters worse, did Mum have any idea why I left? If so, did she know I was innocent, at least in her heart?

Weaving precariously, I made my way to the biffy but ended up vomiting miserably in the bushes near the stable. I felt somewhat better after that and managed to piss where it was more appropriate.

Sarah met me on the back porch with a large glass of water and a blanket. I shivered like an aspen in the wind. As I tipped back the icy water, she simply patted me on the back and said, "This is not the first hangover I've seen. Come in and go to bed, James. You've had a nasty shock. I'm so sorry, dear."

So I had told her about Da, then. Again, the previous day was something of a blur.

"I'll owe you a bit for the whiskey," I said. "I'm sorry, Sarah."

She waved her hand in the air. "These things happen. Go to bed, James."

I gave her a shaky smile and determined to apologize properly after a few hours' sleep. I had never been so drunk in my life and swore — as so many hungover men have over history — that I would never do it again.

I lurched up the stairs to my room, washed my face and drank another cup of water before moving to the window, both to close it and to pull the curtain. It was dark in the room, which turned out to be a blessing because under the moon, half-hidden under a low-hanging branch, sat a man on a horse.

I heard the horse snort quietly or I would not have noticed Riley. He sat astride his beast, barely moving, not smoking, not drinking, not doing much but breathing. Watching. I wondered if he had seen me stumble off the porch, and if so why he had not followed me.

I drew my head back, leaving the window and curtain as they were. I watched him too, for an hour. He finally turned his horse's head and quietly rode away.

He either knew or suspected I was staying with Bert and Sarah. He had been on a reconnaissance mission, checking where the openings to the home were, counting the rooms to the best of his ability, watching for any late-night activity.

He was coming for me. Soon. I had to leave. As soon as possible.

•   •   •

"I have to move out, Sarah. Today."

"You'll be no safer in your new home. Less so, if anything."

"I'm aware of that. But you'll be safer. Jones and Clancy will stay and keep an eye out, right, boys?"

"You're half right," Jones said. "I'm coming with you. Clancy and Angus will stay here."

I started to protest but Sarah put a gentle finger on my lips, which rather belied her next words.

"For the love of God, James, don't be an idiot. We talked about this before you came down. It's the only thing to do. You can't stay there alone, and that's flat."

"But what if he comes here first, tearing the place apart to look for me? And what if he finds Buck? He'll recognize my horse, for certain."

"That's why Clancy and Angus will stay," she said, rolling her eyes as if to emphasize my idiotic status. "You must move after dark. All that bustle will certainly attract attention. Let's see, now, what will you need? What can we lend you?"

The conversation turned to necessary household items. A pot and a pan, two forks and two knives, some blankets and an old cot and a small sofa, regrettably with its springs beginning to pop through the upholstery. But beggars cannot be choosers, and after a smack on the back of the head courtesy of Bert, I gratefully accepted the bits of things he and Sarah could do without.

Sarah clapped her hands and rose, a signal to leap into action. She instructed me and the other men to gather the large pieces and pile them in the living room after moving aside the furnishings. Sarah herself went into the kitchen, where we could hear her banging cupboard doors and clattering cutlery.

Once all the items were gathered, I returned to my room and packed up my few and sorry items. I needed new dungarees and certainly a warm coat. That would have to wait until I had made some money and had sorted out this . . . situation.

The sun hangs in the sky until late during a prairie June. Solstice crept toward us, and the horizon remained a soft blue until ten. At eleven, darkness softly covered the street. Angus had gone off and brought back a cart along with Jim. Buck was none too happy about becoming a temporary dray, but he calmed down once we had him hitched and gave him apples as a treat.

We loaded the cart in less than half an hour and unloaded without incident half an hour later. There were few enough items and more than enough men. When Jim brought out the whiskey bottle, though, I demurred. I had had quite enough last night and stuck to water as the other men toasted my new home.

"To James," Jim said, raising his glass. "May the rest of his life be slightly less eventful."

"Amen," I muttered. "Amen."

CHAPTER THIRTY-FOUR

Two weeks later

She quivered with fear and rage as she stood in the doorway, rifle trained on my chest but eyes focused on the unconscious man lying on my dining room table.

She had already threatened to kill me, but only if the man died. I was certainly hoping for his recovery.

"Steady, there," I said, raising my hands slowly. "Ma'am. Is this your husband?"

"No," she said, her voice quivering along with the rest of her. "He's my brother. Alexander. What the hell happened to him? What have you done to him? Tell me!"

"Ma'am . . . uh, what is your name?"

"Abby. Abigail Pearce. You may call me Miss Pearce. Who in the name of God are you? Are you some sort of doctor?"

"Not exactly," I admitted. "But I guess I've had a little doctoring practice. I'm afraid your brother was shot in the street, ma'am . . . Miss Pearce. There was an altercation. I wasn't there. Jim and Angus and Charlie . . . do you know who I mean?" I paused, and she nodded. "They came running for me, hoping I could do something for him. But his leg — I'm sorry, but it was gone. He would have died of sepsis or blood loss if we hadn't . . . ah . . ." I could not bring myself to say the word "amputated."

Miss Pearce was clearly not the sort of woman given to vapours. Even so, her knees buckled, and forgetting myself — and the gun — I lurched toward her as she tried to regain her balance.

"Easy now. Would you like to take a seat?" I directed her to the sofa with the popping springs. Best I could do.

She still held the gun with an iron grip, but the business end now pointed at the floor instead of at me. Progress. And she did allow me to guide her to the sofa.

"Oh my God," she whispered, as she sank onto the upholstery. "Was it Garrison? His men?"

"I don't know, I'm sorry. Do you have a quarrel with Garrison, miss?"

She gave a slightly unladylike snort.

"You could call it that. The bastard. He wants our land. We farm just south of the new rail line; close enough to abut the track, and a sliver is wanted for the rights-of-way. The railroad company wants a small building there; not sure what. Maybe barracks for the workers, or a siding? We've said no countless times. But Garrison wants it. He thinks he can make a bundle by delivering our farm to the railway. I'm sure he's right."

"He's speculating? Out here?" I was not all that surprised. Garrison would literally do anything for a dollar. Another thought occurred to me. "Is he here, himself?"

"If he's not, he's on his way. Or so they say. His raiders sure as hell are and have been for a while."

This information possibly explained why I had not yet had a visit from Riley. I thought he just had not found me, but more likely he was busy trying to wrest land away from decent farmers like Abby and Alexander Pearce.

"Have you met Trevor Riley?" I asked, my voice betraying bitterness.

"I certainly have. Several times. I expect he set fire to our stable, as well. Didn't catch him at it, unfortunately."

"Oh no. Were any of your animals hurt?"

"Alex ran for it when he saw the smoke. Good thing he was out back at the time. He got the horses out before it burst into full flame. All but one." At this, she hung her head for a moment, and clasped her shaking hands together. I wanted with all my soul, and definitely with my body, to wrap my arms around her. But I did not. She still had that gun beside her.

Her head snapped up a moment later, and she emitted a heart-rending sob.

"He wouldn't be able to do that now," she said through the clouds in her throat. "Oh no, Alex. My poor Alex."

She rose and dashed for the table, Garrison and me forgotten, and threw her arms around her brother's shoulders, her own chest heaving. Thank God she did not slip on the still-bloody floor.

Alex, apparently roused by his sister's hug or her weeping, opened one crusty eyelid — for which I was exceedingly grateful. It was proof positive that the man was indeed still alive. It was then that I realized I had seen him before. Alexander had touched my shoulder in sympathy at the telegraph office. That moment of kindness came back to me in a rush, and I was doubly glad I had — thus far — saved his life.

"Abby?" he croaked.

"It's me, Alex. It's me. How do you feel?"

"Like bloody hell. God, so much . . . pain. They took my leg, Abby."

"I know, honey. I know. I'm sorry. The main thing is you're still alive. I couldn't possibly do without you. We'll manage, don't you worry. Just try to get better." Her eyes implored me to help him, and I responded by upending the laudanum vial, containing the final few drops of painkiller left in Moose Jaw, over his mouth.

"Try to stay still, Alex," I muttered. "I know it hurts like hell. This will help a bit. Try to breathe."

He slipped back into blessed unconsciousness a minute later. Not knowing what his sister wanted to do next, I suggested she sit down again to rest while Bert and I cleaned up the gory mess in the dining area.

"Or you could sit on the porch? Maybe you don't need to see this," I added.

"No. I'm staying right here. I want to be here when Alex awakens." She paused, and when she spoke again, her tone had changed. "If that is all right with you."

"Yes, of course."

The process of scrubbing several pints of blood off a floor is not for the faint of heart. I had just amputated a man's lower leg but still found it horrific. The blood stained the wood and seeped through the cracks between the planks; it would be a while before it became unnoticeable, if ever. Bert helped, to the extent possible; at least he did not have to see it.

"Thank God you were at the shop, Bert," I said under my breath. "I couldn't have done this without you."

"You could, actually," Bert said. "But I'm glad I could help. What will we do with him? He can't very well stay on your table for two weeks or however long it will take to start healing."

"We could put him on the cot in Doc Arlington's old office. But someone would have to stay with him."

"No," said Abby, overhearing. "I'm taking him home with me. As soon as possible. I'll need to get a cart, though."

"You can't go anywhere alone right now," I said, a bit too loudly. "Garrison's men haven't left. God knows what plans they have for you. No. I will get Angus to bring his cart. But is it wise for you and a sick man to be alone? Is anyone else on the farm?"

She shook her head. "Our parents died a couple years back. It's just Alex and me. I'll be fine. If anyone comes near him, or me, I'll shoot the bastard."

"Miss Pearce, there may be more than one bastard."

Those periwinkle eyes looked up at me with a distressed expression that pierced my heart. She knew I was right. I could see it. And she said it.

"You're right. I'm not . . . thinking clearly. But where will we go?"

"Alexander could stay here. I have a second bedroom. Bert? Any thoughts on where we could put Miss Pearce?"

"Abby," she said.

Ah.

"Abby, then."

"Well, we could plunk Clancy on the couch for now, and she could have your old room at our place. 'Tisn't far," Bert said.

I turned back to Abby. "What do you think? There is a lady of the house, and she'd make sure you're all right."

"You mean Sarah?"

"Yes. You know her?"

"Of course. Everyone knows Sarah in these parts. And I've met Mr. Thompson, too. Maybe he doesn't remember."

Bert thought for a moment, and a light seemed to appear over his head.

"Of course. I'm sorry, Miss Pearce. My eyesight being what it is . . . you came in to have a horse shod some time ago, didn't you?"

"Yes. I'm pleased you recall. Sarah and I have had conversations a few times. Mr. Thompson, if you think that would be all right . . ."

Bert nodded. "Safest place for you. We have a couple of gentlemen keeping an eye on our place, and James here has Jones staying the night. Where is Jones, anyway?"

"He got a few hours working on the railbed. He'll be back at nightfall." A horrified look crossed Abby's face as I spoke. "What's the matter, Abby?"

"I haven't even asked you your name. And you saved Alexander. At least, I think you did. I apologize for my rudeness. It's James, then?"

"James Sinclair. I'm very pleased to meet you, although the circumstances are strange, to say the least." I attempted a crooked grin.

"To say the least." She offered me her hand. "Thank you, James."

She touched my hand, said my name, beamed at me . . . and I stood in admiration of the brave, quivering, rifle-toting, beautiful Abigail Pearce.

Chapter Thirty-five

One thing was for damn sure: hell was coming. I just did not know when.

Anyone who would burn down the stable of poor farmers and shoot down an innocent man in the street was capable of anything.

Meanwhile, I had a sick man living in my house. I took one bedroom, Alex the other, and poor old Jones had to make do on the couch. I was deeply grateful for him. Having another able-bodied person around the place at least allowed me to get some sleep.

Occasionally. Alex sweated and moaned and thrashed, awake or asleep, and I worried about him incessantly. We needed more painkillers. I asked Jim, who seemed able to source pretty much anything, to find some more laudanum.

"We need a fucking doctor around here," I said when he came over to see how Alex was doing. "Is there any hope of getting him to Pile of Bones, do you think? They have a doc, right? It'd be a grim journey, though. Forget I asked. I need laudanum, Jim. And for now, whiskey."

"I brought you some. It's hanging on the beast outside. I'll see what I can do about the opiate. Hard to get that stuff."

"Okay. What in hell happened out there? Did you actually see it, or did you just find Alex bleeding in the dust?"

"I didn't see it, but I heard it — yelling, then Alex hollering back. I gather he thought that was the end of it, but then someone shot him. Heard that, I can tell you. Came running and there he was. As you say, lying in a spreading pool of his own blood, right in the middle of the street. Angus was already bending over him when I got there. Then Charlie and Henry came out. We hightailed it over here so you could take a look at him."

"How in hell did I become the doctor in residence?" I asked, teetering on the edge of panic. I did not know what the hell I was doing. How many more medical emergencies would I, a blacksmith and goldsmith for the love of God, be forced to take on?

"You have to ask? There was that baby episode, you know."

"Sarah told me what to do. It wasn't me."

"That's as may be, but you actually brought the little squaller into the world. Heard a rumour you saved the Métis leader's leg, too. True?"

I nodded before the implications of that question hit me.

"How did you know that?"

Jim grinned and shook his head at me. "This may be Moose Jaw, but there is a grapevine. Where do you think I get my whiskey?"

"Ah." I let that sink in for a moment.

"So? Is it true?

I admitted to having played a role in saving Michel Dumas' leg. "But his wife was right there with me."

Jim threw his head back and roared.

"You're in a pile of trouble, my friend," he said, wiping his eyes, when he could speak again. "Dr. Sinclair."

"Don't say that!"

"Well, that's the way it is for now. Listen, I'll put out some feelers on that laudanum. Set you up like a real doctor. By the way, there's some kid looking for you."

"Some kid? What do you mean, looking for me?"

"Hit town night before last. Don't know where he's staying, but he's been asking questions. Knew you by name. Described Buck, too. I'm sorry it hasn't come up; thought you may have your hands full."

Who the hell could be looking for me?

"How old is this kid?"

"Not sure. Skinny little fella. Younger than you. Sixteen, seventeen, maybe?"

"Did he say what he wanted?"

"No. Well, not to me. You might want to ask John. Barkeep always knows more than the rest of us."

"What did you tell him?"

"Nothing, of course. I don't know who this kid is. Maybe he's one of Garrison's spies. But we better figure out who he is, and sharply."

Alex screamed.

"I'd better go check on my patient," I said, turning toward the bedroom.

"There you go, James. You're getting the hang of this doctoring already." He roared again as he left but returned wearing a more sober expression and bearing a large bottle of whiskey.

"Thanks, Jim."

"Whatever I can do. You haven't, by chance, had a letter yet?"

"Sorry, no. I expect it'll take another few days. It's a long way."

"Right."

This time he really did leave. But the door had not hit him on the backside before it swung open again, this time revealing Abby.

Flowing blonde-red hair draped her shoulders, covered in a soft blue shawl worn over a flowered blue-and-white dress. I took in every detail. I almost emitted a gasp at the sight of her but managed to swallow it.

"May I come in?" she asked. "Good morning, James."

"Of course. I'm sure you want to check on your brother. Come in, come in. May I make you some tea?"

"Can I have a swig of that?" she asked, pointing at the bottle I still held.

I admit I was surprised; it was morning, after all, but I knew little about women living frontier lives. I smiled, nodded, and wrenched out the cork.

"Maybe in a glass would be better," I suggested. I went into my tiny kitchen and rapidly washed two of the four dirty cups still sitting on the counter. Pouring a finger into each, I returned and handed her the liquid courage.

"I really must give Alex some of this right away," I said. "He's in . . . some pain, I think."

"Can I see him?" she said. I heard a plaintive note in her question.

"Yes, of course. Just let me check on him first." I smiled again, reassuringly, hoping he would not yell and scare hell out of his sister before I could get to him.

I quickly ducked through the curtain and into his room. His skin was as snow-white as I had ever seen on a human being and sweat poured off his face like rain. Poor bugger.

"Here, Alex, drink a bit of this." I raised his head and tipped the cup to his lips. "I'm going to find you some more medicine. I promise. Won't be long now."

Alex spluttered but got some of the alcohol down his neck. I went to the basin, drenched a towel in cool water, and sponged him off best I could. Then I peeked at his leg. All things considered, it didn't look too bad, and by that I mean infection had not set in. Not yet, anyway.

"Are you up to seeing Abby? She's come by to check on you."

"God, James, I don't want her to see me like this."

"It'll be some time before you see her, then. I think she's pretty tough. What do you say?"

"All right. When you put it that way."

I patted his arm and went out to tell Abby she could go in. She gave me a shaky smile, squared her shoulders and walked in there like a queen.

Leaving them alone to talk, I went out to the porch and had a sip of the whiskey myself. In addition to the sturdy dining room-come-operating table, I had also banged together a few chairs, including two for the front porch. From there, the vista was not just beautiful but also wide. I could see the back of the blacksmith's shop, as well as anyone coming from quite a distance. From the back, it was pretty much bald prairie; but again, it allowed me to detect the clouds of dust that accompanied anyone on horseback.

I sat staring at nothing and wondering what more I could do for Alex. The occasional yelp and sob emanated from inside, but I left brother and sister to it. They were a team. They obviously loved each other. They needed some time.

I did not expect anyone else to appear that day. Bert knew I would not be in the shop, as did Alexander's rescue party, because of my patient; but no one else would. I was therefore surprised and on high alert when a small cloud of dust did rise on the horizon.

I plunged into the house to grab my gun and returned to the porch, standing in wait for my visitor.

It was a kid. A slim, wiry little teenager. I had seen him before.

Tom. The stable boy who loved horses, hated Riley, and saved my backside in Pile of Bones.

I put the gun down, stepped off the porch, and went to meet him.

Chapter Thirty-six

"What are you doing here, Tom?" I asked once we were settled on the porch with a bite to eat and a drop of that whiskey.

Alex had finally fallen asleep, and Abby napped on the sofa. We had time to catch up.

"You said if I was ever in trouble, I could come and find you. That you'd just be a ways down the road. So I did."

"Damn, what's up? What's happened?"

"That Riley man. He came back to the stable after you left and asked where you'd gone. I guess he figured out that you'd been there, and obviously Buck had disappeared, so that was kind of a sign. Where is Buck? Is he okay?"

"He's fine. He's out in the stable. I'll take you to see him later. Then what happened?"

"He told me that if he found out I'd helped you and lied to him, there'd be hell to pay. I believed him."

"Rightly so," I put in.

"I thought I'd better leave. And I thought I'd better warn you. He's out to get you."

"I know. He's out to get everyone, or so it seems. Tom, I'm sorry to say Riley is here. Somewhere. He, I think, just shot a man in the leg. That man is inside." I flicked my head toward the house.

"Bastard."

"Yeah." I took a bite of my sandwich. "You have to stay out of sight until all of this gets resolved. But I have a full house. Not just the sick man, but another friend called Jones. He's trying to keep me alive."

"I could stay in the stable, maybe?" Tom asked hopefully.

"I was just going to suggest it. When we're finished our lunch, we'll go visit Buck. He'll be happy to see you. And I'm sure he won't kick you out. Do you have a bedroll?"

Tom did. I took him to the stable, gave him two apples, and let him get reacquainted with my trusty horse. Buck gobbled up the fruit and nuzzled Tom's hand for more; I could see they were still friends.

"Get settled in," I suggested. "Come on up to the house when you're ready, but for God's sake, be careful. Keep an eye out always."

"I will. Thank you."

Returning to the house, I quietly opened the door and saw Abby still unconscious on the sofa. I heard no rustling or moaning from Alex's bedroom, and figured the whiskey had knocked him out.

Just as well, because I'd stopped in my tracks at the sight of sleeping beauty. She had curled up on her side, hair softly surrounding her face. One arm draped across her stomach, gently pushing on her breasts so that the tops just peeked out from the neckline of her dress. Mesmerized, I just stood there and gazed at her.

Sensing me, no doubt, she stirred a moment later; I quickly looked away and moved toward the bedroom, as if I had just arrived.

"James?"

"Yes, it's me. I'm sorry; did I awaken you?"

She scrambled up into a sitting position, pushing that sunshine mane out of her eyes.

"No. I don't think so. I'm sorry I fell asleep. I didn't sleep very well last night, I'm afraid. And, of course, the whiskey . . . silly of me . . ."

"Not at all. It has been a very difficult couple of days. Would you like some tea or something?"

"That would be lovely."

The coals in the stove's firebox were still glowing, so I fed them with a few splinters of wood until they roared back into life. Pouring water from the pail into the pot, I set it to boil and scoured the cupboards for anything that might serve as a snack.

I had forgotten that my sweet former landlady had packed some raisin cookies in my saddlebag the last time I had visited. Still tightly wrapped, they were fairly fresh and I slid them onto a small plate.

Abby slipped onto one of the kitchen chairs and watched me perform my domestic tasks.

"James, I have to ask you something."

"Shoot."

"I'm sorry, but I have to know. Was it absolutely necessary to amputate part of Alex's leg? Can you tell me about it?"

"It's . . . very gory and shocking, Abby." I turned from the pot to look at her with an intense warning expression. "Are you sure?"

"Yes," she said, although the word wavered in the air. "I am."

I sighed. How could I explain how the leg looked without traumatizing her? I bought myself some time by putting black tea leaves into a teapot and pouring hot water over them. I slowly brought the pot, sugar bowl, two cups and the plate of cookies to the table, and finally sat down.

"He was losing a lot of blood," I began carefully. "It was a large calibre bullet, and it had wrecked a big artery. It also hit the shin bone, or possibly another bullet did. I don't really want to explain that part."

"It's all right, I understand what you mean. Go on."

"Well, basically, the bone and the artery were done for. We had to figure out a way to stop the bleeding and save the rest of the leg."

"And his life."

"Yes, I think so. I hope so."

Before I knew what was happening, Abby put down her cup, got up from her chair, took my hands and pulled me to my feet. Her intense blue eyes looked into mine for a second; she then rose onto her tiptoes and threw her arms around my neck.

"Thank you," she whispered in my ear. "I am so sorry I offered to shoot you."

"You didn't know," I stammered, as I wrapped my own arms around her. "Ah, you're welcome. And I'll make him a good sturdy leg. I promise . . ."

The last word was smothered by her soft lips gently pressing against mine. If I had not already been entranced by this slip of a woman, that kiss would have done it instantly. I waited for a moment, unsure if this was simply a gesture of thanks; but her mouth remained in this highly arousing position and I gave up.

Grasping her more tightly, I kissed her back somewhat less gently, and her lips parted with a small sigh. That was all the invitation I needed to engage my tongue in exploring her further, and in seconds we were both panting and holding each other, madly kissing as if our lives depended on it.

So it felt. Our world spun around us with uncertainty. We were potential victims of a power-mad and wealthy man who wanted her land and my life in forfeit for his daughter's. But it had also brought her to me. Fate had intervened in this unlikely and beautiful way amid the danger.

My body warned me that I had better back away. Apart from the growing and obvious issue, the blood was thrumming in my head so loudly I could not think straight.

"Abby," I said breathlessly, untangling myself enough so I could put my hands on her shoulders and see her face. What was she thinking? Feeling?

She said nothing — just stood there staring at me, breathing as if she had been running, her lips bright red and slightly swollen. Holy God . . .

I could not help myself. I kissed her again. So much for self-restraint. My hands moved down her back, and hers slipped up mine. I was in serious trouble.

I do not know where this might have gone had Jones not decided to show up early. I heard him stomp onto the porch and drop his tools. Abby and I, apparently hearing him simultaneously, sprang apart and looked somewhat guiltily at the door.

"Oh, hello," Jones said as he entered. "Afternoon. Who's your friend, James?" He had lovely manners for a hobo, I thought wildly.

"This is Miss Pearce, Alexander's sister. Miss Pearce, please meet Jones. He's a friend of mine, staying here to keep an eye out for Garrison's men when he's not toiling for the railway."

"Pleased to meet you," Abby said rather meekly. "I should check on Alexander." And she dashed into the bedroom.

Jones gave me a pointed look and grinned; he could not say much, since the house was far too small for secrets. He turned his thumbs up and mouthed the word "sorry." I threw a cookie at him but could not help grinning back.

CHAPTER THIRTY-SEVEN

Abby stayed with Alexander for the rest of the afternoon, and then quietly left for the Thompsons' after saying a subdued goodbye. I hoped her quietude was simply a result of Jones' presence.

But I could not let it go at that. Leaving a woman — especially this one — to walk down a twilit street alone didn't agree with my sense of gallantry; and under the circumstances, I was deeply concerned for her safety. Just as urgently, I had to know what she was thinking.

I pulled on a jacket and ran out the door after her.

"Abby, wait. Wait for me."

She walked on for a few more steps, but then stopped, turned and ran back toward me. And flung herself into my arms.

"Why did you follow me?" she asked, her voice soft in my ear.

Into the top of her head I said, "I . . . I guess I wanted to thank you for the kiss. And for forgiving me."

"For what?" She sounded surprised.

"For Alexander's leg."

"You saved my brother's life. I am so grateful."

"Is that why you kissed me, Abby? Because you're grateful?"

"No. I . . . wanted to. Was it all right to do that?"

"Oh, God, Abby . . ."

I held her face between both hands and this time I initiated, taking her mouth with as much control as I could muster. It fell away from me as she reciprocated, and suddenly we were holding each other and pressing our bodies together in the still, gathering darkness. In that embrace, I would have given everything I had — house, horse, life itself — for Abby Pearce.

I was reeling, but so was she; I could feel her pounding heart against my chest. Passion notwithstanding, I had to get her home, inside and safe, before too much longer.

"Abby, beautiful Abby," I finally said. "Let me take you home now."

"I don't want to go," she said, a little petulantly.

"I don't either. But your safety comes first. Who knows where these bastards are? We can't stay out here."

"I know." She sniffled a little. "I want to kiss you some more."

"I'll kiss you good night when we reach Bert and Sarah's."

I did. Madly. Then I saw her safely inside, said hello to the Thompsons, and tore myself away.

It was not so much a rustle as a presence. A sensation of not-quite-stillness. An impression of being watched, the catch of quieted breathing. It could have been an animal, but I knew it was not. Whoever lurked in the semi-darkness had seen me leave the Thompson home, and may have seen me with Abby.

Several options presented themselves. I could pretend I had not perceived his presence and walk on — although to where, I had no idea. I could not allow him to follow me home. He may not yet know where I lived. I could return to the Thompson house, but that had obvious potential repercussions.

Or I could confront the son of a bitch.

No longer did I leave my property unarmed. Carrying the carbine concealed was impossible, so I had procured a smaller, nine-shot LeMat revolver via Jim's helpful if convoluted supply chain.

I walked slowly down the street, mulling over what to do. I could not have him threatening Abby or Sarah or Bert. I would not lead him to where Alexander lay helpless, where Tom hid in the barn, where Jones was kindly posted as sentry.

No. This waiting game had gone on long enough.

I reached the end of the street, abruptly turned left and doubled back, pulling the gun out of its holster as I crept through the dense bush. Dry grasses crackled underfoot, but soon I could just see a dirt path weaving through the underbrush. I hardly breathed as I neared the man, hoping to surprise him. He was still there, likely watching the house.

A match flared. He lit a cigarette, and in that second of divided attention and the snap of sulphur meeting flint, I strode the last few steps and jammed the gun's barrel into his back.

"Hello, Riley. We finally meet again. But do not turn around. Our reunion doesn't have to be face to face. Get your hands up." He did not comply, so I snicked the hammer. "Now."

He snorted. "You're not going to shoot me in the back in cold blood, now are you, Mr. Sinclair?" His words dripped with contempt.

Rage overcame me. I rammed my knee into the back of his and rapped the back of his head with my gun. He fell onto all fours, but I pushed him the rest of the way down until he lay sprawled in the dust, me straddling his back. It felt good. Extremely so.

"Don't count on it," I said in delayed reply, panting with fury and exertion as I searched him with my free hand. "I hear you've been looking for me. Well, you found me. Now tell me why. Exactly why."

"You know why," he gasped, his face mashed sideways into the earth. But the contempt had not left his voice.

"Tell me anyway."

"You messed with that girl. Your life is over."

"First of all, I did not. Secondly, if you're so anxious to kill me, why haven't you already done so?"

"You've been a little hard to find," he admitted, which shocked me. I had little confidence that moving to the edge of town and staying off Main Street would keep me from being discovered. "Besides, the boss wants to be here, to see you go down. I'm just making sure you don't leave town."

"So the boss is coming. I wondered." A thought crashed into my brain. "You did it. Didn't you? You want to make sure I take the fall for getting Alice Garrison pregnant. Is that what's going on?"

"No!" he said, more violently than I had expected. "It wasn't me. It was you."

I was not sure whether to believe him, but oddly, I was inclined to. His denial was loud, swift and vehement.

"She died, you know," he said unexpectedly.

"Yes. I do know. Tragic."

"It was."

How was this becoming a relatively normal conversation? Having removed his gun, I slid off his back and sat next to him.

"I didn't do it," I said flatly, motioning with my gun for him to sit up. "I'll kill the bastard who did if I ever find him. For the poor girl, but also for myself. And let me add that if anything happens to any of the people in the house you were watching, you're dead too. I guarantee it."

He sneered, but then stopped. I obviously had him at an extreme disadvantage. He seemed to realize that I could indeed kill him. Right now.

"You'll have to get yourself another gun," I added, getting up. "I'll be keeping this one. And don't follow me. I will shoot you in cold blood if you do. Hear me?"

He nodded, a barely visible gesture in the darkness. He must have pulled himself together, though, because as I left him, he called:

"Garrison is coming. Soon. Then all bets are off."

Chapter Thirty-eight

Riley did not follow me. I did not think he would, temporarily unarmed as he was, but I slept restlessly just the same.

Alex only yelled once for more 'painkiller' and slipped back into the arms of Morpheus. He seemed to be healing, or at least showed no signs of infection. A miracle, really.

I finally fell deeply into slumber at perhaps three in the morning, but by the time the sun came over the eastern horizon I was dreaming hard. Abby had come to me in the night; I could not resist her and was breathing like an overused horse as I slipped her dress from her shoulders, revealing perfect satin skin that glowed in the moonlight. She threw her head back just as I heard a crash. The door had been kicked in, and more men than I could count streamed into my tiny home. I leapt in front of a mostly-naked Abby and confronted the interlopers, but I knew it was hopeless. Even with Jones in the front room, we were seriously outmanned and outgunned.

Riley's paw reached around me to grab Abby by the shoulder and I screamed . . .

I awakened bathed in sweat, still screaming, and sat bolt upright staring at the bedroom curtain as Jones came running in. Thank God he came in yelling my name or I might have killed him.

"What the hell, James. Are you all right?"

"I think so. Bad dream." I panted the words out of spasming lungs, trying to understand that it had just been a nightmare. To end all nightmares.

"Sounds like it was a doozy."

"It was. Jones, we have to get out to the Pearce farm. Today or tomorrow. They have livestock, and I don't know if they've finished seeding."

"Must've. It's June already."

"Right." I was not keeping up with time at all. June? "They usually seed in May in these parts?"

"Yep. But you're right. Worth getting out there to check on the beasts. I'm on the railbed today but we could go tomorrow. We'll have to take the young lady, though. Hard to find the place otherwise."

"I expect she'll come to check on Alex today. I'll talk to her about it then."

"I 'spect she'll come to check on you, as well," Jones said with a sly smile. "Seems she's taken a shine to you."

I harrumphed at first, but I could feel my mouth twisting into a dopey lovesick smile. Jones patted me on the shoulder. "I'll see you later. Y'sure you're all right?"

"Yes. I'm fine, thanks. I'll see you later."

"Yep. Back around six."

It occurred to me that if Jones could make it back to my place by dinnertime, that track was not too far out. I was running out of time. And so were Abby and Alex.

· · ·

Abby did come. Before she could duck through to a still-sleeping Alex's bedroom, I swept her into the kitchen, finger on my lips to hush her, and kissed her thoroughly.

"Hello," I whispered. "How was your night?"

"Fine." She looked at me with her eyebrows raised. "Yours?"

"Fine," I lied. "Alex is doing pretty well, really. Abby, I have to tell you something."

I did not tell her about the nightmare. But I did have to tell her about Riley.

"I don't know if you're safe at Bert and Sarah's," I said. "He's watching the house. Maybe he'll stop, now he knows I'm not staying there; but he's keeping an eye on you, too. And you can't go back to the farm alone, obviously."

She bristled. "Why not? I've often been on my land alone and I'm a damn good shot."

"This is a bit different, Abby, for God's sake. These men . . . I don't know what they might do. They've already burned your stable; I think they're capable of anything. Their boss is, for certain."

"I have to get back there soon, James. My animals; I left them with some food and water, but I didn't know I wouldn't be back for two days. And I can take care of myself." She straightened her shoulders and lifted her chin defiantly. I melted inside, but felt I had to push the point.

"They might try to . . ." I could not get the words out. "You know."

"What, hurt me? They already have. They shot Alex, burned my barn, and they're trying to take my farm. Could it get any worse?"

"I meant personally."

Long silence.

"Oh." She dropped her eyes to her lap.

The thought of Riley's rough hands on Abby's silken body drove home just how much I already cared for her. I would have been enraged at such violence against any woman, but my heart told me this was different. Her courage somehow intoxicated me, and I could not bear the idea of a man deflating or destroying it.

But Abby was not my lover nor my wife, and I had little to say about her actions. Not legitimately. I suggested what Jones and I had discussed earlier.

"Would the livestock be all right until tomorrow, do you think? Or should you and I just go today? That doesn't solve the problem of staying at the Thompsons', though."

"Where will I stay, then?" she asked. "I won't run, James. I won't. I can't let them scare me off. This is my life. This is my land. That," she added, pointing to the bedroom, "is my brother. What do you want me to do? Give in?"

No, I did not, if she was going to put it that way. There had to be a solution, but I could not think of one. I opened my mouth to argue, but no words came; and I was saved by a rap at the front door.

My eyes met Abby's in alarm until it occurred to me that a rampaging raider would not have knocked. Just the same, I snatched my gun off the kitchen counter and went to the door. Yelling 'come in' was out of the question.

"Who is it?"

"Jim. Let me in, dammit."

"It's open," I admitted. From now on, I would lock the door. The lock could always be shot off, but at least I would have warning.

Jim's face was a study in conflicting emotions: fear, wonderment, excitement.

"Maybe you should sit down," I suggested. "You know Abby Pearce, of course."

He nodded and gave Abby a sweet, respectful little bow. "Miss Abby. Nice to see you."

"You too, Jim. Been a wee while. How are you?"

"I'm well. Ah, I have something for you, James. Came with the last wagon train." His eyes widened in silent question: was it all right for Abby to see what he brought? I gave him an almost imperceptible nod.

He handed me a letter.

I snatched it out of his hand. It was simply addressed to James Sinclair Jr., Moose Jaw, North-West Territories. Not Mum's handwriting, I noticed with a twist in my chest. Hannah.

"Maybe you should sit down," I said again. Jim nodded dumbly and collapsed onto a chair.

Abby watched all of this with concern and intense curiosity written on her face, but she said nothing and went to the cupboard to get out the box of tea.

My own legs were none too steady, so I sat down almost as hard as Jim had and ripped open the envelope.

There were four sheets of paper inside. I started reading.

> Dearest James,
>
> I find that it is beyond me to express how astonished I am that you have found my James. The fourth sheet of paper in this envelope, folded twice, is for him. I trust and know that you will give it to him as soon as this arrives.

I stopped reading for a second and handed it over. Jim took it with shaking fingers.

I have loved only two men in my life. I thought both were dead. I thank you from the bottom of my heart for this possibly great gift, should James still consider me dear to him.

I could not send a telegram to tell you what follows. This story is far too long, and I couldn't risk anyone else seeing it. Forgive me for the delay. I hope I am not too late, and that you took my earlier warning to heart.

As you know, poor Alice Garrison died after a miscarriage. In her last few days, my Connie — do you remember her? — attended her often. They were friends when they were wee girls, before George Garrison decided that Connie, as a paid servant, was beneath his daughter. But Alice's mother took pity on them and slipped Connie in to see her friend two or perhaps three times.

Alice was very ill, of course, but she was also lucid — until the very end, at least. On her death bed, she spoke to Connie. She said she kissed you and begged you to take her away, there in the alley that day. You declined. With no real alternative, and unable to tell anyone what was happening, she was forced to stay at home. Please understand, I do not blame you for that at all. I do not believe Alice blamed you, either.

Alice forced her own miscarriage. Do you know how dangerous that is? Well, you do now. She lost the child but was left with sepsis. The doctor tried to save her, but by the time Mrs. Garrison realized how sick her child was, it was far too late.

One night, as she lay dying, she reached for Connie's hand and said she had to tell her something before she no longer could.

James, brace yourself, dear.

Alice told Connie that the child was her father's, and that she couldn't bear a babe conceived in incest.

That bastard had been abusing and raping her for three years. Now you know why he was so desperate to lay the blame for her pregnancy on you. Why he chose you personally, I don't know. It may have something to do with Alice's obvious admiration for you, which supported the theory that you were an item, as well as the fact that you were not in their social circle.

It doesn't matter much now. He's coming for you soon, James. Very soon. He must ensure that you are publicly denounced for impregnating and essentially killing his daughter. Perhaps he suspects that someone knows something; I'm quite sure that Graham Tattersall had an inkling. Or perhaps Garrison is simply being careful. But you will pay the price if this goes badly.

Please, James. Protect yourself. Run if you must. I could not bear it if something happened to you at Garrison's hands.

Connie and I are considering what we can do at this end, but we have little money and no real influence. Whatever we arrive at, it might be too late; I'm told Garrison has left the city.

Take care, my dear. I hope very much to see you again. Reasonably soon.

Yours,

Hannah

Chapter Thirty-nine

Jim looked up from his letter just as I raised my head and our eyes locked. He cleared his throat.

"I brought laudanum too."

"Thank you."

He stretched his arm across the table, hand open, toward me and I grasped it. Overcome, he could not say any more, which pretty much told me what his missive contained.

Abby brought the by-now brewed tea to the table, along with the rest of Sarah's cookies unearthed from my cluttered cupboard.

"So," she said conversationally. "Are you two going to tell me what the hell is going on?"

I mulled over her request for a moment. I had to tell her at least the basic information. She knew nothing of my desperate flight out of Toronto, nor what had spurred it. She also needed to know the news about Garrison. I handed her my letter, poured the tea and waited.

Moments later, she carefully folded the paper and put it on the table. I could see her throat flex as she swallowed hard. Then she rose, took my hands, pulled me to my feet and threw her arms around my neck — right there in front of Jim, who tactfully averted his eyes.

She held me hard, and I could feel her body quaking with repressed sobs as I laced my own arms around her. I soon became aware that my shirt was rather wet and broke the embrace enough to see her face.

"Hey, now, don't cry," I said, wiping her tears with my thumbs. "It's very sad about Alice, I know, but don't cry."

"That's not why I'm crying," Abby said with a hiccup. "Well, not the only reason. I'm glad to know what's happened and why you showed up out of nowhere. I wondered. I'm so sorry about it all, James. I am so sorry." She kissed me, but then seemed to realize Jim was still in the room. She gave him a quick look and asked, "But who is Hannah?"

"Hannah was my landlady," I explained. "She helped me escape Toronto by following the remnants of the Underground Railroad. The same way she helped Jim escape bounty hunters twenty years ago." I stopped for a moment; a thought struck me, and I wondered why it had not occurred to me before. "It's strange, isn't it? The Underground Railroad led me to the end of the rail line."

"You're such a philosopher," Jim said, having finally found his voice. "All of this is well and good, but we have a problem. What are we going to do about Garrison? Pretty rare to see the law around here, and would the mounted police believe us anyway?"

This really did pose a challenge. We could not very well just shoot the man in the street without provocation, even if we could find him. And Jim was right; getting Garrison arrested was next to impossible.

"We may have to wait for him to come to us," I said in a low voice. "I don't know what else to do. But we can't hide forever."

"No," Abby put in emphatically.

"Well, we can't allow Garrison to murder you and burn out the Pearces," Jim said. "And God knows what else. I'll bet Miss Abby and Alex aren't the only farmers he's messing with."

"Jim, for the love of God, just call me Abby."

He smiled and gave her another little bow. I was starting to really love that man.

We fell into a contemplative silence. I knew in my heart we needed help, but I did not want to ask. Jones, Clancy and Angus had already supported us by keeping watch at my home and at the Thompsons'. Tom was just a wee kid. Charlie was a new father. And Jim had done enough for me. More than enough.

"We have to build a little army," he said out of the blue, as if reading my thoughts. "There's no other way. We'll have to keep watch and our ears to the ground. I'll see who I can rustle up in town; you can talk to the boys," he added, meaning the hobos, "and Angus."

"I can't have all these men risking their lives for me," I protested. "Maybe it would be best if I left town."

"No!" Abby shouted. "No, James. If you leave, they'll hunt you forever. We have to make a stand. And you're not alone in this."

True. If I left, if we did not face Garrison, what would happen to Abby and her farm? What would happen to my heart? It would surely break if I could never see her again. Like Hannah's and Jim's hearts had.

Alex started to howl at that juncture, and Jim produced the small bottle of laudanum from his pocket. Abby reached for it and went into the bedroom.

"There are no other options, my friend," Jim said. "We'll see this through."

He stood and said, "Together."

•   •   •

I took the opportunity to check on Tom and Buck. I slipped out the back door and walked to the stable, trying to peer into the future. For the life of me, I could not foresee what would happen, nor when. I was damned uncomfortable at having my friends risk their lives for me. But I could not see any other options.

Tom lay sprawled in the hay, evidently having a conversation with my horse. Buck nickered as I neared, and Tom bolted upright.

"Is everything all right?" he asked.

"For now, yes. But I'm afraid Riley's boss, a Mr. Garrison, is on his way to deal with me and with a couple of nearby farmers. You have to stay hidden."

"No way, Mister. No way. If something's coming, I'm a gonna help you. Besides, that Mr. Riley wants my hide too."

"We'll argue about it over dinner, Tom. Just stay hidden for now, all right? Please."

"Yessir."

"Come back to the house for now. You must be hungry."

"I am. Starving."

"Pull your hat down low."

I threw a few more oats in Buck's manger and gave him a pat. Then we hurried back to the house, to find Abby warming soup on the stove.

"Alex," she announced before I could say anything, "is hungry." She beamed at me like the sun in full glory.

"That is a good sign," I said, grinning back. "This young man is too. Abigail Pearce, Tom . . . I don't know your last name."

"Jarvis. Pleased to meet you, miss. Uh, ma'am."

She laughed. "Abby is fine, Tom. Pleased to meet you too."

She roamed my kitchen then, remarkably at home, finding bowls and spoons and knives. Before long, we were eating beef and barley soup, thick with celery and carrots, and warm slices of whole wheat bread with butter. I assumed the creator of this delicious meal was Sarah and asked the question.

"Well, I guess it was a team effort," Abby said. "We've been cooking up a storm over there. Never know when you're going to need some hot soup or stew."

Tom wolfed it down before wiping his mouth on the back of sleeve. "Thank you, ma'am. Uh, Abby. That hit the spot."

"My pleasure, Tom. I'm off to give Alex his lunch. Wheee!"

I stopped her gently as she approached the bedroom.

"I'm no doctor," I began, and Abby laughed again. I had to join in, but then warned her to go slowly. "He hasn't consumed much but whiskey over the last while. His stomach might be a bit tender. We don't want it coming right back up again."

"Yes sir, Dr. Sinclair," she said teasingly, and went off bearing the bowl and plate.

• • •

Tom took himself away after a while, and I went out to the back porch to think while Abby fed and chatted with Alex.

Alice Garrison and Meg Blackwood were on my mind. I felt awful about Alice, but I had no idea she was in such desperate straits; and had I known, what would I have done? Leaving the city with a young woman of minority age would have been disastrous. That bastard of a father. He had ruined her innocence, her happiness, her body, and destroyed her life. I planned to make him pay.

And Meg. Beautiful Meg. I had known her so briefly, but she had a profound effect on me. I wondered how she was, and what she thought of me. I hoped I could explain one day.

I also thought of Beth, the lovely girl who burned with desire and gave me my first real erotic experience. I smiled at the memory and felt it in my groin.

And now, Abby. The woman was a warrior. I added her to the list of powerful, beautiful women in my life, including my mother and Hannah. A tear came to my eye as I thought of Mum, and I wondered how she was coping after Da's death. I would send her money as soon as possible.

I heard a step behind me and turned to see Abby. Her face, alight with the promise of Alex's survival, changed when she looked down into my eyes. She bent over and thumbed away the tear that had apparently travelled down to my cheek.

"What is wrong, James?" Crouching, she took my hands in hers. "Why is there a tear on your face?"

Embarrassed, I turned away.

"I was just thinking of my mum. Not to worry, Abby. I'm all right."

"You miss her."

"I do."

"What's she like?"

"Strong," was the first word that left my lips. "Incredibly hard-working. Beautiful. Loving. Something like you."

I did not mean to say that last bit. It simply popped out of my mouth; after all, I had just been thinking it.

"Do . . . do you think I'm beautiful?" Abby gasped, dropping her gaze. "Really?"

"I do, Abby." Might as well admit it. "Your hair; it's like spun sunshine at early evening with those threads of gold and red. Your eyes are as bright as bluebells." Oh my God, I was waxing poetic. But I could not stop. "And your skin is like satin. But I think your heart is just as beautiful."

I did not quite get that last word out; she had thrown her arms around my neck as she pressed her lips against mine.

"I think you're beautiful too," she whispered and placed her hand on my chest, right over my pounding heart.

She would have had my undivided attention had I not seen, over her gleaming head, a puff of dust partly obscuring the northwestern horizon.

Chapter Forty

"Abby, quick, go inside," I said, leaping to my feet.

"Whatever's wrong?" She was clearly both alarmed and offended, judging by her raised eyebrows and downturned lips.

"Someone is coming. Likely more than one someone. Abby, please. Go inside."

She rose, turned on her heel and marched through the door. I grabbed the carbine, which was rarely far from my reach. Ducking behind the porch's support pillar, I peered at the rising dust, now more a cloud than a puff. Hell. It was not one lonely rider coming toward me, nor two, nor three. How many were there?

I heard a snick before I saw Abby. In a flash, she was right beside me, rifle aimed at the oncoming cloud, which grew with each passing second.

"Who do you think that is?" she asked.

"I don't know. Could be Garrison's raiders. There are several of them — at least. We can't fight them. We have to get out of here."

"What about Alex?"

"We'll have to take him as well. Tom, too. And we'll have to hurry. Tom can help us with Alex."

I turned to go inside, guiding Abby ahead of me, and was just going to holler for the youngster in the barn when I heard something. My head snapped back around to the west, and I put a finger to my lips. Abby froze.

An odd noise emanated from the encroaching dust cloud and it was not gunfire. Before long, it developed into an unearthly squealing as though —

if I did not know better — monsters were howling for our blood. But it was not that. I knew that sound. It was the deafening rubbing of wooden wheels on ungreased wooden axles. Red River carts.

"You can put the gun down, Abby."

She nodded, the muscles in her jaw relaxing. "Métis."

Relief overcame me, and once she had balanced the rifle against the wall (did she carry that thing everywhere she went? It seemed so) I swung her into my arms and spun her around in a wild little dance.

"Thank God," she said, breathlessly.

"Amen to that."

We were not entirely in the clear. While certain that Métis traders would not come in shooting or looting, I still felt a second's trepidation. What did they want? Or was it simply coincidence they were coming toward my home from that direction?

I doubted it was Dumas. He was not expected back in these southern parts for at least another two or three months. I held my gaze on the ear-shattering carts and tried to see through the dust, but it was hopeless.

I thought we should go inside just to be safe, but in that moment a rider detached himself from the group and rode hell-for-leather toward me. Before long, I recognized Clément Pelletier, Michel's lead scout.

He pulled up and swung out of his saddle. I did not expect a smile from the quiet man and did not get one; but he did hold out his hand in greeting.

"It is good to see you, Sinclair. Alive and apparently well."

"It's very good to see you, Pelletier. But what the hell are you doing here?"

"I will let Michel explain. He asked me to ride ahead and reassure you that you had nothing to fear."

"Very kind. It was a bit of a shock at first, to see the dust on the horizon."

"Yes. I am sure. But all is well."

He nodded at Abby, remounted and returned to the cloud. It finally began to settle as the carts slowed, then stopped near the creek behind the stable. I could hear Dumas shouting orders and soon saw him emerge in the clearing air — standing upright, pointing, directing and explaining where to set up camp. That meant he was staying, at least for the night. It also meant his leg had healed.

"They're friends of yours?" Abby asked.

"They are. Michel Dumas and his people. I rode with them for a while on my way west. We had quite a battle with Garrison's men; several of the Métis men died that day, but we must have killed ten of the raiders, maybe more. And Michel was shot, but he seems to be doing well."

Abby's eyes widened at this explanation. "We, James? 'We' killed ten of them? You were part of the fight?"

I had not considered that my initiation into gunfights on the plains would have been surprising, but it clearly was, at least in Abby's eyes. I nodded.

"You're a bit of a dark horse, James Sinclair. I suppose you helped dress Michel's wound, as well. Less, ah, aggressively than Alex's." I nodded again. Her lips curled into an expression I could not exactly read. "Perhaps I should get to know you a bit better." She shook her head in something like disbelief as Michel came striding toward us.

"Michel," I yelled. "What the hell are you doing here?"

He said nothing, at first, but wrapped his arms around me in a powerful embrace for several seconds before stepping back.

"James. It is good to see you too. Will you introduce me?"

"This is Miss Abigail Pearce. She and her brother have a farm nearby. Her brother, I'm afraid, is inside and missing part of his leg."

"I see. I'm very sorry, Miss Pearce, but happy to meet you." Abby responded with a little bow and a pleased-to-meet-you-too. "What happened?"

"One of Garrison's men shot him a few days ago. Garrison wants their land and hopes to make a killing on it by reselling it to the railway. I'm still not entirely sure why he was gunned down in the street."

"So things are escalating."

"Yes."

"I had heard something like that. I am glad I am not too late."

"For what?"

"For what is to come."

"Come in, Michel. I have some whiskey and some tea. What do you know? And how did you make it back here so quickly? I thought you'd be well up north by now."

Michel and Abby took chairs as I boiled water and brought the whiskey to the table.

Michel explained that he and his group had remained in the Qu'Appelle Valley for a week as his leg healed. Finally, he decided they could not abide any longer and they headed north, making it as far as Battleford. Trading was brisk with both the First Nations and the white communities, small as they were; but they were also growing, and Michel had been surprised at how quickly his wares were snapped up. People were starving for alcohol, food, building supplies and news.

With little left for sale, Michel decided to make one last foray further northwest before turning back; but a rider caught up to them. He bore the information that Garrison himself was travelling west, destination Moose Jaw, and that he had James Sinclair and unnamed farmers in his sights.

"That would be you and your brother, I assume, Miss Pearce."

"Abby, please. Yes. Although there are others."

"Michel, who was this rider?"

"I did not know him. But I know who sent him."

I felt my brow furrowing for a moment. Who would that be? Then the light went on.

"Jim."

"Yes. I have a good relationship with the hardware owner. Let's just say we have a mutually beneficial business arrangement. Not to mention we share a sense of brotherhood."

"He's asked for your help, hasn't he?"

"Yes. Which I am more than honoured to provide. We will make camp by your creek, James, and will stay until this is over." I opened my mouth to protest, but he held up a commanding hand. "I needed you, although I did not know it. Now you need me. That is all there is to say."

As I blinked dumbly at my friend, Abby rose, came around the table and put a tentative hand on Michel's arm. He looked up at her with a slightly baffled expression but did not object to her familiarity. To my complete surprise, she leaned down and kissed the powerful and daunting man on the cheek. Even Michel seemed dumbstruck.

"What . . . thank you," he finally choked out.

Abby went pink but collected herself. "No, Michel. Thank you. I think I speak for James as well as myself and Alex when I say thank you, with all my heart."

"Well," Michel said, clearing his throat. "As I said, I am honoured to assist. We must have a council of war. Tonight. I will send Clément into town; you cannot go, James. Nor you, Miss Pearce. He will speak to Jim and arrange matters. And I will see you in a few hours." He tipped back the remainder of his tea and whiskey and left to rejoin his camp.

I gathered Abby into my arms, and we stood in a long, silent, grateful embrace.

• • •

By nine that night, my tiny home was filled with a great many large men and two very tough women. When Jim arrived, Michel went out to the porch and held out his hand. The two stood there, not letting go, for some minutes before ducking inside.

Sarah and Abby sat, hands entwined, on the sofa, with Bert beside Sarah. Pelletier leaned nonchalantly against the rough wall, chewing a long blade of prairie grass. Jones and Clancy stood as if joined at the hip in the entryway to the kitchen. Jim, Angus and Charlie had taken three of the kitchen chairs and placed them in the living room; John, the barkeep, and Tom, my stable tenant, were behind them. There was barely elbow space left for Michel and me.

We talked deep into the night, sipping Dumas' whiskey.

This was my army, along with the Métis warriors. As I looked around the room, I wondered how many of us — and which of us — would survive the coming fray.

CHAPTER FORTY-ONE

The animals on the Pearce farm restively lowed and whinnied when Abby, Jones and I appeared the next morning, rather later than we had planned. The night had been long and none of us crawled out of our beds before seven-thirty.

The ride was shorter than I had expected, but it made sense when I thought about it. Abby's farm abutted the railyards, already in the development phase, although the homestead was at the southern end of the spread — many acres from the townsite. She and Alex had rebuffed all entreaties to sell the northern piece to the railway, but Garrison, of course, felt he could persuade them to turn the land over to him for a tidier sum; he would then hold the railway to ransom. The Pearces had declined his offer, as well.

I could see why. The farm was presently verdant, and certainly large enough to support a family or two in good years. Wheat had long since sprouted and seemed to be thriving in the warm summer sun, supported by recent night rains.

The barn and charred remnants of the stable stood to the east of the surprisingly large two-storey frame house. It had originally been home to six Pearces, Abby explained: herself and Alex, their deceased parents, and two other siblings — one dead, one a teacher living in Pile of Bones.

Buck clearly enjoyed the trip; it had been too long since I had taken him out for a solid canter. I dismounted, held my arms out to Abby as she slipped down from her horse, and the three of us tentatively checked out the home, guns drawn, before heading for the barn. Relief washed over me as I realized no one had broken in. No one awaited us.

Abby took over in the barn, showing us where the feed was kept and the pump was housed. Cattle snorted and nodded their cumbersome heads in apparent appreciation for being fed and watered; the horses nickered and stamped their hooves. I regarded the size of the herd with astonishment; Abby and Alex ran quite the operation.

"Thirty head," Abby said rather proudly, seeing me count the beasts. "Not including the calves. And six horses, including Noble. I hope to send them out to pasture soon, but under the circumstances, I can't have them out there. Not when I'm not around."

"No, I can see why. Have you had trouble with rustlers?"

"Not much. But I don't trust Garrison. He did burn the stable. God knows what he'd do to my livestock in the field."

Not that the cattle and horses were much safer in the barn, I mused, but I did not say it out loud. But what else could she do? It is hard to hide forty enormous animals.

I could see the broken stable through the window. It had not entirely burned down, due to Alexander's hasty actions, but it was in terrible condition. That explained why so many of the beasts were crammed into this building. Having a roof truss or beam come down on them would be disastrous.

Once the animals were comfortable, we shovelled shit for an hour and put down new straw. By now, the sun had risen high in the sky and we were as hungry as the cattle had been.

Buck, Noble and Jones's horse also duly fed, we made our way back to the house. My eyes flicked in all directions, but I saw nothing threatening on any horizon. We would not be here long, so I relaxed. My growling stomach diverted my attention once inside, and Abby set to finding something edible in her pantry. Her garden had been planted, but it was too early for fresh produce.

Soon we feasted on dried meat, relatively fresh bread and preserved vegetables of various kinds: pickled beets and carrots, blanched beans, and finally the most delicious spiced apples I'd ever eaten.

Jones then voiced what I had been planning to mention.

"Abby," he said. "Is there anywhere else we could take your animals?"

"Does anyone around here have extra stable space?" I asked.

"Not that I know of," Abby said.

"Look. At least we can take three of the horses back with us. My stable's big enough."

"Could we? That would be a start. Thank you, James."

"Of course. And we could ask around. It'd be an unholy job moving them, probably to a number of farms, but we could try."

"We could, I suppose. I'd hate to ask; it's hard enough for farmers to look after their own cattle. For how long, do you think?"

"I don't know," I admitted. "Days? Weeks?"

"Well, you two talk about it. I'll go and get the horses reined up," Jones put in. "Bridles are in the barn, Abby?"

"Yes. Thanks, Jones. I really have to water the garden before we go, so don't hurry."

The garden, just west of the house, did look a little peaked. Wheat, a tough crop, could manage with evening rains, but the snap beans, lettuces and other vegetables needed daily watering. We pumped icy well water into buckets and lugged them to the garden, pail after pail dousing the dry dirt. I watched Abby work out of the corner of my eye; the muscles in her neck and arms strained but were fully up to the task. Having abandoned her dress, she was instead clad in a man's boots, britches and a shirt with the sleeves rolled up to expose sun-kissed skin. I was beginning to think there was nothing she could not do.

Snorts and hoofbeats could be heard coming from the east, signalling Jones' return with some of the horses. I looked up at the sound and there, directly to the south and perhaps seventy metres away, loomed the most enormous animal I had ever seen.

A buffalo. He slowly shook his massive, furry head, and exhaled loudly through extended nostrils. Bison were scant on the plains, having been largely hunted out by rotten bastards sometimes supported in their murderous quest by the government; nonetheless, I had expected to encounter one before now. But I had not. And there he stood, pawing the ground, alone and majestic against the bright blue sky.

"Abby, look."

She raised her head from the potato patch and said, "Oh my God."

The monstrous beast grunted and charged. I grabbed Abby's hand and we ran for shelter, yelling at Jones to get back to the barn; but the bison suddenly turned to his left, clearly not interested in us. My blood froze in my veins as my gut turned over.

"Jones!" I screamed. "Get in the barn! Grab your gun!"

Judging by her oath, Abby had the same instinct. The bison had been culled from his herd and driven to the hill. He was not the threat. He was the inadvertent warning. Abby had no fear of the beast itself, but what followed it.

We were almost at the porch when we heard the thundering hooves. Seconds later, a line of riders crested the low hill south of us, dark and menacing against the sun. They had no interest in the bison's hide. They were coming for us.

Abby dove through the door with me right behind her. I snatched my carbine, propped by the front door, while Abby — white with fear, face blotched red with fury — crawled across the room for her rifle. Together we crouched below the window, peering over the sill.

"How many?" she panted.

"Six? Seven? That I can see."

"Where's Jones?"

"I don't know. I hope he's in the barn with the horses. They may not have seen him, but they know we're here. They must have seen us running."

The raiders by now had fanned out, likely hoping to trap us inside. I had no idea what the hell to do; firing first would cause chaos and give them the opening to fire back, while revealing our location.

"Sinclair! Come out!" someone yelled. "Come out or we'll come in. Or burn you out. You and the lady. Your choice."

I began to rise but Abby cried "No!" and grabbed me by the shirt. "No. They might kill you. You can't go out there, James."

"What's the option? You heard them. They're coming in if I don't come out. I have to go, Abby . . ."

A gunshot cracked. Wildly, I looked around me; where did the shot come from?

"Are you all right?" I asked Abby. "Are you hit?"

"No," she said. "Jones?"

I got to my feet and in a crouch hurried toward the back door. I opened it just enough to see Jones partly hidden behind a barrel, shooting at the invaders.

"Jones! Stop!" I yelled, but there was already one raider lying on the ground. His horse was also down, legs flailing over the man's bleeding body.

Bullets began to rain on the barrel, and Jones flattened himself on the earth, still shooting. Soon enough, he was out of ammunition and stuck out there alone, wriggling on his belly toward the house.

One of the raiders leaped out of his saddle and marched over to Jones, a sickening sneer on his filthy face. I raised my carbine but not in time. The man had already aimed at the middle of Jones' back and fired.

Blood spurted from the wound as Jones screamed in pain, just before his body went limp. He lay sprawled on the ground, only three metres from where I huddled in the doorway. He had almost made it.

In helpless fury, I shot the raider dead where he stood, seconds after he fired on Jones.

If my friend was alive, he was barely so and I could do nothing to help him. But he had helped me. The partly-open door of the barn slowly swung wide and before I saw them, I heard them stomping, bawling and crashing. The livestock churned into the yard in a disorganized, maddened throng, turning this way and that, kicking up dust and bellowing in fear. Jones had opened as many of the pens as he had had time for. Cattle and horses, terrified by the gunfire, abandoned the barn and ran.

I had no time to contemplate. It was either take on the raiders, four or perhaps five of them against us two, or try to flee in the chaotic rampage. I yelled at Jones, hoping he would respond, but no answer came. I looked at the widening pool of blood surrounding him and knew he was dead.

Sorrow gripped my heart, followed immediately by panic as I thought of Abby. I turned back into the house and ran toward the living room, frantically calling her name. She did not call back.

Hollering alerted her to my imminent arrival, but it also warned the large man holding her around the waist, his other hand clamped over her mouth. *No.*

"Let her go," I said, aiming at his head; but Abby was in front of him. "Now."

"Well, well," he drawled. "Seems like I have ya both where I want ya. Pretty fond of this little filly, ain't ya?"

I gritted my teeth and said nothing. Denial was pointless, but neither could I admit to my feelings for Abby. It would only make matters worse.

"Cat got yer tongue, Sinclair?"

"Let. Her. Go."

"Or ya'll do what, exactly? Put the gun down, Sinclair."

When I did not, his hand left her waist and moved upward, curling around her breast. She made a strangled sound of disgust and fury, wriggling powerfully in his grasp. But he was, of course, so much stronger, it had little effect.

Her eyes then flicked toward the window and widened in shock. Several of the cattle charged around the corner of the house and streamed past the window. They also caught the eye of her captor.

"Whut the hell?" he said, turning his head.

Abby reached up with an arm loosened slightly by his attention to her breast and viciously scratched his face before elbowing him in the gut. He howled in pain and anger; I saw his eyes narrow as he bent at the waist, still holding Abby with one arm; but she flopped forward like a rag doll and screamed, "Shoot him, James! Now!"

I did. Just below the throat. He made the most revolting gurgling noise as his hand struggled upward to stanch the flow of blood, even as his eyes goggled at me. Finally, he released his grip on the woman I now knew I loved, but in the next second fell heavily on top of her, driving her body flat onto the floor.

I leaped at him and dragged him off her. Three down, I thought wildly, as I gathered Abby — covered in the bastard's blood — into my arms and lifted her to her feet.

"I want to hold you, Abby, but we have to go. Right now. Can you do it?"

She shook like an aspen sapling but nodded.

"Let's try to go out the back way. Maybe there's a horse that hasn't run off."

"We d-don't know wh-where the other men are," she pointed out as we rushed down the hallway.

"No. But we have to give it a try."

She gave a small cry when we peered out the back door and saw Jones lying on the ground, with the man I had killed sprawled nearby.

"What . . ."

"I'll explain later."

Buck, bless his stalwart heart, reared and whinnied by the stable, and came toward us at a gallop when he spied me. Terrified that he would be shot by the remaining raiders, but unable to stop him, I held my breath until he arrived at the porch. Quickly, I scanned the area for the other men; but I could not see them and wondered if they had been stalled by the stampeding cattle.

"Jump on," I told Abby, but her legs would not co-operate. I lifted her into the saddle and leaped on behind her. Buck needed no instruction. The minute I landed on his back, he was off as if the hounds of hell were after him, plunging toward the northwest.

Abby and I hunched forward to reduce the bulk of target available to the raiders. I covered most of her shivering body in this pose, but a moment later I risked a look backward.

The cattle had done their job, thanks to Jones. Three of the horsemen were wildly reining their spooked mounts, surrounded by stampeding livestock. Three up. Three down. Were there only six? I hoped so.

We had made our decision to flee. All we could do now was escape as fast as Buck could fly.

Chapter Forty-two

The relief of dodging the remaining raiders, at least temporarily, was soon replaced by panic rising like bile in my throat. This was not the end of it.

We rode hard, not speaking, until Buck drew up exhausted at his own stable behind my house. I helped Abby, shaking and soaked in another's blood, slip down and we walked quickly into the outbuilding.

Buck headed straight for his stall and began to gulp water from the trough as I finally held Abby, weeping and gasping for air, in the circle of my arms.

"Oh God, Jones," she said brokenly into my chest. "He saved our lives, didn't he?"

"Yes." I gulped my own sob back. "I'd never have thought of releasing the livestock. He died saving us. Oh God . . ." And then the tables turned, and it was Abby clutching me closely, her arms around my neck, muttering soft nonsensical sounds of comfort.

I would have to learn to live with Jones' blood on my hands. I was not sure how. And I would have to tell Clancy. At the moment, I thought I'd prefer death over imparting that news.

Finally, knowing that more of our clan would be in danger if we did not get moving, we broke apart. The sight of Abby's bloody clothing made me sick, but I gave her a crooked grin and suggested we do something about it.

"My shirts will be a bit big for you."

"Much too big."

"I'll lend you a belt, too."

Before we left the stable, I gave Buck some oats, apples and a passionate hug around his thick neck. He nuzzled me back, as if to say it's okay. You're welcome.

Best horse in the world.

I peered cautiously out the stable's man door and, seeing nothing out of the ordinary, took Abby's hand and dashed for the house. I walked in to see Alexander Pearce sitting in the kitchen, bathed in sweat, alarm contorting his face.

"Abby," he breathed. "Oh, Abby. Thank God." Then he took in her clothing. "Oh no, are you hurt? Where are you hurt? You're covered in blood! James!" He tried to stand, bracing himself on the chair. "Do something!"

I lunged for him, fearing he would fall, and took him under the armpits to steady him. Abby cried out in the same moment.

"Alex, be careful! I'm all right, I'm all right. It's not my blood. Please, sit down."

That was when I sensed another human being in the room. I turned my head to see Jim looming right behind me. He dove forward and helped me lower Alex to his seat.

"Jim," I said. "Don't take this the wrong way, but what are you doing here? Why is Alex out of bed? What is going on?"

"Henry came by the store an hour ago. He brought this."

Jim held out a slip of paper, upon which were scrawled the words:

T. Riley: Arriving Wednesday. Get started. Be ready. Garrison. Stop.

Wednesday. Tomorrow.

"Henry intercepted this, then, and copied it," I said.

"Yes. Michel and Clément are out looking for you. We didn't know what 'get started' meant, but we had an idea. Tom is with them."

That explained why he was not in the stable, although I had not thought of it until now.

"He's just a kid," I said.

"He was adamant."

I raised my shoulders. Nothing I could do about it now.

"I stayed because . . ." Jim mouthed the words and tipped his head toward Alex, who by now was clasped in a warm if sticky sisterly embrace.

"Ugh," I said of the bloody mess without thinking, then pulled my brain cells back together. "Abby, why don't we gentlemen go into the living room? Give you some privacy to get, ah, washed up. I'll find you a clean shirt."

She pulled away from her brother, looked down and made a face. "Ugh, indeed. Yes, please, if you would."

She had stopped shaking and spoke with a steady voice. I smiled at her in admiration.

Jim awkwardly helped Alex onto the sofa — reminding me that I had promised my patient a new leg — as I pumped fresh water and put a pot on to boil. Abby needed hot water and soap to get that blood off.

"I'll be back in a second with the shirt," I told her and left the kitchen, drawing the curtain behind me.

I ducked into my room, found a shirt I thought might work — fresh breeches were out; they would not stay up on her slim hips and flat stomach — and hurried back.

She had drawn the window shade and stood before the sink, naked to the waist, hair spilling down her back, hands placed lightly on the counter. My breath caught noisily; I should have backed out of the room, but I could not. Transfixed, I stared at the curve of her waist, the slight swell of her left breast, the promise of hip, the gleam of white shoulder.

She must have heard me, but for a moment she stood like a marble statue before the faint light seeping through the shade. Slowly, she turned her head.

"James," she said, her voice husky and low. "Please put the shirt on the chair. When this is over, I will want you to . . . to touch me. If you want to."

Too aroused to speak, I placed the garment on the chair, locked my eyes on hers and gave her one slow, emphatic nod. She nodded back and turned to the sink.

I had touched her many times. I had kissed her passionately many times. I had held her and smoothed her hair. This was different, and my soul expanded within me. I would protect her with my life and I would survive to love her into exhaustion.

In the living room, I was met by Jim's anxious expression.

"What happened out there?" was the first thing he said.

Quickly, I described the morning's events, but my words caught when I came to Jones' part in saving our lives, for which he had paid with his own.

"I have no idea what's happened to the cattle or the buildings," I added. "We have to get back out there. And where are Dumas and Pelletier? And Tom? We have to find them. What if they've been caught . . . or . . . or worse?"

"Garrison won't take hostages," Jim said grimly. "And Dumas won't allow himself to be taken anyway."

True, I thought.

"I didn't see Riley out there," I added. "Where the hell is he?"

"I don't know. Preparing for the boss's arrival, I expect."

"I can't leave Abby and Alex here alone. What are we going to do?" My little army was already disintegrating. Jones was dead, Dumas was God knew where, and I could hardly command the rest of the Métis men. That left Clancy, Angus, John and Charlie.

Heavy steps on the porch. Jim and I leapt up and seized our weapons as I hissed at Alex to stay down. We crawled toward the window as a voice called, "James. It's Bert. Let us in."

I threw the door open and was astonished to see Clancy there beside him, eyes huge in his head.

"One of Riley's gang came to the blacksmith shop," Bert said. "Looking for you. Pretty dark in there; he couldn't see me, but I could feel him. I gave him a good smack with a poker and he's unconscious. But Riley's on the move. Thought you should know. Thank God Clancy came on by with my lunch, helped me get over here."

"Sarah?" I breathed.

"At home. We have to get over there."

"Yes," I said. "Now."

Chapter Forty-three

The problem, of course, was Alex. Abby we could take along, but Alex was stuck. No way he could get on a horse.

I raced down to the creek and found Jeanne Dumas cooking something that smelled delicious over an open fire.

"Jeanne," I greeted her, panting out the name. "Do you have a travois I can borrow? And would you be so kind as to take care of Alex — the man with the missing leg — just for a while? We have to go find Michel and check on Sarah." I realized she did not know who Sarah was. "The blacksmith's wife."

She straightened and swept her hands over her apron. "Of course. Come, there is one behind my tent."

"Do you know where Michel went?"

"To find you. A farm somewhere?"

"Right." No time to tell her what had happened; nor did I want to frighten her. "I'll bring Alex back and then we're off. Thank you, Jeanne. I'm beholden."

"As I am to you. Wait. Let me gather some men to join you. You may need help."

"I can manage with Alex . . ."

"I'm sure you can. I meant to ride with you."

"I . . . thank you. I can't say no. We need all the help we can get."

"All right. Hurry back, James."

I grabbed the travois, collected Alex and a bottle of laudanum, and with Jim's help dragged him down to the Métis encampment. We placed him cozily in Jeanne's tent and raced back to the house.

"We need horses," I told Jim breathlessly. "Where's yours? Abby's is still out on the farm. At least, I hope he's still there."

Jim put two fingers in the corners of his mouth and let loose with a piercing whistle. His horse loped over almost immediately.

"You'll have to take Abby on yours, at least over to the Thompsons'," he said. "We can borrow a couple there. Bert and Clancy, though . . . they'll have to walk over."

But Bert and Clancy were already gone. Abby paced in the front room.

"Bert couldn't wait," she said as we entered. "Too scared for Sarah. Let's get the hell out of here."

I retrieved my poor tired Buck and up we went again. The three of us tore madly through the short streets and pulled up at the Thompsons', having passed Bert half a block away. By the time we arrived, we realized we had been closely followed by four of Dumas' men. One of them led a fifth horse.

"In case you needed another mount," one of them said. "I am Michel's nephew, Lucien."

"Thank you, merci, Lucien. Good thinking."

And so we were nine as we stepped onto the porch, Bert and Clancy having caught up to us. Jim had a word with Bert and moved him to the side, out of view of the street and the windows. Just then, I heard a crash from inside, and Bert emitted a cry.

"Sarah!"

Jim tried the door, but it was either locked or barricaded. I gestured to Lucien to head for the back door, and he and another man ran silently around the house. Judging by the crash, though, it was much too late to try a surprise entry.

"Nothing for it," I muttered to Jim. "Go."

Jim unloaded his considerable weight onto the door — the man amazed me every day; he must've had nearly thirty years on me — and thank God it came off the frame and slammed to the floor. He gave me a quick satisfied grin and lurched inside, hollering his head off, with me following him and Abby right behind. I would have stopped her if I could.

The first thing we saw, straight ahead in the hallway, was Lucien, who had promptly broken in the back way when he heard the crash from the front. The second thing was one of Riley's men, who stepped out from the kitchen, gun at his side, to evaluate the hullabaloo.

Lucien was closer. He leapt forward, raised his rifle with a howl and crashed the butt into the back of the man's head. Good move, I thought fleetingly; if he had fired and missed, one of us would be dead.

The man sprawled face down on the floor was not alone. Scraping noises and mutterings came from the kitchen, where I assumed they were holding and possibly interrogating Sarah.

I cocked my head toward the room and was rewarded by nods from my new army. Snick. Snick.

We poured in, guns held high, yelling at the top of our lungs. Chairs were overturned in the small room, indicating that Sarah had not capitulated easily. She was, however, gagged and tied to the remaining upright chair. Hot blood rose through my body and I strode to the man on the right, gun pointed at his chest even as his weapon pointed at mine.

"You're outnumbered," I yelled into his face. "If I die, you die." I heard the echo of the first words Abby had ever said to me and would have grinned under other circumstances. "Drop the gun."

Faced by a furious Jim and four other steaming men, as well as one very grumpy woman, he did. So did the other one. They really had no choice.

We lunged at them and held their arms tightly behind their backs. "Rope in the stable," I managed to get out. One of Lucien's men ran out and returned with two long loops.

Abby went to Sarah, removed her gag and cut her bonds. "Are you all right? Have they hurt you?"

"N-no, not really," she said, rubbing her sore wrists. "I'm mightily glad to see you." Her entire demeanour changed as she came off her chair. "Where is Bert? Where is he? Is he all right?"

"He's right outside," Abby soothed her. "I'll get him. You stay here and just take some deep breaths, okay?"

She nodded, relieved, then turned to me. "I didn't tell them anything. Nothing. But here you are, anyway."

Just in time, too.

"Were there just the three men, Sarah?"

"Yes. Well, I only saw three."

Three, of course, should have been sufficient to restrain a middle-aged lady. Bert had done the right thing in coming to get us instead of returning home; he and Clancy could not possibly have overcome these three large young men.

We could not leave the invaders here with Bert and Sarah, I thought, as I watched their tender, tearful reunion. There was no local constabulary and contacting the North West Mounted Police might take some time.

"This bloody town needs a sheriff," I muttered angrily. Jim nodded in agreement. "Where are we going to put them?"

"Where's Angus?" he asked suddenly. "Must be at work. Let's take them downtown, see if anyone's got a locked room we can borrow."

"We have to hurry. God knows what's happening out there with Dumas."

"Look. Why don't I take them into town, with Clancy riding shotgun? You head for the Pearce farm and I'll meet you there as fast as I can. I'll get Angus and the other boys to come along."

I could not think of a better plan. We wrestled those boys out of the Thompson home and onto their horses, hidden behind the stable. Jim tied the whole train together and Clancy came behind, gun trained on the trussed-up men. Lucien, his crew, Abby and I mounted and followed Jim into the street and up to the corner, where we would part ways.

"Wait," I said. "Jim, do you know where Abby's farm is?"

He turned to answer me, and I followed his eyes as they looked over my head into the distance. They widened, then, and I turned too.

"I'm afraid," he said, pointing, "I do now."

A billow of smoke rose from the near south. Abby gasped and kicked her borrowed horse into a gallop.

CHAPTER FORTY-FOUR

Buck needed no further encouragement. He took off after Abby at top speed.

I spent the brief trip wondering why Garrison would want to raze the buildings, but I supposed it made sense. Garrison only wanted the land. If the house and barns were gone, Abby and Alex might capitulate and sell. The expense of starting over would be considerable.

And if they did not give in? It did not bear thinking about.

Smoke filled the sky as we drew nearer. Half a mile out, we saw flames licking below the grim, grey cloud. These bastards were serious, and I knew now what Garrison meant by 'get started.' Riley had been charged with frightening Abby off her land. Garrison was coming for me.

I yelled at Abby to slow the hell down, but she either did not hear me over the pounding hooves or ignored my plea. At the northern edge of the homestead quarter, we began to understand the scale of devastation. The barn was in full flame, and I prayed the remaining cattle had escaped. The house had not yet quite taken; the north wall was charred, but I saw no active fire.

Abby did draw up then; her posture told me she was frozen in shock. I guided Buck close to her and found I had no words of comfort.

"We'll get them, Abby," I said instead, my throat constricting from fury and smoke. "We'll help you rebuild. We'll start over."

She answered with a sob and a nod. "What now?"

"We're going in."

Lucien and his men were by now right behind us. "Where's Michel?"

"I don't know. I can't see through all the smoke. We'll get as close as we can, dismount and stay low; maybe we can see underneath the cloud."

A few more metres ahead, we tied the horses to trees, loosely enough to encourage them to stay put but not hobble them if they had to run. The smoke was both a blessing and a curse; we could see little, but that meant Garrison's gang could not see us either. I hoped. Ducking as I ran, I headed for the house; it offered cover and was the best place to make a battle plan.

Shots rang out around us and we dropped to the ground, wriggling like snakes to the back porch. A bullet sang out from a window, and I suddenly understood why the house had not yet burned. Michel, Clément and Tom were barricaded inside, doing their damnedest to keep the villains far enough away to prevent accurate firebombing.

"Michel," I called over the din. "It's James. Can you hear me?"

I took a breath and rapped at the door, hoping he would not shoot me.

"Michel!" I said again, more loudly. No response.

But a head popped out from the upper story and ducked back in. I heard a faint clatter of boots on the interior stairs, and the door opened to reveal Tom.

"Hurry," was all he said, and we lunged inside.

I saw Michel hunched below the broken living room window, rifle in full cry. Clément stood alongside the dining room window; Tom clearly had been fighting from an upstairs bedroom. I raced over to Michel and slid to my knees beside him.

"How many?"

"Too many," he replied. "A dozen, at least."

"Taken any down?"

"Of course," he said, a touch insulted. "Four, maybe five."

"Is Riley here?"

"Yes. Well, I think so. Although with the dust, smoke and crazed cattle, it's hard to tell. They all look alike."

The livestock had largely blundered off, but errant cows and bulls continued to lurch and bellow in the yard. Bursts of gunfire cracked over the animals' noise. Shadowy figures vaguely emerged from the dust and smoke and faded back into the murk. It looked like a small war, and it sure as hell felt like it.

Michel returned fire, still trying to keep the invaders at bay. I joined him; then a cacophony erupted from Lucien and his men, and probably Abby. Hard to know if we were making any dent in their numbers, but we had little choice but to keep shooting while trying to miss Abby's livestock.

I more sensed than saw the oncoming rider. With little concern for personal survival, he thundered past the window Michel and I defended and hurled a flaming bottle, stuffed with a rag, right at us.

Michel uttered a French curse I did not understand and aimed at the rider as I jumped to extinguish the bomb. Filled with an accelerant, dirt was required to put it out and I ran to find a shovel. Abby stood in the hallway, shaking with anger and fear as she saw the growing fire.

"Quick," I said. "Shovel. Something."

That took two of us out of the fight, as we scrambled to collect enough earth for the job. We barely made it back inside before a rider, yelling oaths at the top of his lungs, barrelled toward us and flung another bomb onto the porch.

"Leave it. The one inside is more important," I said.

"I'll deal with this one. You go in."

"He'll be back."

"I'll hurry."

I did not want to leave her out there but saw no choice. By the time I had returned to the living room, the fire had spread, of course; Michel was doing his best with his boots and the log scuttle, which he had thrown over the bottle to starve the fire of oxygen. I kicked away the metal scuttle and dumped the pail of dirt over the flames, then began stamping out embers in the carpet.

"They're gaining advantage," I said, coughing. My eyes stung and watered.

"I know," Michel said. "We have to abandon the house, damn it, and get out there. We have to chase them down."

He was right, but my heart ached for Abby. She would likely lose her house as well as the barn, but we had to take the battle to the raiders. We were sitting ducks here.

The fire sputtered and smoked; I had made it in time. Michel bent over and rubbed his fingers in the charred wood, then leaned over and smeared the soot on my face before applying more to his own forehead, cheekbones and nose.

"Let us at least scare hell out of them," he said.

Right. "Lucien!" I yelled. "We're heading out."

Michel and I met him in the hallway, where they briefly acknowledged each other, and we all surged outside.

"Tom, stay here with Abby. Keep well covered. Only leave in case of fire. Plenty of places to hide. Got it? Someone has to keep an eye on the house," I argued.

"James, no. It's too dangerous to go out there," Abby said, her eyes pleading. She did not mention my blackened face.

"We have to beat them, Abby. There's no choice. Please, go inside."

No time for embraces. Michel, Lucien, their men and I plunged off the porch and off to get our horses; the occasional bullet sang overhead, but we stayed low.

"Seven, you think?" I asked Michel as we mounted.

"Maybe eight."

Still outnumbered, but it was better than twelve.

"We'll ride together, horizontal line, until we get an idea of where they are," I said. "Then shoot to maim or kill."

The wind had risen and shifted. The smoke from the burning barn now blew north, and by the time we rounded the corner of the house we could clearly see four men: two were creating more firebombs while the other two crouched behind a wagon, one loading, one shooting. We must have been an awesome sight, we six, because two sets of jaws dropped as their owners' heads swung around.

Michel released a shriek of fury that would have terrified the devil. Clutching his horse between his thighs, he rose slightly in the saddle and fired at one of the fire-makers . . . who dropped the bottle, howling in pain as he sank to the ground. I followed Michel's lead — he was, after all, the seasoned warrior — and spurred Buck toward the shooter, screaming my head off. He looked up in shock, and I shot him in the shoulder.

Lucien took on the reloader with no trouble, and his (I assumed) brother dispatched the fourth man. But where were the other three?

A cracking noise from behind me was immediately followed by a stinging pain that sent my hand up to my ear; a bullet had grazed it. Hell; the others were behind us. I reined Buck sharply left and swung my gun around, yelling to Michel. I missed the bastard, who rapidly gained on me, but I was moving fast enough to avoid being shot again. I aimed at his horse and brought him down, hating myself, but accuracy was impossible.

There were more of them, at least two or three, and they were coming at us from all sides. Six on six, I guessed. They were close to pinning us down in the exposed yard, and we were running out of ammunition.

"Ride for the hill!" Michel yelled. The same hill the raiders had come over earlier that day. The same hill the bison had lumbered over. As we rode, a bullet hit Lucien's brother, who fell from his horse. I reined up to grab him, but Michel cried "Robert!" and bent to pull him up onto the saddle.

We crested the hill, flung ourselves to the ground and slapped the horses' rumps.

"How is he?" I gasped at Michel.

"Not good. Alive."

Damn. At least he was alive.

I had to reload the carbine. Sticky blood mixed with the soot on my jaw; my hands shook with exhaustion and adrenaline. I wondered if I still had the top of my ear but had no time to check.

I peered over the hill to see six riders headed straight for us. We aimed as one unit and started shooting. They had the advantage of being mounted; we had the advantage of cover, but that would not last long.

One of our bullets met its mark. A horse went down with its rider, not more than twenty metres away. They gained on us by the second; but suddenly another rider went down, and another. And another. I was sure I had not hit any of them; maybe Michel had?

Then, to the north, I saw the dust billowing, and five men galloped through the cloud. Reinforcements.

This time, they were ours.

"Get down!" I yelled, and all of us flattened our heads on the ground.

Jim, Angus, Charlie, John and another man looked like angels from heaven to me, but I hoped the raiders saw demons of hell gaining on them. The element of surprise is always the best tactic, and within minutes all the raiders were down or dead.

Jim rode up the hill to meet us, grinning widely until he spied Lucien's bleeding brother.

"They're down," he said. "Are you all right? James, your face?"

"Shot in the ear." I scrambled over to the injured man. He was indeed bleeding profusely, but from the arm, not the chest. "Let's get him back to the house." I had a thought. "Riley? Did you see Riley?"

"No. You didn't get him?"

"No."

"Maybe he's in town."

"Maybe." My stomach flipped. "Maybe not."

I whistled for Buck, jumped on and rode for the house, my heart banging painfully against my ribs.

CHAPTER FORTY-FIVE

Blood spattered the dust in the yard. Shit splotched and deep hoof marks scarred the area. The barn smouldered; the garden was in ruins. Buck stepped over a corpse as we neared the last building standing.

There was no obvious sign of human life.

I came off Buck's back before he drew up and ran for the back porch, where I stopped and listened over the thudding in my ears. Nothing, at first. Then a cry; then a shot. Galvanized, I burst through the door, gun leading the way, yelling Abby's name. No reply came. I knew, then.

Riley stood in the living room, pistol drawn and smoking. Tom lay — dead? — in the corner and Abby once again was held in a tight embrace by a man who was not me. His lip curled in menace as my own mouth tightened in a grim line.

"Welly well. Hello, Sinclair. Excellent timing, I would say."

"What do you want, Riley?"

"I was just chatting with Miss Pearce, here." He quirked his eyebrows. "Seems I can't convince her to take a good price for her land. You see how, ah, unimpressed I was by her response." He jerked his head at Tom. "You really shouldn't leave a boy to do a man's work."

He was right. Why had I not stayed?

"I'm here now." I glanced desperately at Tom, then at Abby. "You really don't want to hurt her, Riley."

"Hmmm. And why not?" He tightened his grip on her throat; Abby made a terrifying choking noise.

"She owns half this farm." I did not know if that was precisely true, but I had to say something. "You need her to sign it over. I doubt the railroad would accept anything other than a properly transferred deed."

"Ha. You don't know those men. They'll take whatever they can get."

I doubted that, but if he believed it, I was in trouble. I had to buy some time.

"Maybe we can make a deal," I said, as Abby's eyes flew open. My own pleaded with her not to object. "The north two quarters. What do you say? That's all you need."

"Maybe, but the railway would prefer to have acquiescent farmers ready to crop for them along the line. Miss Pearce, here, has decided against that."

Abby was indeed hardly acquiescent. Riley gave a small shrug.

"Speaking of need, it would be helpful to persuade Miss Pearce, I agree. But you, Sinclair. You I do not need."

In the moment it took for him to point his pistol at me instead of Abby, I hit the ground like a sack of grain and the bullet lodged itself in the opposite wall.

He should have tied her up before I arrived; maybe he did not have time, or maybe he did not think it necessary. Just a woman, after all.

Abby Pearce, right arm released, hacked at his wrist hard enough to force down his arm. Then she bit him in the other hand, the one that had travelled from her throat to her mouth. He yelled and swung around with the gun-wielding arm to smash her in the face, but she twisted quickly; the gun glanced off her temple, staggering her.

I sprang to my feet and launched myself at him. While help was imminent, we were now in a battle of furies and it would come too late. I knocked both of them over, and they landed heavily on their backs, but Abby's fall was half-cushioned by Riley's body. She rolled over Riley, who was temporarily winded, tore the gun out of his hand and stood above him, one booted foot on his chest.

"You fucking bastard," she spat. "You shot my brother, and why? You ruined his leg and maybe his life. You could have killed him. For what? Why did you do that?" He did not answer. "Why?" she screamed.

"He wouldn't sign," Riley muttered, still winded. "I figured I could persuade him. And you." So Riley had in fact shot Alex. Himself.

"Well, it didn't work. It will not work. Then you tried to burn us out —
twice. What else have you done? What else?" Abby was beside herself, and I
worried that her attention was wandering.

"James. You are trying to kill James. And I won't let you."

Riley's hand was creeping toward a pocket as she spoke, so incensed she
did not notice.

"Abby! He has another gun," I shouted.

In the blur of a few seconds, the gun emerged as I crawled toward it. He
aimed not at me, but up at the furious woman screaming at him. Time stood
still as he drew back the trigger . . . and Abby howled . . . and fired.

Jim crashed through the front door, fear stretching his features, gun at
the ready. Michel was right behind him. They were too late. Riley was dead.
And so was Tom.

• • •

She had likely never killed a man before. Not at close range. Not on her living
room floor. Not with a gun swinging toward her face.

The howl had come from the agony of knowing she would kill this man
or die herself. Self-defence it surely was, but Abby's soul shrivelled within
her as she stared down at Riley's lifeless body. I saw it unmistakably written
on her features and in her posture. I had felt it myself.

Gently, I took the gun out of her hands and caught her before she
pitched over. We sank to our knees and I rocked her like a child, crooning
like a mother. My mother.

"You had no choice, Abby. You did the right thing. It's all right. It will be
all right." Was I even making sense? "I'm glad he's dead. It was him, or it was
you. Or me."

That seemed to get through.

"I couldn't let him. Could I, James? I couldn't, could I?"

"No. Abby, you couldn't."

"And Tom. Oh my God, Tom!" She lurched for the young man as a lump
formed in my throat. Guilt burned in my stomach. It was my fault Tom was
dead; not hers. I tore my thoughts away, needing to deal with the living.

I picked her up and settled her on the sofa, further away from the bodies streaming blood around us. She shook and hiccupped but finally, slowly, gathered her wits as she watched Jim and Michel drag Riley from the room.

"Why," she suddenly asked, "did he threaten to kill you? Wasn't he expected to drag you before the court of Garrison?"

Good point. "I don't know. Maybe he intended to just take me down. Shoot me in the arm? Or something has changed. Or he just couldn't help himself."

Or maybe he wanted you, I thought.

The wounded young Robert came through the door, borne by Lucien, Michel and Jim. He still lived, but his arm was torn up plenty.

"Put him on the kitchen table," Abby instructed, and got to her feet. "The doctor will see him now," she added with a slight curve of her lip.

I followed her and soon had the youngster stripped of his shirt and jacket. Abby poured alcohol on his wound, which was bad enough but neither life nor arm threatening. The bullet, thank God, had gone through, so we thoroughly disinfected and tightly bound him up. He yelled, too, which was a damn good sign.

"We have to get out of here," Michel said, once his nephew showed signs of surviving. "We do not know if there are any others, and we are almost out of bullets. We cannot take another showdown."

He was right. The corpses outside, the disastrous condition of the house, the smoking barn, the escaped cattle and everything else would have to wait. Jim went out back to retrieve Jones' body, followed by a devastated Clancy. I returned to the living room and lifted Tom's poor, wrecked body in my arms, struggling not to weep. He, like Jones, had come to help me and died trying to save Abby. I wrapped his wound in a sheet Abby provided — there had been enough blood — and then his body in a blanket.

All the men gathered outside and lowered their heads in his honour as I carried him to my horse. He would ride home with me.

Chapter Forty-six

We buried Tom and Jones behind the house, far from the creek but close to heaven. The starless night fell heavily. Fury raged in my heart; fear gripped my stomach. I did not know what tomorrow would bring. I could not bear another day of slaughter.

The Métis men returned to their camp after our makeshift funeral. Clancy, head low on his chest, headed for the stable and burrowed into the straw, weeping like a child. Charlie, worried for his wife and babe, went home, as did John who had similar responsibilities. Clancy being immobilized with grief, Angus picked up the proverbial cudgel and returned to the Thompsons; I prayed another band of gangsters had not appeared at Bert and Sarah's. Lucien took up the first watch on my front porch; another cousin sat out back.

I looked around for Jim, but he had disappeared into the night. I worried about that, but I could hardly seek him now. I put an arm around my shivering Abby, and we walked quietly into the house.

Alex was in a right state when Michel and Clément brought him back from Jeanne and Michel's tent, but he calmed somewhat when he saw Abby. She assured him that she was fine, and that I would take care of the bump on her temple. I made him down two fingers of whiskey and helped him from the travois back to bed.

Abby and I were then alone in the kitchen. I washed and daubed her wound with alcohol as she gritted her teeth against the sting. Then she looked up and noticed my ear.

"How is it?" I asked, my hand reaching up to test its wholeness. I still had not had a chance to look.

"Bloody," she said. "Caked with it. Let me see."

She reached for the cloth I had used, rinsed and soaked it, then gently began to wipe away the soot and blood covering my face and ear.

"Nicked," she pronounced, and disinfected it. "That's going to hurt."

"Stay with me, Abby," I whispered in a sudden segue.

"Yes," she said, and placed a hand on my cheek. Then she burst into tears. "I have nowhere else to go."

I let her cry in my arms until her heaving sobs turned into shudders, then led her to the bedroom. Eyes and ears were all around us, but I pulled her close and she finally fell into a troubled sleep.

●   ●   ●

Bang.

The door crashed open before the full dawn. Before my senses screamed danger, my subconscious brain drove me leaping from the bed, scrambling for the carbine. Abby bolted upright, shocked out of sleep, and lunged across the room for her rifle.

They had found me.

Half-clad, I lurched through the curtain to see the enormous bulk of George Garrison standing in the middle of my living room with an evil grin distorting his face. In the same moment, one of his raiders dragged Alex, doped but yelling, out of his room and dumped him on the floor. He screamed, then, as his stump took part of the impact.

Lucien howled on the front porch as two more men bound his wrists and punched him into submission.

"Sinclair," Garrison said. "We finally meet. Get the girl," he said over his shoulder. Another man plunged into the bedroom and came out with Abby, struggling in his arms.

Yelling 'no' was going to get me nowhere. Different tactics were needed. I hoped Lucien's hollering would rouse the small Métis Nation; or were they also being invaded?

"Garrison," I said. "It's about time."

He laughed, a sound that chilled my soul. "I knew I'd find you. Apparently, I had to do it myself." He gave an exaggerated sigh. "But here we are. The only question left is whether you will come quietly or will I have to shoot you where you stand."

"That brings up a third question. Where would I be going?"

"Ah. Back to Toronto, of course, to face the magistrate."

"On what charges?"

"Statutory rape of my beautiful daughter; perhaps manslaughter, as well? And murder, of course. Seven counts, at least. Speaking of that, where is Mr. Riley?"

So he didn't know.

"There have been no murders, except for those of my men," I said. "All of our actions have been in self-defence and you know it."

"Proof of that will be another matter."

"True. Although there are many witnesses. And of course, you will need proof that I ever came near your daughter." Rest in peace, Alice, I thought sadly.

His face stretched mockingly. "I doubt that. The magistrate is, ah, inclined to take my word on such matters."

"So I've heard. But what if I have proof that I never touched Alice?"

His eyes narrowed, but he did not flinch. "I would find that hard to believe."

"Would you." I cocked an eyebrow at him. It was odd that I felt little fear for myself; I was terrified for Abby and Alex, but this was the final act in my own play, regardless of outcome. "I do, though."

"And what form would that proof take?"

"A letter."

"From whom?"

"That doesn't matter. Did you know," I said to the men holding Abby, Alex, and Lucien, who had been dragged inside, "that Alice forced her own miscarriage? And why? Because she would not bear a child conceived in incest."

The men looked baffled, but the blood rose in Garrison's face. I thrust my face forward.

"That child was yours," I said quietly, but my voice shook. "Yours, Garrison. You raped and killed your own daughter."

The howl that emerged from his chest and mouth shook the walls.

"You fucking little bastard!" he screamed. "You lying piece of shit! Kill him! Kill him!"

But the men did not move. They stood, frozen, still holding their hostages, and as one turned to gaze at their leader.

"You useless idiots!" he bellowed, fumbling for his own gun, holstered inside his jacket. It was all I needed. I raised the carbine and held it focused on his chest.

"It's true, and I can prove it. Don't move, Garrison."

"Or what? You'll shoot me right here?"

"If I have to."

"Another murder on your hands?" He was beside himself. "Don't listen to him, boys. He's just trying to get himself out of this spot." He calmed a bit, as the men did not move. "Get him."

They did not. Neither did they release Abby, Alex and Lucien, but they did not move.

Stalemate. Garrison was right; I would not shoot him unless a gun was trained on Abby's head. Or Alex's. Or Lucien's. But I had had enough.

How long we stood there, my gun trained on Garrison and his bloodshot eyes trained on me, I do not know. It felt much like forever. Until Michel came barrelling through the back door, rifle first, with Clément behind him.

"Do not move!" Michel said loudly in his most threatening baritone. "James. What do you want to do? Should I shoot him now?"

"No," I said. "I want him to admit he raped his daughter."

"Never," Garrison spluttered.

Michel pointed his gun at Garrison's head as I continued to cover his dark heart. Clément gestured to the other Garrison men to stand down just as two more of Michel's clan burst through the door.

The first raider to give in was the one holding Abby. He released her and dropped his head.

"I didn't know," he said.

"No one did," I told him. "With two exceptions. Maybe three," I added, thinking of Tattersall.

Garrison then did raise his gun despite his abandonment, but the old man was no match for a Métis hunter. Michel shot him in the arm; squealing like a pig, Garrison dropped to his knees.

Clément tore the gun from his hand as Michel and I grabbed Garrison and marched him into the kitchen. We tied him securely to a chair; but then, of course, I could not help myself. I disinfected and pressed a towel to his wound, as Michel smirked at me over our prisoner's head.

"What will we do with him?" he asked.

"Good question. Are the other men behaving?"

"Yes. Lucien, Clément and the others are watching them."

"Michel. I am . . ."

"I know what you are going to say. Stop, Sinclair. We are even now."

"Hardly. And . . ."

The rest of my speech of gratitude was interrupted by another sign of chaos coming from out front. Great thumps sounded on the porch; Abby cried out and Alex, true to form, hollered. The door swung open, and one at a time, three huge men ducked under the frame and stood in a horizontal line, barring escape. One of them . . . unmistakable . . .

"James!" bellowed my friend.

"Jim," I said, coming through the curtain to meet him. "I'm glad to see you; where did you disappear to? And who are your friends?"

"North West Mounted Police," he said, grimly. "Took me all night to track these fellows down."

The men were not wearing uniforms, and I gave them a slightly suspicious once-over.

"Off duty," Jim explained. "I recognized them."

"Sergeant Miller," said the one clearly in charge, "and Constable Perry. Is George Garrison here?"

"I explained on the way. To pass the time," Jim said with a half-smile. "Is he here?"

"Yes. This way, Sergeant."

Miller and Perry followed me into the kitchen, where they beheld a bleeding and bound Garrison. They were clearly unimpressed.

"What's happened here?" Miller asked gruffly.

"Mr. Garrison and three of the, ah, gentlemen in the living room entered my home this morning without welcome or warning," I said. "They then took Mr. Alexander Pearce and Miss Abigail Pearce, as well as Mr. Lucien Dumas, hostage. Mich . . . uh, I felt I had no choice but to disarm him. He was reaching for his gun." I wanted to keep Dumas out of this, to the extent possible.

Miller looked slightly baffled, but his stance softened.

"Why was he here in the first place?"

"Mr. Garrison accused me several months ago of raping his daughter. He has evidently been searching for me ever since, and finally found me."

"And you claim you did not assault his daughter?"

"I did not. He did."

Miller was not a trained police officer for nothing, but the expression in his eyes gave away his surprise.

"Do you have any proof of this?"

"I do. Would you excuse me for a moment? Or come with me. I don't care either way."

Miller jerked his head at Perry, who followed me into the bedroom. I had carefully hidden Hannah's letter in a metal box, which was tied securely to the frame under my mattress. Best I could do. There was not yet a bank in town.

I unearthed it, opened the box — which made Perry twitch; he likely thought I had a pistol inside — and drew out three sheets of paper bearing Hannah's large but tidy hand.

We returned to the kitchen and I handed them to Miller.

"Third page," I said.

He shuffled the sheets and read the damning few paragraphs, then gave me another searing look.

"Who is Hannah?"

I explained.

"Would she testify to this in court? Or this . . . ah, Connie?"

"She would," Jim said, with force. I furrowed my brow at him. "Hannah said so in my letter."

Garrison, perhaps a bit woozy from loss of blood and shock, turned an unbecoming green and vomited on my kitchen floor.

"Hell," I muttered, and moved for the mop, but Michel waved me away.

"I'll handle this. Tell him the rest," he said.

And I did.

About Riley shooting Alex's leg halfway off. About the two raids on the Pearce farm. About Garrison's plot to take their land away, whether by purchase or by pain. About Jones and Tom. I told Miller everything, and in the afternoon, after hours of talk and questioning, he took Garrison and his men away.

CHAPTER FORTY-SEVEN

It turned out that several other Garrison men on that fateful day had, in fact, stormed the Métis camp before Michel and Clément came to save my skin. They must have been Toronto men, unaccustomed to the talents and ferocity of my Métis friends. They did not get very far. Michel's scout had seen them coming.

After the funerals for Jones and Tom, Jim said he had had enough. He would find the law or die trying, but damned if he would tell me so.

"You'd have just come out after me, and then what would've happened to Abby and Alex?" he argued. He had a point.

The NWMP's medic gave Garrison a good going over. He would be all right, we were informed a few days later. He would be taken back to Toronto on the first train out of Pile of Bones to face charges of speculation, murder, conspiracy and rape. They did not want to wait for the rail line to reach Moose Jaw.

I wondered about compensation for the dire damage done to the Pearce farm but unfortunately, Miller informed me, that would take some time. Garrison would have to be tried first.

Therefore, the entire Métis and Moose Jaw community came out to the farm a couple of weekends later. As a community, we raised a new barn, built new fences and repaired the damaged house. Sarah, Abby, Jeanne, Isabelle, Ellie (by now fully healed from the difficult birth), and John's wife Martha all cooked like fiends to keep us fed. Bert came along too, for moral support. He cuddled that sweet Preston baby every chance he got. Alex, by now sporting his new leg, pitched in as much as he could, but the stump pained him. Abby tried to persuade him to rest, but he would have nothing of it.

Abby, for her part, had gone home and stayed at the farm after Garrison was taken away. There was so much to do; her garden was ravaged, but the root vegetables survived. Jim, Angus and I were able to round up some of her cattle, which had taken to the grassy fields to crop and cope. Many were dead, but there were enough to restart the herd.

The NWMP dealt with the corpses.

My ear healed, and so did Abby's bump on the temple. But she was distant, and I worried about it incessantly. Maybe she did not want a killer for a friend or lover. Did she think I dragged trouble behind me everywhere I went? I tried to broach the subject several times, but she danced around it — and me.

A month went by. The crops grew, the rail line came nearer, the blacksmith's shop was busy.

One day, Michel came to see me.

"It's time," he said. "Time to say farewell, my friend. But not goodbye. We will be back every year; we will visit and raise a glass to our fallen and to each other. I have enough business with Jim to make Moose Jaw a worthwhile stop, as well. Take good care, James. And be sure to marry that girl. She will make you very happy."

"Thank you, Michel, for everything. For fighting, for staying, for risking your life and your people's lives. Come back soon, you hear? My home is yours. Always."

We embraced, I gulped. Michel gave me a small salute and was gone.

I went to my goldsmith's bench and got to work.

• • •

The following night, I took Buck out for a good hard ride before currying him, feeding him and going inside to have a thorough wash. Drying my hair with a towel, I emerged from the kitchen wearing only my breeches to see a puff of dust heading toward me.

Now what? Or rather, who?

The carbine sat propped by the door. I picked it up and peered into the distance, but it was hard to see much in the dusk. Just one rider, though.

I could take him.

I strode to the porch and gazed steadily at the oncomer. Then I lowered my gun.

Abby rode up to the porch, slipped out of the saddle and walked toward me. Her hair was a gorgeous windblown mess of gold and red; her eyes shot sapphire sparks; her body trembled like a flower petal in a storm. I wanted to grab and hold her, but I stood before her unmoving. I could not read her. I was terrified.

I heard her breath catch; she took another step and placed a hand on my bare chest, which immediately heaved in arousal and fear.

"Abby?" I finally said, hoarsely.

"It had to be over," she said, tears spilling down her face. "We had to be safe, James. I had to get Alex settled. I had to save my farm. I had nothing left — not my home, not my animals, not even my right mind — or so I thought. But then I realized: it was a disaster, but you saved my farm. My brother's life. And me. It had to all be behind me for certain before I could come to you. I couldn't have borne it if . . . if you were taken away."

"And now, Abby?"

"Now I want you to touch me. Now. If you want to. Please."

Beyond speech, far beyond control, I grabbed her then, more roughly than I meant to, and my mouth crashed onto hers. Months of longing glued my body and lips to hers, and I whispered, finally, "I will not let you go."

"I don't want you to."

I lifted her and bore her inside; her arms were wrapped around my neck, quivering. When I put her down, we clung to each other for several minutes, feeling each other's heartbeats, reliving the last weeks, incredulous at finally being alone together.

She stepped away from me and slipped out of her breeches and shirt; she still did not wear her dresses. I hoped she could, and would, again someday.

Underneath, she wore little. Her breasts strained against the light fabric of her shift, making my head spin. Her body was lithe but rounded, small but strong. My mouth went dry as I gaped at her; she trembled as she bravely presented herself to my gaze.

"James . . . what is it?" she asked. "Do you not . . . not like . . ."

"Oh, Abby, no. Don't think that. I was just . . . speechless. You are so beautiful."

"So are you." She looked down. "But I don't know what to do," she whispered.

Neither did I, really, although my mother's words rang in my head. When you find a wife, my Jem, be gentle. Go slowly. Ask her if you are in doubt. It will all work out.

Dizzy with desire, I still felt myself led by that long-ago advice. I took the step between us and kissed her as sweetly as I knew how.

"We will figure it out together," I said.

I ran my hands over her shoulders and arms and hips, and then I clasped her soft but muscular buttocks, drawing her closer. I had not counted on her own passion. She moulded her body to mine, thrust her fingers in my hair and parted her lips. Suddenly we were tearing off each other's remaining clothing and, once naked, she ran her tongue down my chest from throat to navel.

I stopped her before she could go any lower.

"Abby, God, stop for a moment."

"No. I won't. I can't." Her hands roved over my body. "Show me what to do next."

We were still in the living room. I took her hand and led her to the bedroom, crazed with passion but afraid of hurting or frightening her.

We fell on the bed, lips and hands everywhere, until the enormity of this act, this first time, this expression of love struck me forcefully in the still-functioning part of my brain. She rose under me, moaning and begging, and I was close to entering her; her hand, now at my groin, was ready to guide me. With the last shred of control, I backed away, and she cried, "No! James, please!"

"Abby. I want you, so much I can hardly stand it. But more than that, I . . . I love you. I don't want to hurt you, and what if . . ." I could not say, what if you become pregnant and haven't yet agreed to be my wife?

"I love you too," she said, so quietly and shyly it almost broke my heart. She was a warrior, but so vulnerable to me in this moment I could hardly bear it.

I crawled off the bed, thinking I must look ridiculous with my erection pointing the way; but she gasped and emitted a little 'oh.'

"Where are you going? Come back, James. I don't understand . . ."

From the shelf I drew down a small box. Returning to the bed, I saw her hair flowing over the pillow, her pink-tipped breasts pointing upward; heard her ragged breathing and felt her trembling. I had never been so sure of anything in my life.

I gave her the box and held my breath. Her eyes widened and eyebrows came together in confusion; then she opened it and drew out the golden band within.

"Marry me, Abby," I said simply. "Make me whole. Make me happy. Be my wife."

Her lips formed an O of astonishment as she held the band between thumb and forefinger before her eyes.

"Yes," she breathed. "Oh yes, James. I will marry you and be the happiest woman on Earth." She slipped the ring on her finger and threw herself at me, weeping and laughing. "I love you, James. Oh, so much," she whispered in my ear.

I laid her back, then, and made love to her; slowly at first, so that she would feel joy and passion without pain. She cried out once and bit her lip, but then raised her hips and pulled me inside. The sensation was exquisite, almost unendurable; and I cried out myself as Abby held me and shuddered in my arms.

EPILOGUE

December 10, 1882

The first passenger train ever to reach Moose Jaw, in what was now known as the Provisional District of Saskatchewan, steamed into the station on an excruciatingly cold December day. I remembered the icy winds blowing off Lake Ontario, blasting Toronto into huddling misery, but winter in the North-West Territories was something else altogether.

Abby and I stood shivering on the platform, holding each other as closely as possible to share our mutual warmth. We wore many layers of clothing under our voluminous hide jackets, but they did little to keep our teeth from chattering.

Jim shivered not only from the cold but from unbearable tension. He held his body erect, arms by his sides, frozen with anticipation and terror. He stared, eyes streaming, as the train chugged toward us, slowed, wheezed, and finally stopped. It seemed to take forever, even to me.

Porters opened doors and conductors shouted. People emerged as shadows from the relative warmth of the train into the vicious atmosphere, the air thick with ice fog and steam. But there was no mistaking the tall woman of regal bearing who stepped off, looked around, and walked directly toward Jim.

He took two stiff and staggering steps and soon they gazed into each other's faces, wonderment written all over Hannah's. She lifted a gloved hand and touched Jim's cheek, and parted her lips to say something. Tears froze into glittering diamonds, and her knees buckled under her.

Jim caught her, held her, his enormous body shaking with emotion. I could not see his face, but I did not need to. In my mind's eye, I envisioned the expression it held; I had seen something like it across my own kitchen table.

When he kissed her, finally, I had to look away. That moment held the passion and longing of twenty years, and it was theirs alone. Abby swept away the tear from my eye and put her arms around me.

"Will our love be like that, James?" she murmured. "Will we fall into each other's arms on train platforms, ignoring the gazes of strangers?"

"Yes. Except we will disembark together. I will never be apart from you for a day, much less twenty years."

Jim and Hannah broke their embrace and came to us. I hugged her ferociously, so happy to see her, so happy to see her reunited with her own James. She wept in my embrace and thanked me repeatedly.

"If you hadn't found him . . ." she said. "If you hadn't known . . ."

"But it's all right now," I soothed her. "Hannah, I want to introduce you to Abby. Hannah Vogel, Abigail Pearce."

Abby opened her arms to Hannah and the two women, who knew each other intimately although they had never met, became instant sisters.

I cleared my throat.

"My mother?" I asked, hesitantly.

"She's coming. In the spring."

"Is she well?"

"She is. Don't worry, dear. You'll see her again soon."

I relaxed. "And the boarding house?"

"I threw my apron at Connie and walked out," Hannah said, laughing. "Well, that's the short story. I'll tell you the rest of it later. Somewhere warmer, I hope?"

"Absolutely." I paused. "Garrison?"

"Convicted on all counts. Wonderful witness, Connie, steady and true on the stand. She deserved the boarding house. She drove the nail into his coffin, James. Garrison was killed in prison not two days later. They don't like men who rape their own daughters inside. Or anywhere."

My knees nearly buckled in relief, but despite all that had happened, a flicker of horror at his undoubtedly grim demise flashed through my brain.

Jim cleared his throat. "It's time to get off this blasted platform before we freeze to death. I'm taking Hannah home with me."

I rolled my eyes at him. Where else would she go, after all this time apart?

"Come for dinner tomorrow," Abby suggested. "I'm sure you and James have a lot of catching up to do."

"Of course we will," Jim said. "Hannah? Right?"

She nodded. "Jim will bring the whiskey."

•   •   •

Later that night, I held Abby close by the fire. Wrapped in several blankets, we shared our body heat until it overcame us and we began to make love, as we did every night she stayed with me in town.

I placed my hands on her breasts, felt their weight and firmness, and began to rise as I always did when she was so near.

I nuzzled them for a moment, but then . . .

"Abby?" I said, propping myself on my elbows. "Are you all right?"

"Yes, love. Never better. Please don't stop." She paused. "Why do you ask?"

"Your breasts. They've changed. Just a bit."

I knew it in a heartbeat.

"You're with child," I gasped. "Why didn't you tell me?"

She smiled. "I intended to once Hannah arrived. I suspected, but I've only known for sure this last week. We wanted her at our wedding, did we not? I didn't want you to worry and rush madly off to get a licence and have it done with. We have time to do it properly. And I don't care what people think. You are mine, and I am yours. That's all that matters."

I buried my head in her shoulder and held her against my heart, speechless with emotion. Then I gave a slightly hysterical whoop.

"The babe," I said. "He'll be one of the first ever to be born in Saskatchewan."

"She," Abby said. "She will be."

"Fine. She. As long as she looks like you."

"I can't promise that."

"You can't promise she will be a she, either."

"Do be quiet, James, and make love to me."

And I did, in the hard-fought peace — however temporary — of my new home.

Acknowledgments

This book would never have been conceived, much less written, if it were not for my better half.

The first chapter emanated, bloody and visceral, from a fevered dream suffered by my husband, Ken Paulson. Two days later, I had written a fictional and slightly gorier form of his nightmare and found I couldn't stop . . . except during the endless hours of research a historical novel demands.

Blood and Dust finally emerged several months later. It is as much Ken's book, in so many ways, as it is mine. I cannot begin to express my gratitude for his patience, plot and research assistance, and indeed the germ of the entire work.

I must also thank my main early readers and reviewers, Jennifer Parsons, Bambi Sommers, Kristin Dahlem-Belfour, Mario Dell'Olio, Jan Lansing and Nancy Grummett for their time, sharp eyes and excellent suggestions. I am eternally grateful for and love you all.

And to my friends and family, my wonderful supporters in the writing community on Twitter, the readers of my Adam and Grace mystery series, the many bloggers and podcasters who have all been so kind: I cannot possibly list you all, but know that you are in my heart and I appreciate every hug and gesture, virtual or personal. You fill my life with love and joy.

About the Author

J.C. Paulson, a Prairie Canadian journalist, has been published in newspapers and magazines for 30 years. Her unquiet brain requested a shift from fact to fiction five years ago, when she started writing mystery novels based in her home province of Saskatchewan. Four have been independently published: *Adam's Witness, Broken Through, Fire Lake* and *Griffin's Cure*, along with a novella, *Two Hundred Bones*.

Note from the Author

Word-of-mouth is crucial for any author to succeed. If you enjoyed *Blood and Dust*, please leave a review online—anywhere you are able. Even if it's just a sentence or two. It would make all the difference and would be very much appreciated.

Thanks!
J.C. Paulson

We hope you enjoyed reading this title from:

BLACK ❀ ROSE
writing™

www.blackrosewriting.com

Subscribe to our mailing list – *The Rosevine* – and receive
FREE books, daily deals, and stay current with news about
upcoming releases and our hottest authors.
Scan the QR code below to sign up.

Already a subscriber? Please accept a sincere thank you for
being a fan of Black Rose Writing authors.

View other Black Rose Writing titles at
www.blackrosewriting.com/books and use promo code
PRINT to receive a **20% discount** when purchasing.

Made in United States
North Haven, CT
27 May 2022

19590116R00157